FOOL FOR LOVE

FOOL FOR LOVE

NEW GAY FICTION

EDITED BY
TIMOTHY J. LAMBERT
AND R. D. COCHRANE

CLEIS
PRESS

Published in the United States by Cleis Press Inc., P.O. Box 14697, San Francisco, California 94114. Printed in the United States.

Cover design: Scott Idleman
Cover photograph: Image Source
Text design: Frank Wiedemann
Cleis logo art: Juana Alicia
First Edition.
10 9 8 7 6 5 4 3 2 1

For Richard Labonté,
who helped these stories find a new home.

Contents

| INTRODUCTION

Not too long ago, I found myself at a writing conference standing before my peers in the awkward position of admitting that if I were an Anne Tyler novel, I might be titled *The Accidental Romance Writer*. If the old adage about writing what you know is true, I might want to consider writing pamphlets. My most successful relationship to date has been with my dog, Rex, and I can attest to his inabilities to master the English language or to feed himself.

Luckily, I write fiction. I don't have to write what I know when I can utilize my vivid imagination. It's not that difficult to envision myself as the sort of person who is not only successful in romance, but can overlook the bad habits of another person—such as waking before noon, being the sort who likes to leave the house and enthusiastically interact with others, or having the need to be verbal—and attribute that to my characters.

Oh, Timothy. You're so cynical. Yes, I hear that a lot from my friends, as well as some of our readers. But it's not entirely true. I write romance because I've known it.

We've had some good times, Romance and I. We first met on a rocky beach in New England and held hands as we walked, not caring that the salty surf soaked our sneakers as the sun set on another summer. Later, we warmed our feet on a hearth made of granite and held each other close as we looked at photographs Romance had taken earlier of majestic pine trees and pairs of seagulls blithely crapping on weathered driftwood.

Romance and I spent a weekend in a bed-and-breakfast together. We giddily laughed whenever someone assumed we were brothers—even though we *were* brothers, in a more general sense of the word. We were comrades in our adoration for each other, celebrating our common ground, while exploring our differences in a candlelit dining room. We hiked through the woods, shuffling through fallen autumn leaves and confessing our secrets. Romance reached for my hand to help me traverse the ruddy terrain, and I blushed.

Romance took me to hear the New York Philharmonic, and on a different occasion, the opera. He didn't mind when I nodded off during Act Two, and he nudged me awake for the curtain call. He teased me about it later when we sat on the lip of the fountain at Lincoln Center. When I became irritable, he begged me not to be upset with him as he pointed to a star overhead and told me its brightness couldn't compare to my smile.

Romance sent me flowers and handwritten cards for no apparent reason.

Romance snuggled next to me in bed and didn't mind when I stared over his shoulder as he read a manuscript, while I mentally catalogued every paragraph that made him laugh or invoked a surprised reaction. Romance always responded honestly to my insecure inquiries about my writing.

Romance kissed me back, even after we'd broken up with each other, and said he still cared about me, even though I'd become doubtful of his place in my life and my own ability to give back. He was regretful, but understanding, and said he'd always be there for me even though we'd be apart.

I still see Romance every now and then, mostly from afar. I see him in magazine ads, promoting certain products. Sometimes he crops up in a movie, more convincing in black-and-white dramas than in modern epics with computerized special effects. However, his roles opposite Sandra Bullock are almost always enjoyable. Even though I am a tad bit jaded, when I spot Romance down on one knee and proposing in a crowded restaurant, I can't help but smile wistfully as I pick up my "to go" order and drive home with nobody but my smiling mutt, Rex, in the passenger seat.

I'm wary of fix ups, because Romance rarely shows his handsome mug on a blind date. But when I was presented with the opportunity to co-edit an anthology of romance stories, I could feel a familiar tingle up my spine that reminded me of the time Romance and I first passed each other on the street and locked eyes, unknowing of the years ahead that we'd spend together. I admit I was doubtful about the endeavor; one of the reasons for my last falling-out with Romance is my need to control my environment. I don't have a telephone, because I don't like surprises.

One of the reasons I sometimes feel derisive toward romance is because of the outcry from those who think that if I fall in love with another man, it will somehow harm the nation and necessitate laws to keep me separate and "less than" the more traditional model. I've been in places where my romances have seemed a precursor to danger, so I'd let go of his hand in public and then feel ashamed that I'd given in to my fear of people who might harm me because of who I loved. Is it better to stand up for my romance and feel pain, or love safely in private? Does it matter to anyone but me? What's the point in being romantic when people want to sweep my version of romance under the carpet and then place a heavy piece of tacky furniture on top of it?

My attitude changed when the stories from our writers began to arrive in our In-box. Some of them made me laugh and remember when Romance and I were in similar circumstances. A few of them reminded me of when Romance and I had been together for a while and needed to remember how lucky we'd been to find each other. Two of them made me cry. On the whole, the vast majority of the stories made me long to find Romance again and not give a damn this time what anybody else thinks about us.

Because of the writers in this collection, I'm less skeptical about fix-ups. I'll always look fondly at this anthology whenever my faith in romance gets shaky and see it as a reminder that love and romance continue to be shaped by our imaginations, our hearts, and our faith in each other.

I want to be a fool for love.

Timothy J. Lambert

THAI ANGEL

David Puterbaugh

From the 2006 *Zagat Survey—New York City Restaurants:*

Thai Angel (Queens)

34-11 Broadway (34th St.) 718-555-1212

Locals swear by this "Astoria must," despite its "fancy new name," which fans say hasn't changed the "delicious food" or "bargain prices." The "old lady in the kitchen" can be "scary," but the "heavenly cuisine" is "worth risking the evil eye."

"Seaweed carbs."

"Huh?"

Sean's pale Irish face turned fire-engine red as he studied the piece of paper in his hand before trying again.

"Um...Sandra Dee Crab?"

"What are you trying to say?" Kama asked, leaning over the counter.

"Hello?" Sean said, looking up hopefully. Then he grinned. "I guess it didn't come out like that, huh?"

"Not exactly. Here, let me take a look."

Sean passed the piece of paper to Kama.

"I found this on a website; it said it was a common Thai phrase. I must have written it down wrong, I guess."

Kama looked at the note. "Well, I don't know what this word is," he said, picking up a pen. "But this is how you say hello. *Sawasdee Khrap*."

"Sawasdee Khrap," Sean repeated. He smiled at Kama. "Cool."

"Why the sudden interest in learning Thai?" Kama asked.

Sean shrugged. "Just figured I come in here enough. Thought it'd be polite if I learned how to say hi."

The kitchen door behind Kama swung open and Kama's mother appeared, bringing with her a small brown bag and a lifetime's worth of prejudices.

"*I told you I don't like police coming in here,*" she said to her son in her native tongue. "*If he keeps coming here, then more will come. Maybe you don't care if this turns into a police hangout, but I do!*"

Sean smiled at Kama's mother. "Sawasdee Khrap, ma'am," the rookie cop said.

Kama's mother looked at Sean like he was something stuck to the bottom of her shoe.

"*What did he say to me?*"

"*You know what he said,*" Kama answered. "*He's learning a few Thai words.*"

"*Why?*"

"*Because he's trying to be friendly. Be nice.*"

Kama's mother stared hard at the policeman. "*Weird,*" she said, handing the bag to her son.

Kama looked at Sean, who was still smiling.

"My mother says hello."

"Plain chicken and brown rice! Only a weird person would come to a Thai restaurant and order plain chicken and brown rice!"

"My mother says she knows your order by heart."

"Yeah, I guess I am kind of predictable," Sean said. Then he laughed. "I guess it's weird for someone to order plain chicken and rice in a Thai restaurant though, huh?"

"Plain food! Why does he come in here and waste our time? Why doesn't he just make it at home?"

"I guess I could just cook at home," Sean said. "But I like to go to the gym before work, and I try to eat some protein and carbs after I work out. And since the precinct's just a couple of blocks away...."

"It's not a problem," Kama said, handing him the bag. "We're more than happy to cook off the menu for our best customers."

"Thanks," Sean said. Then he leaned in close to the counter. "Hey, is your mother mad about something? She looks a little angry."

"What is he saying? Is he talking about me?"

"No, she's fine," Kama said. "The kitchen just gets a little hot sometimes, that's all."

Sean nodded. "Oh, right. Well, I guess I'll be going then. See you later."

He waved good-bye and headed for the door. Kama and his mother watched him go.

"What a weird man."

Kama turned around and looked at his mother. *"I wish you wouldn't say things like that. He's a very nice guy. And a good customer, too."*

"Good customer? You mean weird customer! What will he ask us for next? Donuts for his police friends?"

Kama shook his head. *"I wish you would stop judging people."*

His mother turned around and headed back into the kitchen. *"I know a weird man when I see one. And that is a weird man!"*

A few minutes later, Kama looked up when his sister Mali came hurrying into the restaurant.

"I'm sorry, I'm sorry, I'm sorry."

"It's okay."

"It went a lot longer than I thought it would," Mali said as she stuffed her bag under the counter and pulled on an apron. "Then I had to wait forever for the subway."

"Don't worry about it," Kama said. "As you can see, we're not that busy today. So how did it go?"

A big smile appeared on Mali's face. "Really good, I think. I won't know for a couple of days I guess, but I think they really liked me. They had me do two scenes."

"That's great."

"I know it's off-Broadway. Okay, way, way off-Broadway. But can you imagine if I actually got a part in a play?"

"You've been in plays before."

"Those don't count; that was in school. This is a real play, a real job. God, I want this so bad."

Just then the kitchen door opened again.

"Well, look who's here! It's Elizabeth Taylor! We are so honored that you have decided to grace us with your presence today, Miss Taylor!"

Mali scowled at her mother. *"You really need to get a more current actress, Mother. Elizabeth Taylor is one hundred-fifty-years-old. When's the last time you saw a movie? World War Two?"*

"I don't have time for movies because I am working. Like you should be doing! Do you expect your brother and me to do all the work?"

"Here we go," Mali said.

"You think money just appears like magic? How do you expect us to pay for your brother's fancy new restaurant if nobody works?"

"Mother, it is not my restaurant. It's our restaurant," Kama said. *"And we've been through this already. The changes were necessary in order for us to keep the business profitable."*

"Thai Angel! What a ridiculous name for a restaurant! There was nothing wrong with the other name."

"There was no name!" Mali said. *"The old sign just said* THAI FOOD*!"*

"Exactly!" her mother replied. *"When we first opened the restaurant, your father wanted to spend hundreds of dollars on a fancy sign. Happy Day he wanted to call it. I told him no! Wasting money on a fancy sign? Ridiculous! I told him people will come for the food, not for the sign. And look, where are the people now? You have a fancy new sign, and no one sitting at your fancy new tables."*

"It's Monday night, Mother. You know we're always slow on Mondays," Kama said. *"Did you forget how busy we were this weekend? How we had people waiting for a table?"*

"Of course, because now this is a hangout. No one ever leaves!"

"They will leave if you don't stay in the kitchen!" Mali said.

As if on cue, a crash from the back of the restaurant made them all turn around.

"Do you see now what you have done? Do you see what kind of people you have hired for my kitchen?" Kama's mother said to him. *"Thanks to you, we have no customers in the front and idiots in the back!"*

"You know how some actresses get all choked up when they thank their mothers after winning an Academy Award?" Mali said once her mother had stormed off.

"That will never be a problem for me."

"She doesn't mean what she says," Kama said. "She'll never let on, but I know she's missing Dad. I think she feels like the restaurant is all that she...."

Mali looked up and saw immediately why her brother had stopped talking. One of the cutest guys in Astoria had just walked into the restaurant.

"Ooh, look who's back," Mali said, playfully poking Kama in the side. "Body Too Hottie."

Kama slapped her hand away. "Would you stop?"

"You've got a crush on Body, don't you?"

"Stop," Kama said through clenched teeth.

"Oh, c'mon, admit it. I've seen the way you look at him."

"I don't have a—Hey, how are you?"

Body Too Hottie approached the counter with a smile that would have made the Mona Lisa show her teeth. "Hey, guys," he said. "Slow tonight, huh?"

Kama laughed so hard that Mali jumped. "Mondays," he said, shrugging his shoulders. "What can you do?"

Mali rolled her eyes. "It's even worse than I thought." She looked at Body. "I guess you don't get too many slow days at your job, huh?"

"No, not too many," Body said. "The emergency room was really jumping today."

Body Too Hottie was still wearing his blue nurse's uniform, the only outfit Kama and Mali had ever seen him in. Body was one of those people who would look hot wearing anything, but he looked especially hot in hospital scrubs. Mali had nearly choked on her gum the first time she saw how his uniform clung snugly to his muscular frame.

Kama reached for the order pad on the counter. "The usual?" he asked.

"Nah," Body said, as he put down his backpack and picked up a take-out menu. "I'm not feeling like curry tonight. What else looks good?"

"You in those scrubs," Mali whispered. Kama was not amused.

"How about some Pad Thai?" he suggested. "Or maybe some soup?"

"Eh," Body said.

"I know," Mali said to her brother with a mischievous grin. "You should make him the Enchanted Ocean."

Body Too Hottie looked up. "The Enchanted Ocean? What's that?" He turned over the take-out menu.

"You won't find it on the menu," Mali said. "Not yet, anyway. The Enchanted Ocean is a very special seafood stir fry that my brother has been working on."

"It's not that special," Kama said.

"Not that special? Are you crazy?" Mali turned to Body. "It's got shrimp, lobster, mussels, scallops; and then he mixes it all up with tons of vegetables and his own homemade Thai sauce. Trust me; it will blow your mind."

"You'll have to excuse my sister," Kama said. "She's an *actress*. What about some nice—"

"No, that stir fry thing sounds great actually," Body said. "Can I order that?"

"Of course!" Mali said.

"No!" Kama said. "I mean, it takes so long to prepare. You must be in a hurry to get home."

"It doesn't take that long," Mali said. "I know! We could deliver it to you. Here, write down your address."

"But, but...." Kama stood by helplessly as his sister took Body Too Hottie's info.

"About a half hour, okay?" Mali said.

"Sounds great," Body said, picking up his backpack. He winked at Kama. "Thanks a lot." Then he turned back to them when he reached the door. "Oh, by the way, my name is Ben."

"What the hell was that?" Kama asked when Ben had gone.

"I know," Mali said. "I thought he'd have a much sexier name than Ben."

"Not that! What's all this nonsense about a special order? You know I've never made the Enchanted Ocean for a customer before. And Sunan is out on deliveries. Why make him wait for Sunan to get back when he could have taken his dinner with him?"

"Because Sunan isn't going to deliver his dinner," Mali said. "You are."

"I am? Why would I do that?"

"Because it's been over a year since you and James broke up, and you need to get back out there. It's not healthy for you to spend all your time in this restaurant. *With your mother.*"

"But this is crazy!" Kama said. "We don't know anything about him." Then he lowered his voice. "We don't even know if he's gay."

"Oh, please," Mali said. "He's a nurse."

"That doesn't mean anything," Kama said. "Believe it or not, some male nurses are straight."

"Not this one," Mali said. "Didn't you see the backpack? It was Prada. Besides," she continued, "I saw him wink at you. There was definitely a spark between the two of you."

Kama hesitated. "Do you really think so?"

"Yes!" Mali said. "And don't lie because I know that you like him. So get your ass in that kitchen and make the best goddamn Enchanted Ocean you've ever made."

"But what about Mom? Won't she get suspicious when I go out on a delivery?"

"Oh, crap, I forgot about her," Mali said. "Jeez, if you would just come out to her already." After thinking for a minute, his sister said, "All right, I got it. You start cooking. I'll take care of Mommie Dearest." Mali then left him and headed down to the basement.

Although his sister was three years younger, Kama knew better than to argue with her, and the kitchen was soon filled with delicious smells as he began to add the ingredients of his recipe to a wok.

"Why are you making that?" Kama's mother asked when she came over to investigate.

"Um..."

But before Kama could answer her, there was an ear-shattering scream from the basement.

"RAT!"

"Rat? In my basement?" His mother grabbed a broom and charged downstairs. *"Wait! I'm coming!"*

Kama smiled as he stirred. His sister's ability to transform herself from a meddling matchmaker into a screaming B-movie horror queen in less time than it took most people to brush their teeth was the stuff of Golden Globe nominations. But as he stirred, Kama's smile gradually subsided. He had no idea what Mali thought would come from having him deliver Ben's dinner.

Yes you do, he thought. *And you're thinking the same thing, too. You know you're dying to see just how hottie that body really is!*

Kama added the final ingredients to his special dish and kept stirring. James was supposed to have been the one. The one with whom he could finally be himself. He loved his family, of course. He even loved working at the restaurant. But Kama knew there was something missing for him, something that he'd been searching for a long time. Now twenty-seven, he'd hoped to have already found it.

For that reason, when he finished packaging Ben's dinner, Kama went into the bathroom, took off his apron, and put on a clean T-shirt that he kept in the back. He ran water through his thick dark hair and patted it dry with paper towels. For a moment he wished he had cologne to put on, but then realized it was for the best. His mother would have smelled it immediately.

"Elizabeth Taylor, my ass," Mali said when her brother came out of the bathroom. She handed him the bag of food and Ben's address. "You look great. Now go. And don't worry. She'll be down there for hours."

Kama headed for one of Astoria's most well-known streets and made his way to Ben's apartment. As it turned out, Ben lived in a building only a couple of blocks from the restaurant.

"C'mon up," Ben said after Kama rang his buzzer. Ben's apartment was on the third floor of a six-story building, and Kama found the apartment door ajar when he reached it.

"I'll be right there," Ben called, and a moment later he appeared at the door. He was wearing a pair of old blue jeans and nothing else except a wet towel draped across his shoulders. *If Mali could see this.*

"Oh, hey!" Ben said when he saw Kama standing in the hallway. "I didn't realize you'd be making the delivery yourself. I could have come back and picked it up."

"It's no trouble," Kama said.

"Come in," Ben said, stepping aside. "Excuse me while I grab a shirt. I just got out of the shower."

Kama walked into the kitchen off the entrance and put the bag on the kitchen table. Ben went into his bedroom and came back a moment later. He was still barefoot but was now wearing a tight black T-shirt.

"Wow. That smells great," Ben said. "Oh, shit. I left my wallet in the bedroom. Hang on a sec." He padded back down the hall and returned with his wallet. "Hey listen, do you want a beer or something? I feel bad that you came all the way over here, and you made me this special dinner and all. I'd love it if you stayed a minute while I tried it."

In his head Kama could hear Mali screaming, "I TOLD YOU SO!"

"Sure," he said. "I can stay a minute."

"Great!" Ben said. He winked at Kama again. "Please, have a seat."

Kama sat at the table as Ben pulled a couple of beers out of the refrigerator and took the seat closest to him, filling Kama's nostrils with his soapy clean scent.

"I can't wait to try this," Ben said, tearing open the bag. He didn't even bother to get a plate. He just popped open the food container and dove in with the plastic fork Kama had placed inside the bag.

"Oh, my God, this is amazing!" Ben said, his mouth full of food.

Kama smiled. "I'm glad you like it."

"Really, I mean it. This is frigging incredible. What's in this sauce?"

This time it was Kama who winked at Ben. "It's a family secret."

Ben matched Kama's smile. "Well, it's great, whatever it is." He took a swig of beer. "So your family has owned the restaurant for a while, huh?"

"Almost twenty years," Kama said. "My parents bought it when we first came to New York."

"And you all still work there?" Ben asked, taking another bite.

"Yes. Although it's just my mother and sister and me now. My father passed away last year."

"I'm sorry to hear that."

"Thanks. It's been tough on my mother. She doesn't handle change very well."

"Speaking of change, I love what you've done with the place," Ben said.

Kama thanked him again and took a sip of his beer. "It's taken some getting used to, but I think we're all adjusting."

"I panicked when I saw that you'd closed," Ben said. "I didn't realize at first that it was only for renovations. For a minute, I thought I might never see you again."

Kama could feel himself blushing. But then he suddenly felt very bold. "Hey, listen," he said as Ben looked up at him from his food. "Would you want to—"

The sound of a key turning in a lock interrupted Kama, and they both looked over as a pretty girl in hospital scrubs came through Ben's door.

"Hey, babe!" Ben said, jumping up. He kissed the girl on the lips. "Kama, this is my fiancée, Heather. Hon, this is Kama. He and his family own the Thai restaurant I'm always talking about."

"Oh, hi!" Heather said, putting out her hand. "Ben loves your food. He's always telling me that I have to try it, but there's never any left by the time I get home!"

As he shook her hand, Kama stared at the girl like someone who'd just seen Bigfoot or a UFO. "Yes, he's one of our best customers," he said, his mouth instinctively stepping in while his brain caught up.

"Here, honey, try this," Ben said, as he cupped his open hand under a fork full of food and guided it carefully into his girl-friend's mouth. "Kama made it special for me."

"That's delicious!" Heather said after she swallowed. "What is it?"

"Isn't it fantastic?" Ben agreed. He looked over at Kama. "What do you call it again?"

Kama wished that he was dead. "The Enchanted Ocean."

"Doesn't that sound great, babe?"

Kama stood up. "I should get going."

"Oh, no. Can't you stay a few more minutes?" Heather asked. "With our crazy schedules at the hospital, we almost never have company."

"Heather's finishing up her residency at my hospital," Ben said, wrapping his arms around Heather's waist. "That's where we met."

"I know what you must be thinking," Heather said. "A doctor and a nurse. How cute is that?"

"You're cute," Ben said, kissing her again.

Kama didn't know how much more of this he could take. "Yeah, I really have to get back to the restaurant."

"No problem; we understand," Ben said. "Oh, wait. I still have to pay you. How much was it?"

Kama shook his head. "Don't worry about it. Consider it a gift for a loyal customer."

"No way," Ben said, opening his wallet. "Here, that should cover it, right?" He handed Kama a twenty.

"Yeah, thanks."

As Kama started down the stairs, he heard Heather call out that they should all get together soon. He smiled up at her but kept walking, and it wasn't until he was almost back at the restaurant that he even looked at the money. He opened his hand, stared down at the twenty-dollar bill, and then crumpled it up and threw it into the sewer.

"I just can't believe that he's straight!" Mali said for the hundredth time the next day. "There are so many gay guys in my drama class. Body Too Hottie had all the signs!"

"I really don't want to talk about it," Kama said. He was working at the front counter, trying his best to ignore her.

"It's these damn metrosexuals," Mali said. "They make everything so confusing." She picked up a tray and went to clear a table in the dining room.

As Mali left the counter, the front door opened, and Kama looked up to see Sean coming into the restaurant. Kama almost didn't recognize him without his police uniform. Today, he was wearing a T-shirt and jeans.

"Hey. You're not working today?" Kama asked.

"No," Sean said. "I was just in the neighborhood."

"Oh, okay," Kama said, not really paying attention. "I'll go put your order in."

"No, don't." Kama stopped and looked at Sean. "I mean, I didn't come in to eat," Sean said.

"Oh?"

Kama watched as Sean reached into his back pocket and unfolded a piece of paper. His hands shook a little as he cleared his throat. *"Would you like to have dinner with me some-time?"*

Kama stared at him for at least a minute before he burst out laughing. "I don't know what you were trying to say that time," he said, "but you just asked me to go out with you."

"Good," Sean said. "I finally got one right."

A huge crash came from behind Sean. Mali had dropped her tray. She and her brother were now both staring at Sean with their mouths wide open.

"What?" Kama said.

Sean walked up to the counter. "The first time I came in here,

I just wanted to get something to eat. Every time since then, it's because I wanted to see you."

Mali gasped, and Kama looked at her before looking back at Sean.

"I know it's crazy," Sean said. "I don't even know if you're gay. And I really hope you won't be offended or anything if you're not. But I figured...."

"Yes," Kama said.

"Yes, what?"

"Yes. I'd love to have dinner with you."

Sean turned a little pink. "Really?"

Kama smiled. "Really."

"Okay, great," Sean said. "How about Friday? Seven o'clock?"

"Sounds good," Kama said.

"Great. I know a good Italian place in the city." Then Sean looked a bit alarmed. "You do eat other food, right?"

Kama laughed. "From time to time."

"Great," Sean repeated. "See you then."

"OH! MY! GOD!" Mali said when Sean left. "I'm so happy for you!" She threw her arms around her brother.

"Would you stop? It's just a date."

"You never know," Mali said. "This could be the one. And look at it this way; if you marry him, he'll be easy to cook for."

Their mother came out of the kitchen. "*What was that crash?*"

"*Nothing,*" Mali said. "*I dropped a tray. Don't worry; I'll clean it up.*"

Her mother shook her head, and then she turned to her son. "*I thought I heard the weird man out here. Didn't he order his weird food?*"

"*No, Mother. He didn't order anything today.*"

"Then what did he want?"

Mali was now standing behind her mother. Kama looked at his sister, and she nodded. He looked back at his mother.

"He came to ask me out on a date, Mother. And I said yes."

For a moment, Kama's mother didn't even appear to be breathing. The only thing about her that still seemed alive were her eyes, which bore into her son like laser beams that had locked onto their target.

Then, suddenly, his mother closed her eyes, took a deep breath, and opened them again. She stood on her tiptoes and kissed her son on the cheek.

"It's okay," she answered, the first and only words her children had ever heard her say in English. *"Your father was a weird man, too."*

LOVE TAPS

Mark G. Harris

There's nothing like a good night's sleep, and that's just what Sullivan got: nothing like it. He had collapsed into his side of the bed the night before around 1 a.m., after listening to the first hour of his boyfriend's radio broadcast. His back stiffened and he wrenched himself out of bed to find that, in a wicked layer between the fitted sheet and the mattress, Chuck had arranged some wire hangers.

Chuck was Sullivan's first and only boyfriend. Despite his limited knowledge of such things as relationships, Sullivan knew that putting clothes hangers in someone's bed wasn't jake. The act struck him as either a declaration of war or a cry for help. Chuck's dad was a plumber, and Chuck knew through osmosis how to fix a leak, as well as change a tire and thumb wrestle, so to Sullivan that ruled out helplessness.

Chuck worked as a disc jockey. They had been forced to move out of state to this town a month ago, when an opening for the graveyard shift offered Chuck that for which he'd been working long and hard, a chance to finally be on-air. Every night since then, sometime during the beginning of his show, he would play a song just for Sullivan. Last night's had been "Truckin'" by the Grateful Dead. It was one of those laid-back, bluesy songs Chuck considered conducive, and in bed he would often let it strum softly in the background while he changed the title in a whisper in Sullivan's ear and trucked Sullivan's brains out.

Conflicting schedules had not allowed the time for much strumming lately. Come dawn, Chuck would return home and crawl into the warm, body-shaped indentation left by Sullivan, while Sullivan showered and left for another day of watering plants at the nursery. It was as if they weren't together anymore. Sullivan was on the verge of becoming one of those widows who talked only to her dead husband's military photo and always made soup for two, the empty chair gazed at through a mist of tears and broth steam.

Three years together, one month of passing each other in the doorway without touching, and now this, a prank fraught with meaning. Rare was the creature who could get decent rest with a word like "fraught" weighing on his mind.

Sullivan rolled his bicycle to the door of their apartment, saw Chuck's keys and reading glasses on the table in the morning light, and thinking of the hangers again, smeared the lenses with his spit-dabbed finger. He had not expected it to make him feel so giddy. He pedaled to work. His smile that day for ladies land-scaping their yards was noted, and his dimples were compli-mented more than one time, which put him in better spirits.

Sullivan came home and spent the evening smelling his boyfriend's shirt. That night's song was Billy Idol's "Dancing with Myself." Then: an hour of sleep before the phone started jangling. Sullivan answered, only to hear the other end hang up. This happened two more times during the night. He star-sixty-nined immediately after the third and was greeted by the worst imitation of an old lady he'd ever heard. It was unconvincing for its falsetto wrongness and for the music playing in the background, which sounded nothing like Benny Goodman, or whatever else Sullivan imagined grandmothers listened to. But then his grandmother, for instance, liked that little mulatto Liza Minnelli, meaning Prince, so there was no telling. He hung up, irate that he'd charged their phone bill fifty cents for something he already knew. He knew who was calling, but the answer as to why wasn't as easily forthcoming, and it nagged like a hangnail.

Cold dread creeped Sullivan out during his stint at work the next morning and continued into his evening alone. He knew, somewhere in town at this moment, Chuck was chatting with Lloyd, the driver of the 6:35 p.m. bus. Lloyd wasn't Charon, and he wasn't ferrying Chuck to the Isle of the Dead, only to the downtown area, so that Chuck could do his preliminary job as a sound engineer before his broadcast shift began. But the shadow of vast separation weighed the same tonight. Sullivan sat in the lotus position on the sofa to catch the tail end of "Wheel of Fortune," his mind looped in scout knots.

"What's it all mean?" he asked the nearby cluster of African violets.

They didn't live with a dog, so Sullivan had only the plant to confide in. Chuck desperately wanted to adopt a puppy, perhaps a boxer. Sullivan had concealed his own yearning and kept shooting down the idea as impractical.

He had reason. While Chuck and he were browsing the local gay bookstore the week before, Sullivan had wandered off to the travel section and started a conversation with a lesbian couple. They had seemed to like him immensely until Chuck joined the party, and then it was all over. Chuck had them cackling and clapping him on the back after only two minutes. Sullivan attempted to butt in and mention that he, too, had always wanted to visit Ibiza, and the women were right, the food was supposed to be incredible, but his voice was not one that carried even under the best circumstances.

The idea of getting a puppy and having him prefer Chuck wasn't something Sullivan was ready for, and it was bound to happen. He wasn't ready for the day when he would gently clasp the dog's warm, little shoulders during a moment alone with him, perhaps while "Judge Judy" was on, and inform him, "I'm sorry, Henry. No, now, no, look at me. Chuck isn't coming home anymore. He's left you. It's just you and me. Now, who wants to play tennis ball? Is it you? It is you, isn't it?!" Perhaps for an hour or two the dog would grow to like him and forget about Chuck, but the betrayal when Chuck's keys sounded and the dog realized he'd been tricked would imply traits about Sullivan that he wanted to remain unknown.

Maybe those traits were showing at last and Chuck had finally caught on. "Dancing with Myself." Why that song? It was the first song that Chuck and Sullivan had danced to, but there was also a strong possibility that playing it was meant to convey a message. Sullivan was insecure. Sullivan was too needy. Three years had rendered Sullivan's charms meager and repetitive and Chuck wanted his freedom. Chuck's career was finally preparing for takeoff, and Sullivan's carry-on exceeded the size restrictions.

"Well, what if I am a little needy?" Sullivan said.

What kind of freak breaks up with his gentle, peace-digging, loyal man via Billy Idol? Stupid Chuck. Stupid name. Means "dispose of." His name is Charles, he should quit hiding it, come on out, he really isn't fooling anyone.

"Wheel of Fortune" was ending, "Jeopardy" was about to start, and revenge was on Sullivan's agenda.

He didn't spend that night on the floor curled up listening to his boyfriend's voice. He twisted the tuner to another station instead and cleaned house. When he went to bed he felt the sense of accomplishment that his Hoover always gave him, and a dull sleep overtook him. It was interrupted around three a.m. when a pizza delivery boy rang the apartment's doorbell. Sullivan opened the door and smiled the deranged smile of one who recognizes that half the battle is won in welcoming it.

"This had better be vegetarian, or I'm going to let loose on his T-shirt collection," Sullivan said.

He went back to the bedroom, located his jeans, found the total and a tip for the delivery boy, and wished him a pleasant rest-of-the-night. Sure enough, the pizza was Sullivan's favorite, but he refused to eat it. He stalked to the kitchen, to the junk drawer, returned with a felt-tip pen, and scrawled HA HA HA on the pizza box. He left the box propped up against the computer, where Chuck couldn't miss it, and went back to bed but couldn't sleep. He got back up, scratched out what he'd written, replaced it with YOUR DICK'S AS JUVENILE AS THIS JOKE, and felt better about the whole thing.

The next day, after babysitting the impatiens, Sullivan stopped off at the grocery store for some last-minute supplies, packed them inside his knapsack, and headed home. Tonight was Chuck's night off. Weekly, since the big move, they had set up a routine on this night. They competed with each other while watching "Jeopardy" and then took two beers in little brown lunch bags to the park across the street from their building and shot baskets. They rounded off the night with dinner and the choice of either a movie or a few matches of pool at the straight watering hole on the corner.

But tonight they were having new friends over for a late sit-down supper for six: themselves, the lesbian couple, and the young marrieds Sullivan was fond of who lived across the breezeway. All week, Sullivan had tried to figure out where to seat everybody and to come up with a flavorful menu. Anything but think about what was about to happen inside after he parked his bicycle. The parting hug he would receive any day now.

Sullivan opened the door and tried to resist giving in to a grand mal. The living room he'd so diligently cleaned the night before was now a mess worthy of a stiff drink and a rethinking of his life. CDs lay scattered on the floor. A bag of weed and three clean, white joints spilled out of the little malachite box on the coffee table. The now-embarrassing lid from the pizza box was taped to the wall over the stereo like art.

Chuck emerged from the bathroom, Q-tipping his ears. He was wearing his reading glasses and was James Deaning it this evening in a white T-shirt and sagging jeans, his hair damp and smelling of Prell, his feet bare and beautiful and padding to where Sullivan stood.

"What's up, man?" Chuck said. "Help you?" He laid his glasses and the Q-tip on the little doorside table, no doubt realizing what effect laying the used cotton swab on the furniture would have on his boyfriend. "I know you?"

"It's been a while, but your name's on the tip of my tongue."

Chuck wrapped Sullivan in his arms and began something close to what the courts in their state would construe as molestation. "Sull. My little Sully."

The long, tiring days seeped from Sullivan. The listening to the granular gravel as he stepped on it. The untangling of the hose as he watered the green fronds and leaves and flowers. They were replaced with quiltlike sensations akin to snacking between meals while revisiting a faithful, favorite book. Memory bathed him at the right temperature. He remembered why he'd written so passionately in his journal the night he and Chuck had met.

He remembered Chuck teaching him how to bowl. He remembered how, when he and Chuck went to protests, Chuck would always, between shouted slogans, mutter under his breath asides to him. Things like *I love you more than my snooze button,* or *I could eat you with a spork.*

Sullivan had long since ceased to actually see Chuck. Some strange sense, like bat sonar, guided him now and rendered what he saw as superfluous and obsolete. It was the same as when he watched "I Dream of Jeannie" and found Jeannie more attractive than her sister, even though they were played by the same actress. Chuck's aura of love had slowly overridden Chuck's appearance to the point that if he were to come home missing his nose, Sullivan wouldn't notice, or love him any less. And Chuck's nose was killer.

It was more than a little unfair that Chuck had lifted him up for so long and was tiring of the burden. Perhaps it was unfair of Sullivan to think the thought, too. He pulled himself away from Chuck's embrace.

"So what's going on in here?" Sullivan said. "Too neat for you?"

Chuck went and sat in the eye of the CD hurricane. "Getting the music together for tonight."

"Ah."

"Yeah."

"What's the DJ got planned, then?" Sullivan set his knapsack on the kitchen counter and began delivering forth the bottles of red wine, chickpeas, and that incense Chuck liked.

"When everybody gets here, not sure if we should have Guster or Ryan Adams playing."

"Guster, please."

"During dinner, Charlie Parker."

"*Massey Hall* or *The Essential*?"

"*Savoy and Dial.*"

"Please don't leave me." Sullivan looked down and fiddled with his belt loops. "I blurted. Sorry. I'm a blurter. You knew that when we first met each—"

"Okay, I won't." Chuck had his serious face on.

"You won't what?"

"Work on Maggie's farm no more. Sheesh. I won't leave you." Chuck began stacking his music and putting it away. "I've got an idea."

"Yeah, what?"

"Meet me on the couch. Say, now-ish."

Sullivan sat next to Chuck and waited. Chuck didn't say anything.

Sullivan picked up the joints. "What are these for?"

"For tonight. Figured, why not just leave them out? We're going to wind up sparking up anyway, if these people are going to be friends of ours."

"Chuck—"

"What? It's our house, for Pete's sake."

"All right, all right. You can at least arrange them nice." Sullivan placed one joint in front of the sofa where he'd planned on seating the lesbians, another in front of the mismatched easy chairs where the married couple would sit, and the last where he planned to sit with Chuck, facing the group on the hillbillyesque rag rug that Chuck's mom had given them years ago as a moving-in present. "Well, it was very nice of you to roll them. You're grade-A."

"You think I want to leave you."

Sullivan put the bag back into the malachite box and lidded it. "Yeah. I do."

"Man, Sull, are you dumb."

"I—"

"You're lucky I've got a thing for licking your dimples, because you're not getting far with me on your brains."

"Well, at least I've always known where pickles come from. You thought they grew on curly vines, back when I met you."

"Sully, what makes you think I would want to break up?"

"Well, what am I supposed to think? You're putting hangers in the bed."

"Right."

"You keep calling and hanging up on me. Make me get out of bed to pay for some pizza I didn't order."

"I don't like you sleeping without me, when I'm not here."

"Okay, well, I can't sleep at work. Why are you pranking on me? What did I ever do?"

"At least you're the one I'm pranking on. I'm not pranking on anybody else."

"That's the same logic a guy who abuses his wife uses, only he says, 'beating.'"

"I miss you," Chuck said. "Okay? I'll quit my job if I have to, but I can't keep not seeing you, or spending time with you, or sleeping next to you, every day like this. I can't. I'll get another job, so I can be on your schedule. But what I really wish is you'd just quit yours, and get on mine. It makes more sense that way... money-wise. You can't understand that?" He made for Sullivan's neck, which was of the sensitive variety. "Aw, Sulli-man. Snooze Button. I miss you."

Amid the slurping, Sullivan said, "Oh," and understood.

And a reassuring vision parted its velvet curtain before Sullivan's mind's eye. In it, the competition would wage on for the rest of their lives together. He and Chuck would eventually agree to the only kind of open relationship the two could tolerate, an endurance heat where each would see which one could remain faithful and resist outside temptation the longest. Sullivan knew he would be able to beat Chuck there and smiled. And the two of them would sit side by side in the retirement home each evening, skipping their meds, watching their game shows, and ridiculing the young doctors and nurses who thought of them as two harmless old men in bathrobes. They would adopt a dog, and likely as not would name him Henry, since Chuck was fixated on that name. Sullivan was already thinking of late-night jobs for which he was qualified, perhaps bar back or supermarket bag boy or janitor. It didn't really matter.

Sullivan looked at his watch and nuzzled the serious head on his chest with his nose. "It's almost time for Alex Trebek. You thirsty?"

"Yeah."

"Me too. Get me some apple juice?"

Chuck groaned and got up to head for the kitchen. While his back was turned, Sullivan checked himself in the mirror over the sofa and saw a fresh, red blotch on his neck that, in front of their new friends tonight, would bloom into an embarrassing, blackberry-colored hickey, one that would be a chore to explain and a chore not to. He imagined he could hear Chuck snickering in the kitchen.

Unluckily for Chuck, Sullivan had a contingency plan. He called out, "Whoever loses tonight on 'Jeopardy' has to cook. Unless you're chicken."

"My knowledge is fearsome, whelp. Best fear it."

Sullivan started the tape he'd made of the previous night's episode. Chuck rejoined him and commented on the graininess of the picture quality, but otherwise had little chance to speak. He lost his shirt as Sullivan proceeded to get every response correct, except two in Civil War Generals and one in Geography, so as not to rend the tender, white fabric of credibility.

Sullivan was the better cook; Chuck hated to cook, but there

was nothing else to be done about it. Besides, Sullivan liked to watch Chuck perform in the kitchen. There was something erotic about it, something as sick yet as thrilling as witnessing a fight, in watching Chuck use the measuring cup like a rookie, or throw a pinch of salt over his shoulder for luck, or dice up green and red and yellow peppers, and garlic and onions, and scoop them up with the blade of his knife, tossing them into the sizzling pan and turning to Sullivan to say something like, *Come on, man, who wouldn't want to eat this.* There was really nothing like it.

MATCHMAKER

Shawn Anniston

I stopped believing in romance in high school. I even knew the exact date: Saturday, May 14, 1994. I was a gawky, seventeen-year-old high school junior at his first formal dance. In the weeks leading up to prom, I decided not to take the easy way out by inviting Caitlin or Jessica or Jennifer. I was going solo for one reason, and his name was Kevin Bundrum.

Kevin had transferred into our school only a few months before, but he and I immediately connected in art class. All the other guys in the class were jocks who took art for an easy credit. The teacher, Mrs. Phillips, was the football coach's wife. But Kevin was serious about painting, and he appreciated my semester project, an ongoing comic strip about a misfit prodigy that was a blatant rip-off of "Calvin and Hobbes" and "FoxTrot."

Art was the only class we had together, but Kevin and I hung out with an eclectic group of friends between classes, after school, and on weekends. Most of us thought of ourselves as misunderstood, creative geniuses, but we were really just awkward teenagers. The best thing about my friends was that none of them cared that I was gay. The subject never came up between Kevin and me. I knew he knew and seemed to take it in stride. I thought Kevin was cute—in fact, I thought that a lot, especially at night when it was lights out at my house—but I just assumed he was straight. He never showed particular interest in anyone, female or male. Until about a month before prom, when he got coy.

"I was thinking," he said one day, his forehead wrinkled as he stared at the watercolor he was working on, "do you think it's geeky to go to prom?"

I shrugged and said, "I don't know. I hadn't thought about it."

"There's someone I've been thinking of asking, but I don't know if that person is interested."

The deliberate lack of a gender in his comment piqued my interest. "All you can do is ask."

"Maybe," he said. "It could be awkward though. I mean, if this person doesn't feel the way I feel, it could screw up our friendship. Also, other people might not..."

When he trailed off, my heart began pounding. He wanted to ask me out, but such a thing would be revolutionary in our school. No guy had ever asked another guy to prom. Would I say yes? Was I that brave? Other than with my close friends, I'd never been all that open about being gay.

I glanced nervously toward the football players scattered around the other tables, being obnoxious as they flirted with the girls while pretending to work on various pathetic projects. Kevin and I weren't even on their radar.

"What we should do," I said, "is get up a group of people. All go together. Safety in numbers, you know? Then if the moment seems right, you can do something to show you think this person's special."

"Like what?" Kevin asked, finally looking up.

Why hadn't I noticed that he wasn't just cute? He was gorgeous. Blue eyes, black lashes, brown hair that curled naturally to his shoulders and that he often pushed off his face. He reminded me of Eddie Vedder. But an Eddie Vedder who could smile. An Eddie Vedder who wasn't all cloaked in flannel angst. An Eddie Vedder who was going to be my secret prom date.

"I don't know. Take a rose. If you sense any interest, offer it to"—sudden dilemma: Should I say *her* or *him?*—"offer it to the object of your affection and ask for a slow dance or something."

"That's kind of romantic," Kevin said thoughtfully.

From then on, we referred to Kevin's potential prom date as "Object." It was our own little flirtatious game, and I pretended to have no idea he was talking about me when he'd say something like, "I wonder if Object would like me better in a suit or a tux?"

"Go all out," I suggested. "Object's worth it. And my mother insists that *I* rent a tux."

The idea of the two of us dressed formally, dancing cheek to check, kept me flying for days.

"Are you sure I should get Object a rose?" he asked one day as we bumped into each other at our lockers. "Maybe that's too pushy. Maybe Object would like something that doesn't scream, 'Couple!' "

"You can never go wrong with a rose," I insisted, thinking of Kevin looking at me with his Eddie Vedder eyes—except not so angry—as he offered me a single, long-stemmed red rose.

Unlike every bad movie I'd ever seen about teenagers, nothing went wrong the day of prom. My tux was a perfect fit. I had no zits. My hair was adequately cool. My parents did nothing stupid. My little sister didn't hide anything or lock me out of the bathroom. It was clearly going to be a perfect night, the most romantic of my life. I had complete faith in that until the moment Kevin crossed the ballroom at the Hilton and offered a single, long-stemmed rose to Caitlin, who blushed, followed him to the dance floor, and transformed me from dumb boy to bitter man.

No wonder Eddie Vedder always looked so pissed off.

Amanda and I met when she was a college student and I was working in her dorm's cafeteria. I'd already graduated and found out that a degree in art history was helpful when dishing out bowls of macaroni and cheese as garishly colored as an Emile Nolde painting. Vegetables too lackluster for anything resembling a James Peale still life. Bland meat so limp that it might have been on a Dali canvas titled *The Resistance of Thyme*.

It didn't really bother me to dish out carbs to bratty college kids. Like the food I served, I was invisible to them. For me, it was a job that paid decently and gave me enough time off to do other things. Weekends, I went out to our local gay club and danced. Weeknights, I frittered away hours online. Sometimes I made a halfhearted attempt at doing something creative. Romance was dead to me, but I still loved art.

Amanda recognized that immediately on a day when I pushed a bowl of salad under the sneeze guard for her and she spotted the tattoo of Rodrigue's *Blue Dog* on my wrist.

"Hey, I've got a poster like that in my room," she said. "I love *Blue Dog*."

I nodded and spooned carrot and raisin salad into a bowl for the next student in line. Amanda moved on. When I got off later, she was standing outside the door of the cafeteria.

"Hey, you want to, I don't know, get coffee or something?"

"I smell like dorm food, and I'm not really—"

"I'm a lesbian," she said. "I'm not asking you out. You're just the first person I've met on this campus who knows about *Blue Dog*."

I had coffee with her that day. Pizza with her that night. We went to a Bogie and Bacall film festival that weekend. Eventually, we were absorbed into each other's groups of friends, apartments, lives. By the time she graduated from college, I had a job archiving the papers of the recently deceased patroness of our city's fine arts museum. Amanda got a job counseling at a free clinic, where she met her girlfriend, Melissa, a nurse. Ultimately, the three of us became roommates.

While Amanda could be capricious, Melissa was a rock. Even though I'd known Amanda first, I liked them equally. The longer they were together, the more alike they became, with their dyed black hair, jangling silver jewelry, multiple ear piercings, and funky dresses worn over clunky boots. They even had companion tattoos: Peppermint Patty on Melissa's left arm and Marcy on Amanda's right arm, so when they stood side by side, it was a lesbian "Peanuts" festival. They even called each other "Peanut" and were often referred to as "the Peanuts" by our friends.

It didn't bother me when they got all mushy with each other. Romance seemed the rightful domain of women. I asked only two things of them: that they not rope me into their sentimental nonsense and that roses never be part of the picture.

"You're like that character in *Tales of the City*," Melissa once said. "The one who got mixed up with the religious cannibals."

"Ha. Cannibalism is right," I said. "Romance eats you from the inside out. Romance is the big lie. The first and final stage of a disease that attacks your mental health and then—"

"I think you protest too much," Amanda said. "Just wait. One day, I'll introduce you to a man who changes your mind about hearts and flowers."

"I can find my own men, thanks," I said.

It was true, too. It was rarely hard to get a first date. If he didn't want a second, that was all good. Men who tried to go beyond three or four dates found that my heart had turned to granite. In the best cases, my dates who didn't end up as tricks became friends.

Things went along fine, until Amanda's big announcement on my twenty-ninth birthday.

"What do you mean, you're pregnant?" I demanded. "Lesbians don't get pregnant!"

Melissa's expression was deadpan as Amanda said, "You know how moronic that sounds, right?"

"What—When—How'd you get pregnant?" I sputtered.

"First, an angel appeared in a flash of light."

"Seriously. If you did that whole turkey baster thing, how come I wasn't included? Or at least informed?"

"No kitchen gadgets were involved," Amanda said. "I got pregnant the old-fashioned way."

When I looked at Melissa with mock awe, she said, "Don't be ridiculous. I've never even been near a penis except in a medical capacity. But she has. With my blessing."

I stared at them, my silence reaching like tentacles into their secretive little souls, until Amanda said, "Christmas. When we went to my parents' house. Remember I told you I saw Frederick?"

"Your middle school boyfriend? You had sex with *him?*" She nodded. "With the intention of getting pregnant?" Another nod. "Why Frederick?"

"You mean why not you, don't you?" Melissa asked.

"We thought it would complicate things if we picked you," Amanda said. "Frederick was willing, and he's moving to Vancouver, which geographically eliminates him as a complication in the baby's life."

I managed to choke out something congratulatory before I offended Amanda and her careening hormones, but inside I was thinking, *Baby? Baby! What kind of complication will a baby be in* my *life?* It wasn't my best moment, probably, but putting one's self first was, as far as I was concerned, what any sane person did.

Sometime around Amanda's fifth month, I began to pick up subtle signals from her. Subtle in the way of a screaming jet engine.

"I met the nicest man at the clinic today," she said.

"Crabs, syphilis, or herpes?" I asked.

"He's a drug rep," Amanda said. Her voice was sulky, but I didn't dare accuse her of a bad mood. The more victimized she was by her hormones, the more she insisted that it was everyone else, not her, whose moods shifted like a liar's eyes. "Todd. Tall. Blond. Great ass."

"Frederick really changed you," I said, peeling the apple I took from a bowl of fruit on the kitchen counter.

"Todd's gay, you idiot. I gave him your number."

"Oh, no, you didn't," I said.

"I hate it when you do that," Melissa said as she walked into the kitchen. "You sound like a cross between Rosie Perez and Rose Marie."

"Who's Rose Marie?"

"Never mind that," Amanda said. "Seriously, would it kill you to go on one date with the guy?"

"He *is* nice," Melissa said. "He has a great apartment in one of those mid-rises they renovated downtown."

"Fine," I said.

I'd been having a dry spell lately. It wouldn't hurt to meet this Todd.

"Todd's first mistake," I complained to my friend Mick on the phone, "was opening the door for me when I walked out to the BMW Z4 Roadster parked at the curb. Too much car, too much money, too much chivalry. He had the temerity to pull out my chair in the restaurant!"

"That bastard," Mick said.

"There were candles on the table. And linen napkins."

"I hope you gave him a piece of—"

"My mind? Of course not. I was the perfect gentleman. I just blocked his number from my phone."

"Smart move," Mick said. "How inconsiderate for the Peanuts to subject you to that."

"I know," I said. "It better not happen again."

Melissa made her move two weeks later. We were sharing a bag of microwave popcorn and watching "The Facts of Life" on Nickelodeon when she said, "Did I tell you that my cousin finally got moved in?"

"What cousin? Moved in where?"

"My cousin Charlie. The one with the Siamese cat. The lawyer?"

"I've never heard of this person in my life."

"You never listen. I'm always talking about cousin Charlie."

My inner alarm was triggered, and I made a wild guess. "Is he the gay cousin?"

"That's him! Anyway, you know those new condos out on River Road? He's leasing one with an option to buy. Those things are huge! We should take a ride out there sometime."

"Uh-huh," I said and stared at the TV, pretending to be riveted by Blair's cousin Geri, an aspiring comic with cerebral palsy. "The Facts of Life" wasn't just entertainment; it was a public service announcement.

I wasn't at all surprised a couple of days later when Melissa and Amanda suggested a detour on the way back from the grocery store. Nor was I surprised that cousin Charlie just happened to be home, had a couple of bottles of wine chilling in the fridge, and even whipped a dish of stuffed mushrooms out of the oven. Wasn't everyone similarly prepared for drop-in guests?

"So they wanted you to meet him," Mick said. "And he was nice enough to provide munchies. What's wrong with that? Is it because he's a lawyer? Not *all* lawyers are bad."

"He's a lawyer who had cut flowers on his dining room table," I said.

"Shameful."

Spitting out one word at a time for emphasis, I said, "He put a rosebud in a buttonhole of my shirt as I was leaving."

"God, did Melissa have to sedate you?"

"Sarcasm is one of the least appealing qualities in any friend," I said.

"At least I don't bring you flowers," Mick said.

And so it went. Week after week. Even in the third trimester of her pregnancy, Amanda had an unerring instinct for finding single gay men. Craig wanted to go for a moonlight swim in the pool behind his suburban ranch full of Berber carpet. Damian invited me to dinner at his garden home and surprised me with tickets to a local theater production. Arnie's entire upper-floor apartment in a restored Victorian contained an extensive DVD library with every romantic comedy featuring Julia Roberts, Drew Barrymore, and Sandra Bullock. Will's split-level located deep within a gated community overlooked a pond that had actual swans. The swans intrigued me, so I consented to a second date. It ended badly when he wanted to give me a full body massage with scented oils.

"What the hell is wrong with these men?" I demanded of Mick. "Have they no pride? Can't they just scratch their balls and offer me a can of Budweiser? Why must I be always tormented with moonlight and roses?"

"You poor lamb," Mick said.

I should have known Mick wouldn't sympathize. I'd actually introduced him to Paul, the engineer with his own sailboat and a cabin on the water, and they were already planning to move in together.

Was there no place in the world for a clear-eyed realist?

The first snag at the Buffy Benning Birthing Center was the news that Amanda's doctor was out of town.

"But she knew the baby might come a few days early," Amanda growled, looking a lot like a *Jurassic Park* raptor.

"It'll be fine," Melissa said soothingly.

"It will be," the admissions clerk told her. "Dr. Fannin has delivered hundreds of babies. You couldn't be in better hands."

Amanda was slightly mollified until Dr. Fannin actually visited her in the birth room.

"You're a man," she hissed, her eyes glowing with reptilian menace.

I would have looked for evidence of a raptor egg, but I was trying not to drool as I stared at Dr. Fannin. I didn't know why he was having that effect on me. He was tall and slim and nothing close to my type. I had a thing for smooth chests, and the *V* of his scrubs showed a dusting of dark hair. I was attracted to men with light eyes, and his were brown. Messy hair appealed to me, and his was buzz cut. I liked big hands, but his fingers were slender, almost delicate. The mouths I most enjoyed kissing had full lips; his were average. I couldn't really check out his ass because of the lab coat, but his narrow hips didn't offer much promise in the way of the fleshy melons hyped in porn novels.

"When your pains are closer together, you won't care what gender I am," Dr. Fannin said. "Let's take a look."

Melissa directed a pointed stare my way. I smiled sweetly and said, "I wouldn't dream of leaving my little Peanut at a time like this."

I had no idea what time it was when I finally staggered out of Amanda's birthing suite. The sun had gone down. The preceding hours had been among the most grueling of my life. There was nothing I could do to draw Dr. Fannin's attention to me when Amanda was making such a production of yelling, dilating, panting, and cussing, and I was exhausted from trying. If Amanda hadn't finally pushed her daughter into the world, I would have gone in after her.

In the space of an afternoon, I'd become a man possessed. I'd moved beyond Dr. Fannin's many physical shortcomings to catalog his other flaws. What kind of freak kept a sense of humor when women were screaming at him? His polite professionalism in the face of natal carnage surely indicated he was on serious mood stabilizers or had no soul. My own nerves were shattered, and I *liked* the Peanuts.

The doctor's only redeeming feature was revealed when a nurse came in to tell him that he had a call from his framing contractor. When he came back to the birth room visibly annoyed, Melissa attempted small talk by asking if everything was okay.

"Never build a house," he said. "Apparently there's a problem with my foundation. I'll be lucky if I'm not stuck in my efficiency apartment another year."

Amanda's bellows cut the conversation short, and Susannah Lynn finally made her appearance.

There was a different clerk in admissions, and I asked if she knew where I could find Dr. Fannin so I could thank him.

"Well, I shouldn't tell you," she said with a guilty look around. She dropped her voice and said, "If you go out the side door and follow the path, you'll come to a gazebo. He's probably there smoking."

Even though I didn't smoke, the fact that he did made me happy, because yet another flaw made him more approachable.

The pea gravel crunched under my feet, so he was forewarned of my arrival.

"I wasn't sure if I said thank you," I answered his inquisitive look.

"All in a day's work," he said. "The baby is—"

"Not mine," I said firmly. "Amanda and Melissa are my roommates. I'm a virgin. With women, I mean."

"Ah," he said.

I couldn't think of a single sensible comment, so instead I said, "I don't suppose you have another cigarette?"

He held out a pack of Parliaments and his lighter. I tried not to cough when I lit my cigarette, but smoking was never one of my charms. I could only hope I also had Bette Davis eyes as I spit puffs of smoke.

"How many kids do you have?" I asked.

"None."

"Oh, well, I'm sure there's plenty of time for you and your wife—"

"I'm single," he said. Whatever happened on my face made him smile. "I'm not a virgin with women."

"Ah," I mimicked him and tried not to look crestfallen.

He smiled again and said, "I'm not a virgin with men, either."

I couldn't stop the stupid grin that spread across my face as I said, "Would you like to go out sometime?"

"This is very common," he said. "You're caught up in the moment. You see me as a powerful part of the miracle of life. After a few weeks of soggy diapers, smelly formula, and sleepless nights, all thoughts of romance will vanish."

"Oh, I already don't believe in romance," I assured him.

"One month," he said.

"Pardon?"

"Give it one month. If you still want to go out, call me, and we'll talk."

"It's a date."

I lasted three days before I called him, opening with, "I like to plan ahead. What kinds of things do you enjoy doing in your spare time?"

"I'm a doctor," he said. "I don't have spare time."

"Would you happen to have a spare hour? You know, for a predate interview."

After a pause, he said, "Thursday at noon. I have one hour. That's all." He gave me directions to his office.

On Thursday, Melissa came home for lunch as I was packing a picnic basket from Pier One that she and Amanda always took to free outdoor concerts. Her eyebrows shot up, and she asked, "What the hell are you doing?"

"I'm taking my lunch to the lake. I have a folder of Mrs. Delisle's notes and correspondence to read and catalog," I lied, "but it's too nice a day to work inside."

"I wish I had that option," she said. She grabbed an orange and started picking at it. "Sorry if the baby kept waking you up last night. She was really fussy."

"I never heard a thing," I assured her. "Slept like a rock."

"Lucky you," she said, and left the kitchen to hang out with Amanda and the baby raptor.

We sat cross-legged on top of a picnic table at the lake and ate the sandwiches I'd made.

"I can't believe I let you talk me into this," Dr. Fannin said.

"It's for the best," I insisted. "Taking a break refreshes you. You could probably find a cure for cancer if you spent less time in the office."

"Not my field," he said.

"Then you can discover a cure for having babies."

"I warned you it's not easy living with an infant," he reminded me.

"It's a big house," I said. "I barely know she's there."

We did a little of the backstory thing while we ate. He was from a big family. His mother was also a doctor. His father was an architect. His brothers and sisters were scattered all over the country. He wanted a big house so his family could visit occasionally, especially his nieces and nephews.

Our conversation was satisfying proof that he was the wrong man for me. Too stable. Too lovable. Any minute he'd tell me he had a golden retriever and memberships in book clubs, the symphony, and Big Brothers.

As we were climbing down from the table so I could drive him back to work, our heads almost bumped, and he kissed me.

I decided his lips weren't so average after all.

Not calling him or seeing him for a month was a good idea. It would give me time to get over my senseless fixation.

Four days later, I called him late in the afternoon to see if he wanted to eat sushi.

"It's not a date," I said. "My favorite sushi place is a hole in the wall. I'd never take a date there. It's just that I have to eat, and I figured you do, too."

"I like sushi," he said. "But I'm supposed to meet my contractor at the house site. Why don't I pick you up after that?"

"Why don't I pick you up now and go to the site with you?" I asked. I wasn't ready to relinquish the driver's seat.

Later, I walked around his property while he smoked and talked to men in hard hats. I'd figured him for some ritzy subdivision where everyone made at least ten times my annual income, but his property was miles outside the city. I spotted pecan trees, oaks, thirteen potentially rabid squirrels, and poison ivy.

"You probably won't even break out," he said later as I sat on the kitchen counter in his tiny apartment while he rubbed calamine lotion on my bare arms. "This is just a precaution."

"So you said about the hot shower," I said, "but I think you just wanted to see me in a towel."

"It's a good look for you," he said. "Seriously, though, the hot water cure has always worked for me. You can't wear your clothes again until you've washed them. I just need to find something around here that you can fit into."

He glanced up in time to catch my smile.

"Well, there *is* that," he conceded. "But I was thinking of hospital scrubs."

"Getting into your scrubs was my plan from the start," I said.

The Peanuts were beginning to get suspicious about my unexplained absences and air of distraction. I wasn't about to divulge any information regarding the good doctor. I was afraid they'd start putting up *Little Mermaid* wallpaper in my bedroom.

"That's insane," Mick said when I called to complain about that. I was sure he sounded impatient because of his frustration with some project at work.

"No, it's not. Why do you think they spent months introducing me to men whose best features were residential? They've been trying to push me out of their nest ever since Amanda peed on her pregnancy test strip."

"No, I meant *Little Mermaid* wallpaper. Melissa hates that movie. She believes it contains a message to girls that they should give up everything for a man."

"Okay, maybe they'll paper the room with *Ms.* magazine covers. But I'm not going anywhere."

"Not even for Dr.—does he have a first name?"

"I prefer that we continue to call him Dr. Fannin," I said. "It maintains the proper distance between us."

"What distance?"

Disgruntled, I cut the call short. Mick's perception had been distorted ever since he'd moved in with Paul. I'd only seen Dr. Fannin a few times. It wasn't like I was pursuing him. But just in case anyone else was getting that impression, I resolved to go beyond the monthlong waiting period before I called him again. If I called him again.

It felt liberating to be dancing at the club again. Though it wasn't late, many of us had already pulled off our T-shirts as we gyrated among the crowd of tanned, sweaty bodies. I'd caught the eye of a cute blond who hooked a finger in the waist of my jeans and pulled me toward him.

I waved my arms over my head and gave him my most suggestive look. He grinned and yelled, "Let's get out of here."

"Really?" I asked. I was having a good time. I wasn't sure I was interested in leaving to trick.

He leaned close, licked the edge of my ear, and asked, "Why not? You know what you want. I know what I want. What's the point of wasting time with conversation, flirtation, and suggestion? Why cut *to* the chase when you can cut *out* the chase and get right to a satisfying ending?"

Amanda and Melissa were snuggled up on the couch watching TV when I got home.

"Wow, you're back early," Melissa said.

"It was boring," I said. I still couldn't believe I'd passed up the chance to go home with a hot guy. Maybe I was coming down with something. I felt okay, though.

Amanda patted the space next to her and said, "You can have a wild and crazy time with us. We're watching a 'Full House' marathon."

"All right, all right, I get it," I huffed. When they stared blankly at me, I said, "You don't have to talk about how miserable I must be when Susannah cries all night. Or how sorry you are that the trash reeks of dirty diapers. You don't have to apologize every time I open the refrigerator and see your expressed milk on the top shelf. You don't have to make veiled comments about *full houses*. You want me to move out so you can be a happy little family. I'll start looking for my own place next week."

"Are you high?" Melissa asked.

"*You're* our happy little family," Amanda added.

"Then why'd you keep trying to fix me up with men by telling me what great houses they had?"

"Is it possible that you heard things we weren't saying?" Amanda asked. "Nobody wants you to move out."

"Seriously?"

They both nodded vigorously, and I said, "Good. Because... Because good. That's all."

I flopped down on the couch, and Amanda rested her head on my shoulder while Melissa turned up the volume on "Full House." Unfortunately, we were just in time to see D.J. catch her boyfriend Steve kissing his ex-girlfriend Rachel at the prom.

"Oops," Amanda said.

"Please," I said. "It was twelve years ago. I'm over it." Melissa snorted. "I am!"

Now that I knew my home was safely mine as long as I wanted it to be, I worked to make it better. When I wasn't sharing baby duty, I put new caulking around the windows and doors before the weather got too cold. We turned what had once been our junk room into a nursery, and Amanda and I together painted murals on the walls: an underwater paradise of fish and bright sea vegetation with no mermaids.

It was nice nesting with the Peanuts, and I stopped going to the club on weekends. Date deadline passed, but I never called Dr. Fannin. Maybe I was hibernating; I'd emerge in the spring to make new conquests.

I was home alone one day when someone knocked on the front door. I opened it to find Dr. Fannin standing on the doorstep with a bouquet of flowers. Including roses. My hackles went up.

"What are those?" I asked, as if he were holding a bag of scorpions.

"Flowers," he said. "Amanda seemed a little blue when she had her checkup yesterday. I thought these might lift her spirits."

I regarded him suspiciously, sure that Amanda had been matchmaking again, and said, "Do you take flowers to all your postpartum depressives?"

"Just the ones with charming roommates who lose my phone number," Dr. Fannin said.

I stared at him. He stared back. I stared harder. He dropped the flowers on the floor as he stepped over the threshold and hugged me. I wasn't sure which of us closed the door, but I knew it had to have been me who led us to my bedroom, since he didn't know the way.

He didn't need any other guidance from me, however, and later, when the lights were back on and the condoms were properly disposed of, he wrapped my quilt around us.

"Don't get too comfortable," I said. "It's not like I invited you to move in. In fact, I don't remember even saying you could walk through the door."

"You owed me a date," he said.

"I changed my mind."

"That's okay. I decided early on that I like the way you don't date me. We can keep not dating, if that's what you want."

I thought it over and finally said, "Yeah. That works for me."

"Good." He kissed me.

"You're not going to turn this into some big romance, are you? Because I don't believe in romance."

"Never," he promised and kissed me again.

A VIEW

Brandon M. Long

It took me a minute to figure out what was going on when my alarm clock started that high-pitched whining noise. Another Monday. The weekend went by entirely too fast. I got a lot done, but it was all housekeeping crap: grocery shopping, laundry. I cleaned the house and got bills mailed off. I went to see a movie with my friends Jen and Dan, but it was so bad that I put a mental block on it and tried to force it out of my memory. The high point of the weekend was sitting in our favorite pub after the movie and laughing at Dan when he tipped his newly delivered pint all over the table. Good times!

After I managed to whack at the alarm clock enough to shut it off, I grumbled as I heaved myself out of bed. One of my feet was tangled in the blanket, and I nearly did a face plant as I stood up. Oh, yeah, it was going to be a great day.

I went down the hall to the kitchen, ricocheting off the walls like a drunk, and hit the button on the coffeemaker. The built-in grinder began to whirl as I headed to the bathroom.

I turned on the shower to get it warmed up and looked at myself in the mirror. Not too bad. My black hair was just starting to get a touch of white at the temples. Other gay men my age might freak out and have it colored, but it wasn't a big deal to me. Despite all the time I spent outside, my skin was fair, and thanks to good genetics, it had always been clear. I spent just enough time at the gym to keep the belly at bay. I gave the chest hair an occasional trim to keep from getting too beastlike, but that was about as far as my vanity went. I realized that it flew in the face of all the stereotypes of the primping fag, but that had never really been my style.

After nodding approval to my reflection, I hopped in the shower and tried to get my body working fast enough that I wouldn't be late for work. Spring was still a few weeks off, so I'd been spending all my time in the lab, and the office workers always made note of who came in late or left early. Busybodies.

The hot water felt really good, so I ended up taking a longer shower than I should have. After brushing my teeth and slapping some gel in my hair, I threw on the first things I found in the closet, grabbed some coffee and a yogurt, and headed out the door.

The freeways around Seattle were always a mess. It didn't matter what time of day or night: a mess. I ended up being fifteen minutes late. The harpy at the front desk shot me a nasty look when I walked in. Oh, well. The caffeine was starting to kick in, and the day was looking up.

I logged onto my computer and checked my email.

"Rats," I said aloud.

My boss had sent me an email late Friday, after I'd left, to let me know there would be a group of potential investors coming through for a tour early Monday. I wondered if he did these things on purpose. Since I was running late, the group would be coming through my lab any minute. I hurriedly ran around trying to organize and tidy up.

I was in the process of cleaning out some sample dishes that had gotten a bit slimy over the weekend when I heard a knock at the door. Without waiting for a response, my boss walked in with four other people in tow: two women and two men. One of the women looked like a professional golfer. The other woman reminded me of a librarian who would sooner shush you than look at you.

Both of the men were wearing suits. The one in the dark suit impressed me as the typical corporate type. Far too busy and important to be doing anything so menial as touring a botanical lab. The other guy had on a light gray suit. Besides his attire, the first thing I noticed about him were gray eyes that seemed a perfect match to the suit. His dark brown hair was cropped fairly short and had a controlled mess thing happening. He wasn't particularly tanned, but his skin wasn't fair, either. His jaw was angular, and I could just make out the shadow of whiskers beneath his skin. His nose was straight and in perfect proportion to his face, and his lips were full and pulled back into something between a smile and a smirk. It was hard to tell his age from his looks, but I guessed that he was maybe a couple of years older than me.

It suddenly occurred to me that I'd been staring and hadn't heard whatever it was my boss was saying. I put the dish in the sink and grabbed a towel to dry my hands.

"What was that?" I asked.

"I was just saying that these are the folks from M. C. Knight Corporation. They're here to take a look around," my boss replied. He was a good man and didn't seem upset that I hadn't been paying attention to him.

I took a couple of steps forward and extended my hand to

the guy in the dark suit. He shook it but didn't say anything. I turned toward the librarian and golfer and shook their hands as well, and they both introduced themselves. I finally made it to the light suit. While he shook my hand, he told me that his name was William Knight.

"As in M. C. Knight, Knight?" I asked with a smile.

"Matthew is my uncle," he replied.

When he smiled back, I saw that his teeth were perfectly straight and bright white. I was a sucker for a nice smile and pretty chompers. He held the handshake a bit longer than was necessary, letting go when Jim, my boss, introduced me as, "Christian Ellsborn, our most talented plant guy."

"Chris, please," I said to the group. "And as far as the plants go, they're already out there; they just need to be found." I gave them my most charming smile.

Jim explained how I spent most of the season in the field identifying plants that might have cosmetic uses. At his urging, I detailed the plant characteristics I looked for and how I collected and processed samples. I made a joke about trying to figure out which extracts made good lotions and which made your nipples fall off. Nobody but the gray suit so much as smiled, but then again, he hadn't quit smiling during my extended monologue.

Jim chimed in to say that when I brought plants back to the lab and checked them out, I sent anything with promise down to the "boys" in the chemistry lab. (All of the "boys" in the chem lab were actually women.) For Jim to say that I was the "most talented plant guy" was a nice compliment, but also simple fact. The only other plant "person" at the company was a woman who dealt with aquatic plants. I figured the guests didn't need to know that tidbit.

The visitors seemed completely bored by all of this, except William, who appeared genuinely interested. He nodded and smiled while I explained the hazards of handling unknown plants. I kept rambling, unsure what to do with my hands.

When Jim finally said, "Let's leave Chris to his work and take a look at the chemistry lab," they followed him from my lab like a line of baby ducks.

I continued to stand there for a minute, feeling like a blithering idiot. I finally went back to washing out my sample containers and fiddling with busywork. I wouldn't really have all that much to do until the weather turned nice enough for me to go in the field again.

After about half an hour, there was a knock at the open door. I turned to see William walking into the lab.

"I'm sorry about that intrusion," he said. "These things are never fun for anybody."

"No biggie," I replied. "I'm pretty slow this time of year anyway."

"I was just wondering," he paused, "if you ever go collecting in the islands?"

"I have a couple of times," I said, "but most of the islands have been so developed that there aren't a lot of native areas left."

He nodded and said, "My family has a place in the San Juans. They bought it before development really started tearing things up. Maybe you'd be interested in taking a look sometime?"

"Definitely," I said. "How big is the lot?"

"Well, actually," he stammered a bit before continuing, "it's the whole island."

All I could come up with was, "Wow."

"It's a small island." He grinned. "If you have a card, I could call you sometime and make the arrangements."

I opened one of the drawers and fished around until I found one of my seldom-used business cards. I handed it to him.

"The number and email address are on there. Thanks," I

continued. "It would be fun to see what it looked like before all the construction."

He glanced at the card before stuffing it into his pants pocket. "I'll definitely be in touch," he said. He shook my hand again and left.

When I got home that night, I called my friend Tim Finn (it was always first *and* last name, didn't know why, some things you didn't question), who wasn't home, but his boyfriend, Noah, answered. I told Noah about the cute guy who'd visited my lab and offered to let me do plant scouting on his island.

Noah seemed intrigued and asked, "Think he's family?"

"Don't know," I replied. "Doesn't matter anyway. Looked a bit too stuffy for me. Damn cute though."

"At the risk of sounding like Jen," Noah said, "do you know that he's stuffy, or is that a projection to deflect your own insecurities?"

I sometimes forgot that Tim Finn had hooked up with a psychologist.

"That does sound like Jennifer," I replied. "And it's even less pretty coming out of you."

Noah just chuckled and said, "Fair enough. You didn't ask for my opinion, so I shouldn't offer it."

"Hey, you can offer any opinion you want, but you ought to know by now that I probably won't listen."

"Again, fair enough," he said.

I heard Tim Finn in the background, but I didn't want to go into the whole thing again. I told Noah to fill him in before we said good-bye.

I changed my clothes and headed to the gym. It wasn't a particularly heavy workout, but then again, it rarely was for me. When I got home, I broiled some fish and ate in front of the TV. There really wasn't anything on, so it wasn't like I could say that

I actually watched anything. I cleaned the kitchen and myself, put on a pair of boxer shorts, and plopped back down on the sofa to play a video game. Boring, and pretty much status quo for a weeknight. I finally dragged myself to bed so I could sleep and start the whole cycle again the following day.

When I got to work the next morning, the light on my phone indicated that I had voice mail. I dialed in to retrieve my one message and heard, "Hey, Chris, it's Will. Will Knight. I was hoping to catch you before you left, but I guess I'll send you an email instead. Later."

The time stamp was Monday at 5:45. Forty-five minutes after I'd left. I logged onto the computer, curious as to what he wanted, and skimmed through my in-box until I spotted e-mail from an external source: WKnight@knightindustries.com. I opened and read through it. I went back and read it again. And then, a third time.

Chris: It was nice meeting you. I hope that you're able to visit the island this spring. I think you'll enjoy all the plant life. Somebody should. Also, I was wondering if you might consider having dinner or drinks with me sometime. Maybe this weekend? I hope that's not too forward, and if I misread the situation, please forgive me, I mean no offense. Hope to hear from you soon. Will.

I really didn't know what to make of it. I stared at the screen for a while. How was I going to respond? Did I want to go out with him? I thought about what Noah had said. Was I projecting something onto Will without knowing it?

The refrain that kept running through my head was, *Way too much thinking this early in the morning.* I needed coffee.

As I sipped my caffeine fix, I kept talking myself back and

forth. On one hand, he was cute, and what would it hurt to have drinks with him? On the other hand, did I really want to start up that kind of potential drama?

I decided that the situation didn't demand an immediate conclusion and mentally set it aside. I more or less coasted through the rest of my day.

When I got home that evening, I called Jennifer. As soon as she answered the phone, I realized my mistake. She was most assuredly not the person to talk to about this. I didn't need another lesson on the symptoms of "Princess Syndrome." This was Jen's belief that I had a fixed set of criteria that I'd romanticized to the point that no one could possibly live up to it. She said that if I couldn't see Prince Charming right off the bat, I didn't even give a man a second look.

I made small talk with her for a bit, invented an excuse to get off the line, and called Dan. If anyone could understand my dilemma, it was Dan.

He didn't answer at home or on his cell, so I left a message. I didn't feel like going to the gym and decided to take a walk around the neighborhood. It was kind of chilly, but the rains had stopped for a while, and I thought it would be nice to get outside.

I wandered down a couple of blocks, cut over to Cedar Avenue, and walked until I got to the park. I stopped at a viewing terrace at the far end, sat down on a bench, and looked out over the Sound. It really was a nice evening. The skies were clear, and I could make out the trees on the islands. The windbreaker I'd put on was enough to keep me comfortable, so I just sat.

My reverie was broken by the sound of "Zip-A-Dee-Doo-Dah" from my cell phone. It was Dan.

"Hey, dude."

"Waz up?" he asked.

"Nada, really. I just wanted your opinion on something."

"I'm here for you, bro. Lay it on me."

He certainly seemed to be in a good mood. I filled him in on the background of my situation with Mr. William Knight. Dan immediately tagged him with the moniker "Billy."

"Did you say anything that might have made Billy think you were interested?" Dan asked.

"No, it was all work stuff. I mean, I was kind of staring a bit, but I don't think it was that overt."

"Was it one of your gaga stares? You know, when your mouth hangs open and your eyes gloss over? Did you go all dyslexic?"

"I don't do that," I replied indignantly.

"Like hell you don't," he shot back. "You do it all the time. Some cute guy talks to you and you go all retarded."

"No, I don't."

"Remember that guy at Louie's a few weeks ago?" he asked. Without waiting for a reply, he continued. "He asked you how to find the bathroom, and you told him, 'Go to the last stair and take a left at the tables.'"

"So I got a little tongue tied. Big deal."

"Cuz he was hot. If he'd been ugly, you wouldn't have given it a second thought. Chris, there are no stairs at Louie's."

"Oh, shut up. That has nothing to do with this. This guy asks me out and I ask your advice. How does that end up as a make-fun-of-Chris session?" I asked.

"Okay, okay. Why is it even an issue? Why *wouldn't* you go out with him?" Dan asked. "He didn't ask you to tie him up and spank him with a Barbie, did he?"

"Look, I don't need this kinda grief. If I wanted to be mocked, I'd call Jen," I replied.

"I'm not mocking you. I just meant that it seems like a no-brainer to me," he said sincerely. "You said he's cute. And rich never hurts."

"That's another thing," I interjected. "Seems like it might be a bit awkward going out with someone like that."

"You rich folks should stick together," Dan said. "Then you can all hang out up there on your pedestals."

"What the hell are you talking about?" I asked. "After paying my bills last weekend, I have seventy-six dollars in my checking account. That hardly constitutes rich."

"Your grandma has money. Your parents have money," he replied.

"Okay? Nana's got money; I don't."

"Yeah, yeah. Rich people never admit to being rich."

"You're nuts," I said.

"So, you gonna date him or what?" Dan asked.

"Well, *you* haven't helped me one whit," I answered. "I guess I might as well have dinner with him. It's not like he has my home number or anything. If it gets too weird...I jump ship."

"There you go!" Dan said. "Go into it with a healthy, positive attitude."

"Shut up."

On the walk home, I considered all the things that could go wrong if I accepted Will's invitation. It finally occurred to me that I was doing exactly what Noah, Dan, and Jen (if I'd given her the chance) had accused me of doing.

I let myself into my condo and immediately logged onto my computer, opened my work account, and replied to his email. I suggested that we meet somewhere on Saturday evening, but I'd let him choose the time and place. I hesitated momentarily before pressing the Send button.

By the time I was finished checking my personal email, there was a response from Will.

Chris: I'm glad you've agreed. Saturday is great. Let's meet at Giovanni's at eight. I'm really looking forward to this. Will.

For better or worse, I'd committed myself to something that simultaneously excited and scared the crap out of me.

I skated through the rest of the week and landed myself at Giovanni's twenty minutes early. I was sitting on a chair in the lobby when the maitre d' walked over to me. "Are you Mr. Ellsborn?"

"Yes. I'm waiting for someone." It occurred to me that he must know that since he knew my name.

"Mr. Knight just phoned and asked that you be seated at his table. He apologizes that he's running a bit behind, but he should be here shortly. Please follow me."

He led me to a table situated near a window that had a terrific view of the city's skyline. I asked my waiter for a very dry martini. I wanted something to sip, but I didn't want to be hammered when Will showed up. I wondered how long he'd be. And why he had his own table at Giovanni's. And what I'd gotten myself into. And if my trousers made me look fat.

I occupied myself sipping my drink and playing with breadsticks that I took from a vase in the center of the table. Will sat down at 8:30.

"I'm so sorry," he said. "This buyout has been a lot more work than anyone anticipated." He paused and smiled at me. "And I've been watching you from the lobby for a couple of minutes."

I had a moment of panic thinking about how ridiculous I must have looked. I just stared blankly.

"I hope this doesn't come across as anything but a compliment, but you are so damned cute," Will said.

The odd thing was that he seemed sincere.

"Huh?" I asked. "Why would you say that? I was sitting here like a dork, using a breadstick as a baton."

I wondered if I looked as embarrassed as I felt.

"Exactly," he said. "Those breadsticks taste horrible. The only thing you *can* do is play with them. But nobody does. Except you. I just thought it was cute, that's all."

"Well, thank you, I guess."

"You want another drink?"

"Not just yet. You need to catch up anyway."

"I'll just have wine with dinner," he said. "I'm not much of a drinker."

When the waiter came to take our orders, Will ordered wine for both of us. I was better at choosing beer, so it was fine with me that he took charge.

"How's the plant business?" Will asked.

"Pretty slow until they start growing again," I replied. "How's the business business?"

"Hopping. The number crunchers are still doing their thing, but it certainly looks like a good buy."

"What does?" I asked. I realized that I had no idea what Will or M. C. Knight Corporation did.

"Parish Cosmetics," he responded with a puzzled look. "Didn't Jim tell you guys?"

"Jim Parish tends to be fairly tight-lipped. So he's selling? I thought he was looking for investors."

"Wow. I guess I shouldn't have said anything. I assumed you all knew from the way he talked about it." He cocked his head to one side and looked at me. "I guess you should probably keep that between us."

I had to admit that it felt like a pallet of bricks had landed on me. I complained about my job; who didn't? But I loved what I did, and the prospect of Jim selling off the company and my being out of work threw me for a loop. I didn't know what to say.

Will was the one who broke the silence. "I'm sorry. I wish I hadn't done that to you. Nothing's final, and nothing's been discussed about employee retention as of yet."

"Not your worry," I replied. "Let's not talk shop anyway."

I was trying to put on my most charming facade and not let him know that he'd freaked me out. But the whole interchange, which took less than three minutes, had driven home the fact that this guy was way out of my league. He was buying the company that I worked for, for Christ's sake.

"Agreed." He smiled. "So what do you do for fun?"

Our conversation flowed so smoothly and effortlessly that by dessert, I'd almost forgotten my earlier trepidation. It might have had something to do with the three glasses of wine on top of the martini, but it definitely had more to do with those gorgeous eyes and beautiful smile. It occurred to me that Will smiled almost constantly, but not in a phony or forced way. He seemed genuinely happy and not at all shy about showing it.

When he finally stood up to leave, I asked, "What about the check?"

"It's taken care of."

I raised an eyebrow. I'd never been to a restaurant that didn't bring out a check. Will just winked at me, took my hand, and prompted me out of the chair. We retrieved our coats and stepped outside.

"I hope it's not too late for you," he said. "There's something I'd like to show you."

I looked at my watch, surprised that it was already eleven. "I've got nothing to do tomorrow. Whatcha got?"

I hadn't meant to sound flirtatious, but he gave me a quirky grin. It seemed almost devious.

"Come on." He walked to a long, dark Rolls Royce and

opened the rear door. I stepped in, and the driver nodded over his shoulder as Will closed the door behind us. "The office, please, Mack."

"I thought no shop talk," I said. He leaned over like he was going to kiss me and for a moment, I panicked again. But he raised a finger and put it to my lips.

"Surprises are no fun if you know what they are," he said.

He dropped his hand from my face and closed it around my hand, which he held during the whole drive. My head was a swirling-twirling mess. I didn't know how I felt about him touching me like that, but I knew that I wasn't about to take my hand away.

We pulled up in front of one of Seattle's tallest buildings. Will opened the car door and stepped out, still holding my hand. After we walked to the entrance, Will knocked. A surly-looking security guard roused himself from the desk and came to the door. He unlocked it when he saw Will.

"Night, Mr. Knight," he said.

I wondered at what age Will had grown tired of the name jokes.

The guard locked the door behind us as we headed toward the bank of elevators. One of the doors opened immediately. When we stepped inside, Will hit the button for the top floor.

We exited into a small lobby. Through the open doors of an office, I could see floor-to-ceiling glass. Will led me inside without turning on any lights.

The view was spectacular, city lights reflecting off the Sound in myriad dancing shimmers. I walked to the window and stared. I could feel Will standing next to me, but he didn't say anything. He just let me take it in. After a while, I turned to him.

"I don't really know what to say," I stammered. "There aren't words to do it justice."

For once, Will wasn't smiling. He stepped closer and gently kissed me. In the moment that his lips brushed mine, I felt exhilaration, eroticism, fear, passion, panic, desire, dread, and longing. My brain was fuzzy. I'd never experienced such a sweep of simultaneous emotion and wasn't sure what to make of it. My knees went weak, cliché be damned. Will slipped his arm around my waist as I started to slump.

"You okay?" he asked.

I straightened up and, without a word, kissed him back. Mine was not the gentle kiss he'd given me. Mine expressed all of the exhilaration, eroticism, passion, desire, and longing, but none of the fear, panic, or dread. He responded in kind. When we finally broke apart, he let out a small gasp. My breathing was a bit labored, too.

"Well, then," he said, smiling again. We stood looking out the window for a while, and then he checked his watch. "As much as I hate to do this, I have a flight to catch. We should probably get you back to your car."

"A flight tonight?"

"Yeah. I delayed it as long as I could so that we could get together, but Matthew Knight will wait only so long."

The guard nodded as we left. "Night, Mr. Knight."

I couldn't suppress a chuckle. Will shot me another crooked grin.

Inside the car, Will took my hand again. "You have no idea how nervous I was about that," he said. "I wasn't sure if I'd read things right, or if you were going to slug me."

"Everything has been amazing. Dinner was great and that view..." I was uncertain how best to continue. "And that kiss—I'm not sure what to say about that."

His smile took in his entire face, and I felt the same odd flood of emotions that I had earlier.

"I've never been able to make anyone lose his balance before," he said. "I'll have to be more careful next time. When can I see you again?"

"When do you get back?" I asked.

"Next Wednesday. Unless I can talk my uncle into coming home early."

"Why don't you give me a call when you get back, and we'll set something up?"

Will took his cell phone from his pocket and began thumbing around the keypad. He asked for my number.

I remembered what I'd said to Dan. Once Will had my home number, things would take a giant leap forward, and that scared me.

"Why don't you call me at work? I'm always easier to reach there."

I felt a strange pang when his smile faltered, but he recovered quickly and said, "Sure. I'll ring you as soon as we touch down."

The rest of the ride was quiet. When Mack stopped where I pointed out my car, Will brushed his lips against my cheek. But it wasn't the same.

I berated myself the entire drive home. I couldn't reconcile my conflicting feelings that I'd preserved my escape route but had made a horrible, monumental mistake.

I spent the next few days thinking a lot about Will: his eyes, his smile, his quiet charm, his easy demeanor. But mostly about the look on his face when he realized that I wouldn't give him my home phone number.

He'd gone out on a limb twice. He'd risked rejection by asking me to have dinner with him, and he'd left himself open by moving in for that kiss. I'd risked nothing. I hadn't put myself out there. I hadn't revealed anything or left myself vulnerable.

Every time I closed my eyes, I saw that look. No matter how I tried to rationalize or convince myself that I hadn't done anything wrong, I couldn't stop seeing the pain in Will's expression. I'd hurt someone who'd done nothing but show me kindness and decency. And worst of all, there'd been no reason for it. After having spent three hours talking to him, I might not have known him well, but I certainly knew that he wasn't going to stalk me. I should have given him the damned number.

I found myself looking forward to his call. I wanted to apologize. I wanted to explain. But mostly, I just wanted to be with him again.

Wednesday morning came, and I stuck close to my lab to hear the phone ring. I checked my email every half hour. I was nervous but more excited than anything else.

I ended up working late that night. I stayed until the night janitors knocked on my door. I hadn't even known that we had night janitors.

I finally went home, halfway hoping that there'd be a message on my phone—which was absurd, since that was what had started the whole mess. I went straight to bed, but I lay awake thinking. I realized that if I'd been in Will's place, I wouldn't have called me either.

Finally, I did something that I didn't remember ever having done. I cried myself to sleep.

When my alarm went off the next morning, I considered calling in sick. I finally decided that moping at the office was just as good as moping at home. I got myself up and ready. I noticed but didn't care about the glares from the front office harpies when I was late. Even though I knew it wouldn't be, I checked to see if the message light was blinking on my phone. I didn't even bother logging onto my computer.

I spent the day finishing preparations for the spring season. I cleaned out all the sample drawers and the cooler. I cleaned equipment and did inventory of the supplies I needed to restock. Just before heading out, I logged on to the computer to email my request for beakers, dishes, and whatnot to the supply gurus.

I was stunned when I saw a message from Will in my in-box. I hesitated, unsure whether I really wanted to open it.

Christian: Have decided to continue working in New York for a bit. I'll contact you upon return about the possibility of another meeting. William.

It had all the warmth of a Popsicle. And we were back to Christian and William. I read through it a couple of more times to make sure that I hadn't misunderstood. Of course, I hadn't. I sent my email to the supply room and left.

After a few days, I managed to convince myself that if Will called me, I'd go out with him again, but if he didn't, well, no biggie. Denial could be a beautiful thing, but I still checked my email more than I had in my three years of working for Parish Cosmetics. I even called my work number from my cell phone to make sure the message light was working. This continued for about two weeks. After that, I checked less frequently. The guilt had quieted, but I still found myself thinking about him.

It was a Tuesday when I logged in to find an email waiting for me.

Christian: Am working in London. Will be in Seattle Saturday. Same time and place? Will.

My heart jumped and I might have momentarily blacked out. I was still Christian, but we were back to Will. And was he actually asking me out again?

I replied instantly:

Will: Definitely!! Chris.

I began to plan how best to apologize. To let him know that I'd just gotten scared and that I hadn't meant to hurt him.

Those thoughts consumed me for the rest of the week. Every time I came up with some way of explaining why I'd panicked, it always led me to the realization that Jen was right. I hadn't been afraid of Will getting weird on me; I feared that he *wouldn't*. The Princess Syndrome had kept me safe my entire adult life. No one could possibly hurt me if I always found something "not right" with him before he got too close. I thought of all of the reasons why I wanted to spend time with Will and couldn't come up with a single legitimate reason why I shouldn't.

I got to Giovanni's a few minutes before eight. The maitre d' lifted his eyebrow and said, "Mr. Ellsborn? May I help you?"

"I'm supposed to meet Will...Mr. Knight," I said.

"We didn't know he was coming in tonight. But we always keep a table open."

I followed him to the same table as before. I eyed the breadsticks but decided against grabbing one. I ordered a martini. After an hour, I ordered another. The last thing I wanted was to be toasted while trying to deliver the eloquent apology that I'd come up with. But the wait was getting to me. My palms were sweating.

I ordered my third martini at a quarter to ten. The realization that Will wasn't coming was finally sinking in. I downed the last of my drink and caught the waiter's attention.

"Another?" he asked.

"Just the check, please." He scrunched up his eyes and looked perplexed. "Actually," I amended, pulling out my wallet, "just put it on this." I handed him my credit card.

Outside the restaurant, I stopped on the curb and felt a rush of melancholy as I looked at the spot where Will's limousine had been parked before. I stood for a while and felt myself sinking deeper into a funk. I glanced at my watch. It was 10:45.

I'd never actually had an epiphany until that moment. I looked at my watch again and wondered. I went to my car and drove as fast as Seattle's mazelike streets would allow, pulling in front of the granite-and-glass-clad building at 11:05.

I could see the same guard sitting inside, but he either didn't hear or ignored me when I rapped my knuckles on the glass door. Once I began pounding, he sauntered over. He looked irritated, but as soon as he recognized my face, he unlocked the door.

"Go ahead," was all he said.

All four of the visible doors were ajar on the top floor, but only the lobby lights were on. There was no sign that anyone else was there. I took a deep breath and steeled myself for another disappointment. When I went into the office with the grand view, it took a moment for my eyes to adjust to the darkness.

He was sitting in a rolling armchair in front of the window and hadn't turned around. He must have heard the elevator and was waiting to see what I'd do. I walked to the chair and put my hands on his shoulders. He didn't flinch and didn't speak. We stayed that way for several minutes.

His tone was level when he finally said, "I'd decided you weren't coming."

"I'm sorry. I guess I'm not the brightest bulb in the box. I took a three-hour detour to Giovanni's."

"I know," he said. "Jean-Pierre called to make sure he could give you my table."

"And you didn't have him tell me that you were here?" I asked.

"I wanted to find out if it meant enough for you to remember. Our meeting wasn't until eleven, remember?"

"Right," I said.

He still hadn't turned around or looked at me.

"I've missed you," I said. I hoped it didn't sound as pitiful as it did in my head.

"When my uncle bought this building and I saw this view, I knew that if I ever fell in love, it would be with a man who had the same reaction that I did." He spoke haltingly, as if revealing a secret he'd never said aloud.

I waited for him to continue, and when he stayed silent, I asked, "And I didn't?"

"No. You seemed even more awed than I was."

"Was I the first?" I asked.

"You're the only. I've never brought anyone else up here."

"Why me?" I asked.

After a pause, he said, "The day we met, your enthusiasm for your work was so evident that I wanted to know you better." He took a deep breath. "But I hadn't decided to bring you here until that night at the restaurant."

"Why then?" I asked.

"Because of the breadsticks."

"The what?"

"Most people would have been rubbernecking. But you were content to conduct your orchestra with a breadstick." I felt myself blushing. "I had a feeling you might be able to see through the crap, for what things really are. The way I hope I do. I'd always been afraid to show this to anyone." He waved his hand toward the window. "I had a feeling that you might be the one who could see it the same way I do."

I spun his chair around. I couldn't read his expression in the dim light, but I took a chance and straddled his legs, sitting but keeping most of my weight on my own legs. He didn't try to draw away.

"I'm sorry," I said again. "I was afraid, too. I didn't...I don't... want to get hurt. And judging by the way I've felt the past few weeks, I think you could definitely be the one to hurt me."

He moved his hands so that they were resting on my hips and said, "Maybe I fall too fast."

"And I don't fall at all," I said. "Aren't we the pair?"

After he kissed me, I said, "Promise that you won't hurt me."

"*Sic volvere Parcas,*" he replied.

"So spin the Fates," I translated. There was enough light for me to see him raise an eyebrow. I shrugged and said, "Private school."

"I can promise you that I'd rather amputate my toes with a butter knife, but I don't know how the Fates will spin any more than anyone else does." He leaned forward and kissed me again. A really good kiss. "I don't know if our threads are being woven together or not, but if more kisses like that are involved, I sure want to find out."

I got to see the sunrise from that vantage. It was almost as good as the lights at night. However, Will smiling at me from the couch, still without his shirt, was an even better view. He looked at me, and I knew that he was right. The Fates might not deign to reveal their designs, but I, too, wanted to find out what might be in store for us.

GRATITUDE

Felice Picano

Both women had stepped away from the table. Lizabeth, his agent, went to the restroom. Andrea Kelton, the editor who'd just said the words to make him float on air while seated still on the big *moderne* banquette, had received a phone call from her office, and had wandered off somewhere at the far end of the restaurant trying to get better wireless reception. Leaving Niels Llewellyn alone to sit and gloat. Around him: the delicate tinkle of crystal and silver against porcelain in the overpriced eatery, and its otherwise artful sonic decor of swirling waters covering the million-dollar deals being proposed and sealed by the industrial and media movers and shakers about the big, posh, water-hushed room.

It was something to savor, as had been Andrea's words: "This is unquestionably your breakthrough book. We're so proud to be involved!" Followed rapidly by further indications of how proud they actually were, including the stunning figures of the enormous first printing the company had settled on, the prepublication acceptance as a "main selection" by the book club, with its own concomitant huge printing, and even—he was to expect it as soon as this week—an unprecedented further advance on his advance of a year past, actual cash, more than double what he'd received, as though confirming the success of a novel not yet in print, never mind one liable to succumb to the vagaries of the marketplace.

Lizabeth returned first and confirmed that the second advance, presale, and huge printing meant there were to be no vagaries of the marketplace at all now. They—she and he, together for twenty-six long years, through wheat and chaff—had been elevated, as though on an enormous dose of morphine, a good half foot or so above the buy-and-sell mentality that had so enclosed them throughout their professional and personal relationship. Niels was now about to become a *personage,* and she, too, at least in the industry, a correlative minipersonage. They toasted each other's good sense and tenacity and lifted a glass edge toward whatever literary gods there still might be in this ghastly age, to help them ever onward.

Then Andrea was back, closing the phone and saying, "The advertisements are set now for a national vend. Six major newspapers and three magazines," and Niels sank back into the banquette and listened almost as though he were not the major reason, but instead some hanger-on, or better yet and ironically, given his age, a child, as the glories of his immediate future were trotted out in all the brightest colors with metaphorical pennants excitedly set to fly in front of him.

He was hardly a child, closer to sixty than fifty. No friend to the reflections of window panes and looking glasses that had a startling way of creeping up and suddenly presenting him to his nowadays always unsuspecting and usually horrified self.

"About time," some would say. His previous agent, gone

into real estate in Gulfstream St. Pete; his sister, an aged thing upon a stick who lived in Middletown, New Jersey, on a government pension and who he still held responsible for his mother's death: responsible by means of her unbending maternal neglect. Was it half a lifetime ago? "About time," a few dusty professors would utter, those not yet retired, who'd gone to college with him, saying it with a bit more fire, a smidgen more respect. "About damned time!" his few pupils over the years would celebrate, wherever they celebrated these days; he expected in their overpriced apartments in the wilds of Queens or Staten Island. After all, who could afford to live in Manhattan except the wealthy and the few like him who actually were more or less rent-controlled unto death?

The celebration was soon over. The women were once more drawn to their cell phones. Someone—he didn't know, he didn't care which—paid for the, of course, overpriced lunch. They all stood, made kissinglike gestures in one another's direction, and slowly slid out of the water-tumbled dining chamber, into a corridor, into a bar, toward a coat-check room, into another corridor and out onto the front foyer where men with suits even he knew were ridiculously expensive—suits he soon could buy should he care to change his look ("Post-Graduate" one magazine had written of his habitual costume)—were entering.

In the spring afternoon sunshine, Lizabeth spotted a taxi, and Andrea mentioned they were going the same way. Touchy kisses this time from the two of them, as the middle-aged women skipped chattering like preteen girls through the mid-Fifties street traffic and into the cab, "No-Noing" another matron foolish enough to try to beat them to it. Then the taxi slid forward, they were gone, and Niels was alone.

"It's April ninth!" Niels found himself saying to three other women, stepping around him without even a look back, headed into the restaurant's foyer. Then he moved out of their way, forward into the noise and grime of a Midtown sidewalk.

"About time!" he repeated to himself with secret joy, wondering with a start how life would be different now. "You're lucky, N," Scott Fortismann had said to him only a few nights ago. "Fate is saving you for last, for when you're ready for it. Unlike poor schmuck me, you'll be able to handle and thus enjoy your fame when it comes." To which Niels had answered, "*If* it comes!" and been clapped on the shoulder and assured all across Riverside Drive and into Scott's hundred-thousand-dollar Merce coupe, that it would, it would, Scott Fortismann knew for sure.

Scott, of course, had become famous early, at twenty-eight, world famous at thirty-four with *Nets*, and so had been famous seemingly forever, and it had ruined him. Scott would reiterate that to Niels during their long (and, on Scott's part, increasingly booze-tinged) meals. And Niels could see for himself: the lengthy, expensive, disgraceful, emotional, first divorce. The seemingly abandoned children who'd come to hate Scott, Nicky nearly murdering his father that insane afternoon on the yacht in Antigua. Brenda in and out of jail or Payne-Whitney or more lately caught up in the bust of the latest escort service to take her in. Scott himself going from wife to wife, girlfriend to girlfriend, even drifting into Niels's territory awhile, with that much younger and somewhat questionable African-American minimalist, what was his name, Nigeria Sands? More disrepute at their very public breakup at the Venice Biennale. Providing ignominious material for half a week of say-anything-just-so-long-as-you-show-everything (and they did!) European scandal sheets. Their few remaining friends, their colleagues certainly, and much of the reading public had come to expect Scott Fortismann's very public romances and breakups so they could afterward savor them, endlessly rehashing them, appreciating them, a great deal more than his dwindling output of serious plays.

Scott Fortismann would probably be the only one left of Niels's so-called circle (long *perdu* thanks to car accidents, air accidents, overdoses, suicide, cancer, and AIDS) who'd be truly happy for Niels now. The others, well, what had Samantha W. mouthed off last week? "For every artist who makes it in this damned country, fifty others have to fall down in front of a bus." No, they wouldn't so much like it, would they? No matter what they would actually say to his face—and who could blame them?

He'd reached the corner of Fifth Avenue, where a complete tangle of traffic appeared to come from two directions. A crowd of pedestrians were gathered under the construction scaffolding, barring Niels from even seeing what was going on in the middle of the intersection—if not from hearing shouted drivers' curses and the incessant honking of car horns.

When he'd passed here earlier on his way to lunch, three construction workers had been sitting just over there, somewhat elevated, chowing down on hero sandwiches and messily drinking out of big thermoses as he'd stepped around the corner. One of them, maybe twenty-six, slab-sided big, with a mess of thick, bark-colored hair and post-twilight blue eyes, had suddenly stood up and stretched himself to his full six feet and two inches, and Niels had stopped short on the sidewalk and just gawked at the big child-god as the fellow's eyes closed and his muscles played along his arms and over his chest, obvious through his thin Metallica Rocks! T-shirt, and his mouth smiled in sheer animal pleasure at such a simple activity as yawning and stretching. Cupid's dart had stung Niels so suddenly then, so utterly, he'd become nauseated. He'd felt such complete, astonished, unmitigated desire and such an opposing instant equal realization of the impossibility of its ever being fulfilled, that he had actually had to turn away and retch.

Andrea and Lizabeth had noticed how pale he was when he'd arrived at their table not long after. They plied him with brandy and fabulous news until he forgot the godling, and his own embarrassment, doubled of course when said deity had noticed Niels about to pitch forward over the two-by-four temporary wooden railing onto the filthy curb. Said deity had rushed forward and grabbed Niels, shouting, "Give me a hand! This old guy's goin' under."

He'd been freshly mortified by the shout, and of course, they'd easily grasped him and pulled him over to where they sat, where the third one had plied him with tepid coffee from a thermos, the three of them clucking over him. "Jeez, we thought you was a goner!" "Is it your ticker?" And worst of all, Adonis-in-construction-boots demanding, "Look me in the eye, so I can see you're all right. C'mon, right in the eye! Udderwize we're calling EMS. C'mon, fella!"

And he'd been forced to actually look close-up at those eyes and so been able to determine their exact shade of semiconductor cobalt, which he now knew so very well he could mix it at any paint store, not to mention the naturally frosted three different tones of browns of his leonine mane, or his complexion like that satin found on century-old Valentines, or the exact cut of his Medici upper lip, the slightly fuzzed depth of his matching dimples. Niels had almost lost it again. He'd gaped, until they declared, "Yawl right, now!" and "Want help inna taxi?" all of which he fended off, with many mumbled thanks and gratefully downcast eyes, getting as far away as fast as he could and then, past the construction site, looking back once, only to be startled by his Adonis's head thrust out over the sidewalk and his somewhat worried face, his big right hand stuck out in a peace sign V, to which Niels at last responded with one of his own, before somehow managing to actually stumble the twenty yards or so to the nearby restaurant.

Niels didn't see any of the three now. Could they have already left for the day? Then he heard one: Adonis himself shouting, and then there he was, in a sort of setback where the boarding had been nicked three feet into the building dig to allow for a temporary enclosed chute, probably for rubble to be dropped from the top of the construction to its collection site far down below. Hidden within the crowd, Niels felt safe in turning and gawking at the perfection of the creature as he waved his hands and shouted up some obscure lingo, possibly to one of his colleagues from before. It was almost amazing watching him.

Niels became aware of the crowd thinning, his cover lessening, and was about to persuade himself that he'd soon be spotted again—but would that be so very bad? He might even go over and thank him for his trouble earlier—when his peripheral vision caught something else.

The enclosed chute next to the construction worker had been shaking from side to side, perhaps as a result of larger pieces tumbling down through it, and at an upper section, he could see a piece of something seemingly caught fast. It bulged suddenly, maybe two feet above the construction god's head, and then more rubble came down into it, finer stuff, and then it moved horizontally maybe four inches on either side. Suddenly it half detached from its lower portion, which swung around a hundred and eighty degrees, revealing, as he'd feared, a good-sized chunk of concrete wedged in tight.

It was the workman's absolute, total failure to see any of it taking place that impelled Niels forward through thinning pedestrians, shouting and knowing he couldn't possibly be heard over the noise of the chute, over the traffic. But he knew he had to do something or it would disgorge directly over, on top of, onto the fellow's head.

Not even realizing what he was doing, all the time keeping his eyes on the broken shaft, Niels dove across the sidewalk. He panicked even further as the construction worker headed under its opening, directly under where more rubble had been dropped down, and where the structure now swung side to side. Niels was yelling, "Get away! Get away!" Yelling loud enough, it turned out, for the worker to turn toward the sound of his voice. A split second of surprised but pleased recognition appeared on his handsome lips, his mouth opening to say something back, as the concrete wedge began to give way, and Niels threw himself directly at the worker's midsection the way he'd seen defensive linemen tackle a quarterback on televised football games, with utter disregard for gravity, himself, or where he might land even. He felt the young fellow's complete astonishment as he caught the blow and tumbled sideways virtually head over heels, Niels all the while thinking, *God! Have I done enough!* just as the noise above him reached a thunderous boom. Niels looked up and his vision seemed closed down to an overhead tunnel of unstoppably charging black rubble, and he understood that he'd succeeded in saving Adonis but that now the ton of concrete was for him alone. There wasn't even time for the next thought before it all went quite dark.

"...so I told him, Tyrone, 'No! I am not going to that restaurant with you! I don't care how many of your friends are waiting there!' Can you believe that? Him telling me that—just to get me to go? What an idiot... Hold on! I think this patient is conscious. Hello, sir? *Sir?* Better get that intern at the desk. *Sir? Hello. Can you hear me?* Can you recognize I'm Tyesha Melton, your nurse? How many fingers am I hold—? There you are, doctor, I was just...Yes, sir, we were about to turn him over like we usually do at this time, and he just now opened..."

Niels registered it all, and with a sigh of relief he thought, *Oh, good! Here I am. It worked. I saved the lovely boy and suffered some little concussion and all will be well.*

The intern, who seemed to be of Middle-Asian origin with untypically bad facial skin but lovely brown eyes simply drenched in several rows of eyelashes, said, "Please, sir. I'm Dr. Kawalor Dohendry. You have had a serious accident and have been out of commission for four days and three nights."

Niels began to say something but nothing came out—he could only croak.

The nurse lifted a little pink cup of water to his mouth, and he sipped, while the doctor looked on benignly, and Niels tried to say something and still nothing came out but frog talk.

"Not to worry, sir," the doctor said. "These things happen. Maybe later we shall speak. Can you nod your head?"

Niels nodded his head, and even he could tell that the motion he made, if it existed at all, was very, very minor.

"Good, sir. Good progress, I think. We will now be able to communicate," the doctor said, smiling fatuously.

Communicate? Niels wondered. *I, who could write a page-long sentence without the need of a single semicolon! You call this communicating?*

"Your son is waiting in the other room. Nurse, get him," Dohendry said.

Son? I have no son.

"He slept over all three nights in this very room, on a narrow cot we brought in. He insisted. What a good son! In my homeland of course this would be unextraordinary, even expected. But in the U.S."—he pronounced it You-Ass—"it is very uncommon for such devotion from a family member. Ah, there you are, sir."

Niels looked up and it was the Adonis from the construction site, unharmed, dressed in different clothing, clean pants and shirt, but the same fellow, more gorgeous than ever. He had his hands together, as though he'd been wringing them, and he looked so sad and yet hopeful, too, now.

"Yes," Dohendry went on to the Adonis, "as I told you would happen, he is fully conscious now." The doctor did something, tucked in a blanket or something, Niels couldn't make out the darting little movement indicative of care. "But as I also told you, he is unable to speak. The trachea, you understand. It is temporary," turning to Niels, "only temporary. It is like a rubber tube that has been given a blow," he illustrated in the air with a karate chop to one forearm, "and it needs now to come back to normal." Turning now to the Adonis. "He is fully conscious and understands. But only in nods can he communicate."

Niels looked with astonishment at the construction worker, who suddenly pushed the little doctor aside, fell upon Niels, and hugged him, sobbing loudly.

"Oh, look, nurse," Dohendry was saying beyond the big clasping body, "such a lovely reconciliation. I take back all the bad things I have said about American fathers and sons. Every word of it." He then turned to the other nurse and rapidly said something in a foreign language Niels had never heard before.

She responded back and it necessitated their going to some machine at the end of the room, while Niels remained unable to do anything but bear the big, young, lovely, clean-smelling head and torso and arms of the Adonis thrown about him, still sobbing, until finally, the big tanned face pulled back, cobalt eyes brimming over with tears, and the quivering Michelangelo lips whispered, "Why'dya do it? Why'dya save my life like that?" Before he resumed hugging him and sobbing.

It was during these moments that Niels had the most bifur-
cated emotions he could have possibly imagined. First, of course,
and obvious, the pleasure of the big delicious fellow all over him,
grateful, delighted, his warmth, his sheer presence; next to that,
opposite it, the absolutely below zero chilling recognition that
Niels's action had not at all resulted in some little concussion
and all would be well, because he was more or less paralyzed,
wasn't he? Paralyzed, unable to speak, unable to move anything
but, he imagined, his head a quarter of an inch, side to side.

Niels Llewellyn died then as he had lived in his previous life,
realizing what his impetuous and altruistic act had cost him. He
felt his spirit leave him and he died. Once again all went black.

But not for long, since he was now in intensive care in a large
Manhattan hospital. And so, he came to again a few minutes
later, only to see Dohendry and hear him saying, doubtless to
the Adonis, "We must expect these little setbacks for the next
few days. The shock. The shock of it all, and the happiness your
father must now feel is naturally the cause of it. He will survive,
believe me. A good son's affection…"

He did survive, with all the complications that ensued. Adonis's
name turned out to be Danny Masini, twenty-nine, of Center
Moriches, Long Island. There was a wife, Sylvia Masini, pretty,
demure, sweet, and a little Danny, aged twenty months, a cupid,
a *putti,* an angel. The other workers from that day came in,
too: Ethan Skavenger and Anastas Doremates. They visited less
often, but often enough, and sometimes with girlfriends. They
lived in Merrick, Long Island. Every visit went on for hours and
was filled with food and balloons, huge pop-up get-well cards,
flowers, music playing, and people talking. In short, a little get-
well party. Soon, the nurses hung around more, to flirt with

Anastas and Ethan and their friends, and so Niels got constant, adoring attention from them all. Doubled by Dohendry, who had appointed himself the little group's guardian, who got Niels into total physical and voice rehab, pulling strings for medicines not yet fully approved by the FDA, and who visited him daily with new methods, ideas, and potions, even when he was moved to a room down the hall and Dohendry was no longer assigned.

Niels made progress. He seemed to have no choice but to make progress. Soon his croaking was more nuanced, comprehensible to the beautiful Danny Masini, who insisted to anyone who asked, despite the difference of their names—for they'd gotten his wallet, his ID, his card for the paltry catastrophic insurance—that they were related. How could anyone doubt it? Soon Niels was moving his fingers on his left hand, and with little Danny playing with him, his fingers on his right hand. Dohendry was there saying, "What did I predict? Not of course, with the spinal damage you sustained in the accident that you should expect anything like a full recovery, but with such loving friends, such a family, such a son, why I think you should expect a wonderful life."

One day, perhaps five weeks later, his agent Lizabeth arrived. She was horrified to see him but hid it quickly. Niels got everyone else out of the room—there always seemed to be at least one of the workers' *cumadres* sitting with him every day, or someone's teenage son helping him do rehab. It was understood by all, and totally approved by all, that he would be living with the Masinis once he got out. On the weekends, various male family members and pals were helping to close in and insulate the sunroom that faced west over the estuary down to the Great South Bay. Danny showed him photos and videos with construction progress reports, and it would all be very beautiful. It was understood by all that Niels was "theirs" now, and they would take care of him, and do whatever was needed, from now on, no matter what it took. He knew they thought he was a bum, without two nickels to rub together, and he was waiting for the appropriate moment, once they were all settled and "at home," to tell Danny the truth: that such virtue had a monetary reward, too. He knew what Danny would say, "Who needs your money? We've got enough! We're family. Family!"

"Who are these people?" Lizabeth asked.

"What's happening with the novel?" he asked carefully and watched her slowly figure out what he was uttering.

"Everything we spoke of, except"—here she almost broke down—"the press we've gotten is astonishing. You saved a man's life. You're a hero. You're a public relations windfall. Andrea's executives decided to print and ship six months early, there's so much demand for your book."

Niels smiled.

She then went on to explain her absence in Europe, at the Frankfurt Book Fair and then on vacation after, which was why it took her so long to find out about him.

"Andrea says photographers from *People* magazine want you," she said, awed. "That's a few hundred thousand copies, right there."

"Good," he croaked.

"Good? Look at you, Niels! What happened? Oh, God, it's all my fault. I should have put you into a taxi, that day. Just look at you!"

She must have become very loud and sounded upset because suddenly the door opened and two people came in: Tania Skavenger, Ethan's sister, and Danny himself, the look on his face saying, *Leave him alone or by God, I'll…*

"What's happened," Niels croaked out the words carefully, quietly, grasping the edge of Liz's sleeve with his crooked (but growing stronger every day) two fingers, "is that I'm happy, Liz."

Lizabeth backed off, all but thrust aside by Danny, who sat down and said, "Look at you, grabbing at ladies! You're something else!" He kissed Niels's mouth, and said to Tania, "Get me some of the green Jell-O." Then to Niels, "How you doing? Danny's here and all is well. Ready for some?"

"Really, really happy for the very first time in my life," Niels muttered as Danny readied the spoon of Jell-O and made airplane buzzing noises.

"Okay, sweetheart! Open up wide! Here it comes."

HAPPY HOUR AT CAFÉ JONES

Rob Byrnes

I hate blind dates. And when I use the term *blind date,* I'm painting with a broad brush. I hate personal ads and Missed Connections and meeting the men my friends think would be perfect for me. I'm the type of man who wants—no, *needs*—to measure up a prospect with his own two eyes before agreeing to anything involving one-on-one interaction, including things as innocuous as dinner, or even coffee.

Anyone would be justified in wondering why I have an account with that well-known Internet date-finder, given my aversion to blind dating.

There are two simple reasons, really. First, because sometimes I just like to look. On one of those long, lonely nights, it puts my mind at ease to know that hundreds of other gay men in the general vicinity of Rochester, New York, are also alone, wondering when their Prince Charming is going to read their online profile and come to their rescue. Yes, I know that they are putting their best foot—or at least best *picture*—forward, but it's still a small comfort to scroll through a sea of generally good-looking men and know that they are also single and, theoretically, also datable for those who don't share my aversion.

And my second reason is because one should never say never. After all, I used to also hate broccoli.

Since my Internet dating account is a free one—I obviously don't take it seriously enough to buy a premium package—it's been a harmless enough diversion. And despite the fact that I hate blind dates, I *have* used it for purposes other than idle scrolling.

Only twice, though.

The first time was when one particular man's picture and profile caught my eye, and—when I couldn't get him out of my head for a few days—I steeled my nerves and sent him an email. After a flirtatious exchange over the next few days, we agreed to meet for a drink. But when he finally appeared, the cute young blond man in the picture turned out to be a washed-out forty-something with jowls and a drinking problem so bad he was already loaded before he arrived for our happy hour drink. I was out of the bar before the thought even occurred to me to order a second round, and vowed to never again so much as talk to another man before seeing him in the flesh.

With that history, I should have learned my lesson. But no, curiosity got the best of me one more time.

I hadn't been to the website in quite a while. It wasn't that I had any real-life action going; I was just in one of those phases when I didn't care much. Ogling the photos of strangers wasn't a priority in my life at the time. Even the fact that I had a profile on the site—a stripped-down free profile, granted, but nevertheless a profile—was almost forgotten, shoved so far back into a dark corner of the dusty attic of my mind that when an email from an unfamiliar name appeared in my in-box I almost thought it was spam and deleted it. I'm still not quite sure what brought me to open it, but I did.

Hi, SouthWedge32.
  Read your profile, saw your picture. You sound like you'd be fun to meet.
  Interested? Write back.
  DavidP195

I closed the email, considered deleting it...and didn't. But I did ignore it for hours, focusing my attention on items relating to work and a particularly inane email conversation with my friends, all of whom seemed to be bored at their respective offices that morning. In fact, it was only after lunch that I returned to the message from DavidP195 and reconsidered it.

Curiosity finally won out.

Please don't take offense, I typed, *but I need you to send me your profile and photo. You've seen mine, so it's only fair, right?* I signed it, *SouthWedge32.*

His response came the next morning. The profile was vague but didn't set off any alarm bells. The picture, on the other hand, seemed too good to be true. A nice-looking face; dark—almost black—hair; piercing brown eyes; a mischievous half-grin that showed off his dimples to their best effect. If I had met him face-to-face, in a bar or at a party or even in the workplace, *and* if he looked anything like his picture, I would have been all over him. But after all those months, the memories of the jowly alcoholic were still vivid to me, and I was determined to exercise caution. Mr. Piercing-Eyes-and-Dimples could very well be a bloated, drug-crazed sociopath, a fact I would be well-advised to keep in mind.

Despite my reservations, I wrote back and asked if it was a current picture. Less than twenty minutes later his response arrived, assuring me it was taken only weeks earlier. He concluded his email with an invitation to meet for a drink sometime, so I could see for myself.

Long story short—because a blow-by-blow account of our lengthy email exchange over the next few days would bore anyone to tears—I finally found my resistance wearing down. I wouldn't commit—DavidP195 hadn't quite won me over to that extent—but I was slowly being charmed by his persistence. I had a lot of questions, but he seemed to have all the answers and a great deal of understanding about my caution. If, that was, he wasn't lying through his teeth, as bloated, drug-crazed sociopaths were wont to do.

Some of those answers were more or less self-explanatory. His name, for example. He assured me it was actually David— the P came from his last name and the 195 from a favored set of numbers that, if I had to bet, would have been part of his address at one time—and that more information would be forthcoming on an as-needed basis. In turn, I confirmed for him that South-Wedge32 was a predictable combination of my neighborhood and age, but that he could call me Brian.

Ever so slowly, I felt my trepidation melt away. His picture was current. He had a college education and worked in a white-collar profession. He didn't smoke but didn't mind smokers. He drank, but only socially. He loved movies, especially the classics. He kept himself in shape but wasn't a health fanatic. He was interested in politics. He even *read. Novels.* He sounded almost too good to be true, which, of course, could be a problem in and of itself. I was starting to wonder what he saw in me that made him feel I was worth pursuing over the course of all those days and messages. I *knew* I wasn't too good to be true.

It took him another week, but he finally got me to agree to a quick phone call. At the pre-appointed time, I dialed the number he provided me, and the phone was answered on the second ring.

"Is this Brian?" There was a confidence in his voice that put me at ease, banishing the nervousness I'd felt as I dialed the phone.

"It is. Which means you're David."

"I am." Which kicked off a delightfully short conversation that was not quite the equivalent of meeting in the flesh, but was close enough that I finally decided to set aside my inhibitions and meet him the following Thursday after work for a quick get-acquainted drink, with no promises beyond that. It seemed to be the safest option.

Thursday morning, we exchanged one last email to confirm the location and share our wardrobes for identification purposes, in case the photos didn't conform to reality. I selected Café Jones, which was a bit of a hole in the wall and had all the distinction of being the bar where I met Stuart, the last man who could be passably termed my boyfriend, but was otherwise a safe choice. I was familiar with it, but it wasn't a regular haunt; meaning that if David turned out to be a bloated, drug-crazed sociopath, I still stood a relatively decent chance of avoiding him in the future by avoiding the bar.

Like most of upstate New York, Rochester had roughly twelve sunny days each year. Unfortunately, that Thursday wasn't one of them. After tucking my car into a nearby municipal lot, I walked the grim block of cracked sidewalk to Café Jones through a light, misty rain falling from forlornly gray skies. I distractedly played with the keys in my pocket and wondered why, exactly, I had thought this meeting was a good idea in the first place.

David was cute in a photo, but I couldn't guarantee it was even him. He was charming in email, but what was he like on the other side of the screen? Even our one phone conversation had been utterly pleasant but incredibly brief. This had the potential for disaster. My only consolation was that I could always leave quickly, and I could most likely avoid Café Jones for the rest of my life without a second thought.

In minutes I reached the building, little more than an extended stucco shack in the middle of a trash-strewn lot painted a gray that matched the sky. The very sight of the exterior—the grimy, chipped facade; the faded sign announcing that the building was indeed Café Jones, and which hadn't been attended to in a decade; the flickering strip of neon advertising Genesee beer through a small rectangular side window—made my spirit heavy.

I took a deep breath and approached the front door, the wood scuffed with the distress of hundreds of combative feet and fists over the years. The aging spring holding the door to the frame creaked to announce my arrival as I pushed it open, revealing a gloom even deeper than that of the Rochester sky. I blinked a few times to adjust my eyes as the door snapped closed behind me, and the seven or eight men lining the bar turned to look at me before returning their attention to the mute television set bolted high on the wall facing the street. They were watching golf, I noted, following the closed-captioning as if they cared. In front of each was a glass or a bottle or sometimes both, and none of them—even the one or two who were probably fairly young—looked passably younger than a sickly fifty in the dreary early evening gloom.

So this is where gay alcoholics come to die, I thought, but then silently reprimanded myself. I was, after all, among them.

I sat a respectful distance from the nearest barfly, and when the bartender finally honored me with his sullen attention, ordered a vodka-soda. Miserable day, miserable place, and even a miserable bartender. This blind date—the date I was dreading—was getting off to an inauspicious start, and the date himself hadn't even arrived yet.

I heard the spring on the front door squeak again and looked expectantly at the entryway, but the silhouette I glimpsed before the door snapped shut again wasn't him. At least not the "him" that I had been led to believe was David. And he wasn't wearing the blue shirt and khakis I had been told to watch for. I returned my attention to my drink and then joined the others in pretending to watch the silenced television.

A few minutes later the spring groaned again, and again I turned expectantly, only to see that it wasn't David coming into the bar. But this time, I knew the man walking through the front door.

I should have. I'd spent three years of my life with him.

"Hey, Brian," he said, spotting me in the gloom and approaching. "What brings you to the Jones? Slumming?"

I gave him a slight nod. It wasn't really a surprise to see him at this bar, but I'd gambled against it. Sometimes when you play the odds, you still lose. "Hello, Stuart. It's been a while."

"Mind if I sit down?" He took the barstool next to mine before I could respond. "It *has* been a while. Maybe we'd see each other more frequently if you bothered to return my calls."

I allowed myself a smile. "You figured that out, did you?"

"I see." He waved for the bartender's attention and was rewarded with a nod of recognition and a decidedly less surly attitude than I had received. In Stuart's case, familiarity apparently didn't breed contempt. At least not with this bartender.

In all honesty, after a year of being apart, I was more or less indifferent to his presence. Yes, the breakup had been his idea; and no, I hadn't seen it coming; and yes, I was bitter for a while, especially when I found out who he'd dumped me for. But time had passed, and the wounds had healed. There were even times when I missed him a bit. Not enough to return his infrequent calls, obviously, but I still felt a little something whenever I picked up his voice mail: a tinge of nostalgia, as memories of the good times crept into the corners of my mind.

Enough not to mind his company for a few minutes while I waited for David, at least.

"So again," he said, after ordering his drink, "what brings you to the Jones?"

"I hope this isn't going to sound rude, but I'm meeting someone here."

A thin smile crossed his lips and he took a long, slow look at the handful of regulars strung along the bar. "Anyone I know?"

"Not even anyone *I* know." He looked at me, not quite comprehending, so I filled in the blanks. "It's a blind date."

Again came the smile. "A blind date?"

I looked away and sighed. "An Internet date. Are you happy now? Your ex-boyfriend is so pathetic that he's meeting someone he's only talked to through email."

Stuart laughed. "Oh, Brian, that's not pathetic. Well...maybe a little. But why are you meeting him here?"

"Because I never come here. If I had him meet me at the Pub, say, he'd know where to stalk me."

"It sounds as if you've already decided that it won't work out."

I shrugged. "It's an Internet date. What could possibly go wrong?" I thought again about those words. "No, he seems perfectly normal. Almost an ideal match, in fact. It's just that...I don't do things like this."

"I know you don't. That's why I'm surprised." He swiveled

a few inches on his barstool, the better to face me. I noticed that he was now cropping his hair much shorter, conceding the battle he was slowly losing against male-pattern baldness. It looked good. "Just let me know if I'm in the way."

"I will. And you will be. The moment he walks through that door."

"Until then?"

"Until then, you can stay." I patted him lightly on the leg. "We can catch up."

"Good." He stirred his drink for a moment with a swizzle stick. "So what have you been up to?"

"Work, home, sleep, work, home, sleep. You know the drill."

"I do."

The awkward banality continued for a few minutes as we struggled for conversation. Although Stuart and I had shared everything during our three years together, the year apart seemed to have made all but the safest topics off-limits. But since even in dreary Rochester there was only so long you could discuss the weather, after a few minutes I bravely decided to shift gears into uncomfortable, but unavoidable, territory. It was either that or we were going to have to stare at each other until David made his entrance.

"Still seeing that guy?" I asked.

"Who?" He thought for a moment. "Randy?"

"I guess so. The realtor?" The fact that he'd left me for him went unsaid.

"Yeah, that was Randy." He didn't seem fazed to talk about him in front of me. "Nah, we broke up a few months ago. He didn't get me."

"What's that supposed to mean?"

Stuart leaned forward, resting his elbows on the bar. "You know how some people get you, and others don't?" I shrugged.

"You, for instance, *got* me. It's just…just the way our personalities meshed when we met."

"And the realtor didn't get you."

"The realtor didn't get me." He flashed a smile. "Here's a good example. Remember how we used to have Pasta Night?"

I remembered. "Sundays. And you'd channel Kool and the Gang and start singing, 'Oh, yes it's Pasta Night, and the feeling's right…'"

He snapped his fingers. "Exactly. The first time I did that in front of Randy he was, like, 'What the fuck?'"

"Oh, God, you didn't." I buried my face in my hands and started laughing. "I can't believe you did that. That song of yours was just so…so *silly.*"

Stuart was laughing, too. "I did. Once. And never again. But that's what I'm talking about, Brian. *You* got it. You got *me.*"

I uncovered my face. "That's because we were both silly idiots. When you think about it, having a Pasta Night song isn't really all that funny, is it?"

"I thought it was. Try it out on your…your…your *date* tonight, and see if *he* thinks it's funny."

"Uh…I think I'll pass." Stuart's mention of my date prompted me to steal a glance at my watch. David was already almost ten minutes late, a fact I mentioned aloud.

"I see you're still stuck on punctuality," he said.

"I'm not anal about it." He rolled his eyes, prompting me to add, "Am I?"

"I think we had this conversation back when I had an investment in it. Now I don't, so I'm going to drop it and offer to buy you another drink, instead."

I looked at the almost-empty glass on the bar in front of me, and then again at my watch. "Okay, but just one. I don't want to be drunk when he gets here."

After catching the bartender's eye, Stuart asked, "So does the date have a name?"

"David."

"Oh, now *that's* original."

I shook my head. "And here I was afraid you'd lost your sarcastic edge. For the record, he says his name is David, and I have no reason to doubt him."

He conceded the point, and when our fresh drinks were in front of us, lifted his glass and said, "Here's to what I hope is a successful first date for you." I was about to join him when he added, "And may it turn out much better than the last first date you had at the Jones."

After a brief pause, I picked up my glass and gently touched it against his, saying, "The last first date didn't turn out all that bad."

He offered me a faint smile. "I guess not. We got three good years out of it, didn't we?"

"We did." The mental image of a slightly younger Stuart, dressed in shorts and a T-shirt, dancing around his apartment while going through what had been his Sunday night routine, made me laugh, and I sang, "Oh, yes, it's Pasta Night…"

"God, we had some good times together," said Stuart, joining in my laughter at the memory. "Why did we let it fall apart?"

"We were young and stupid," I said. "We made a lot of mistakes. And maybe you have to go through things like that to realize which mistakes to avoid in the future."

"Maybe." He paused. "Is that why you don't return my phone calls anymore?"

I sighed but took his hand. "It's not like that, Stuart. I'm not *avoiding* you. But, well… we're moving on with our lives, right?"

"Trying to. I suppose."

I tensed a bit. "This would probably be a more appropriate

conversation at some other time. You know, a time when I'm
not about to go on a date with someone else."

He pulled his hand away from me and held it out defensively.
"I just want us to keep in touch, Brian. You know, we have a
history, and it wasn't all bad. These memories—the Pasta Night
song and everything else—they're something we'll always have
together."

I nodded. "You're right. We will."

"Of course," he said, a sly smile on his face, "if you're never
going to return my calls..."

I made a vague promise to reform, and we settled in for
more conversation: remembering some of the more endearing
quirks of our three years together; catching up on the lives of
friends who were divided like so much community property
after the breakup; asking about each other's families. Soon he
was ordering another round of drinks, and when I glanced at my
watch and saw that David was now more than twenty minutes
late, I made no effort to stop him.

After a short while, I excused myself to use the men's room
and asked Stuart to keep his eyes open for the blue shirt and
khakis. When I returned, he was still sitting alone at the bar, but
seconds later the front door swung open. I strained to get a look
at the new arrival.

"Is that your boy?" Stuart asked.

"Maybe." The man stepped forward, and now that he was
in the light I could see that he was, in fact, wearing the promised
blue shirt and khakis. That part was right, but everything else
was all wrong. He was easily two decades older than the alleg-
edly current picture David had emailed, and his hair, dark and
lustrous in the photo, was thin and lank. I didn't like to think of
myself as superficial, but if this was David it was probably going
to be a very short date.

I excused myself from Stuart and slowly approached the man in the blue shirt and khakis. He looked at me apprehensively as I drew near.

"Are you David?" I asked.

"No, sorry."

I apologized for bothering him and tried not to show my delight as I retreated.

"Short date," said Stuart as I reclaimed my stool.

"The good news is that it wasn't him. The bad news," I stole another glance at my watch, "the bad news is that he's a half-hour late."

"Do you think he's blowing you off?"

"I don't know," I confessed. "He seemed so eager to meet when we were trading email, but, well...not so eager now, it seems."

Stuart was abrupt. "I think you've been stood up."

I shrugged unhappily. "Could be."

"Why don't you let me take you to dinner?" That surprised me, and he must have seen it in my face. "Look, he's a half-hour late. And you don't even know the guy. He could have had second thoughts. Or maybe he's one of those people who gets off on doing things like this." He motioned to the patrons down the bar. "Hell, Brian, one of these trolls could be your David, just sitting there and watching your humiliation. Why don't you come to dinner with me?"

"But if he shows up..."

"Listen to me." One hand clamped down roughly on my shoulder. "He isn't coming. That's the downside of Internet dating, Brian: The anonymity makes it easy for someone to change his mind. Face it, will you? If this David even exists, you're not going to see him tonight. You've been waiting for thirty minutes."

I took another look at my watch. "I have to admit that it doesn't look like it's going to happen, but we made a date and I said I'd be here."

He shook his head and looked away.

It was at that moment when a chilling thought occurred to me. As much as I didn't want to believe it could be the truth...

"You're very sure that he's not coming, Stuart. Is there a reason for that?"

He looked back at me, and I tried to read his expression. It was strange that after four years of knowing him—especially those three years together—I still couldn't pinpoint exactly when he was misleading me, even as I felt strongly that I was being misled. I knew to expect sarcasm from him, and silliness, and maybe a bit too much negativity, but...deception? I didn't want to believe it, but his sudden and firm insistence that David wasn't going to appear made the hair on the back of my neck bristle.

"Let me help you," I added, when it was clear that he wasn't going to answer me. "You know David's not coming because," I hesitated, and then plunged forward, "because there is no David, right?"

Stuart stared at me.

"You made up David because I wasn't returning your calls, and this—you walking into the bar, our conversation, the trip down memory lane—you set up this whole thing."

He held his stare for a few more beats, and then surprised me with a tight-lipped smile. "Is that what you think?"

"I'm not sure. But that's what I'm *beginning* to think. It would explain a lot." Again I tried to read his face; again it was unreadable. "I know it's easy enough to create a fake email account, but who did you get to play him on the phone?"

"You really think that I made this guy up?" I didn't answer, and after a few strained, silent moments he said, "Okay, I know what you want to hear, so if it makes you feel better, I'll give it to you. It looks like you caught me, Brian. All I had to do was send a few charming emails and now here you are, trapped in my lair at Café Jones." He paused for effect. "Clever of me, wasn't it?"

At least I understood Stuart's sarcasm. Still, I held my ground. "I want you to know that if you tricked me into coming here, I'm not mad."

He smiled. "Me, neither." With that, he spun around on his stool and stood. "Now that the game is over, I guess I'd better get home. I only meant to stop for one, after all, and you kept me here past my limit." I didn't answer—I didn't know how to answer—but when he leaned forward to kiss me, I reciprocated. "Take care of yourself. It was fun catching up. And...well, I hope your David walks into your life some day. You deserve it."

Then he was gone.

As I sat alone at the bar, I had a brief moment to reflect. If Stuart had set up this scenario, it was unfortunate, because I now had a glimpse of an ugly aspect to his personality that would be impossible to get past. And that was too bad, really. We'd both screwed up a good relationship, him perhaps more than me, but there was more than enough responsibility to go around. It was funny how seeing him again had made the bad times seem so correctable in retrospect. The good definitely more than outweighed the bad in my mind. I could even see myself returning his phone calls occasionally.

But...the *deception*...

"Excuse me. Are you Brian?"

I looked up at a man I hadn't realized was now standing next to me. A man who looked so familiar, with his dark hair and dark eyes and dimples.

A man in a blue shirt and khakis.

I tried to sustain a smile, but it faltered in my sudden confusion.

"I am," I confessed. "And you're…"

"David. Well, okay, it's really Daniel, but I didn't want to use my real name until I knew if you were legit." He looked me over. "And you certainly seem to be the real thing. You look just like your picture."

"Uh…" My brow felt damp, and my breathing was shallow. "Yeah, I don't play those Internet games."

"Mind if I sit?"

I shook my head. "No, go right ahead."

As he took over the stool, he said, "I'm sorry I was so late. There was an accident on the Inner Loop and I was trapped."

I allowed myself a smile. "You're only a few minutes late," I said. "Hopefully, that's nothing that can't be overcome."

David—I mean *Daniel*—was actually very understanding when I excused myself roughly twelve seconds into our date. Stuart had managed to make it down the block to the parking lot, but not to his car, by the time I caught up with him.

"Congratulations," he said when he saw me. "I crossed paths with the man I assume is your date on the sidewalk. Blue shirt and khakis, right?" I nodded. "So he really exists."

"Uh…yeah. About that…I guess I owe you an apology."

He waved the apology away. "Forget it. You jumped to some strange conclusions, but from my perspective, it was just good to see you again."

The cold mist—or maybe it was the words I was about to utter—made me shiver slightly.

"You want to have dinner?"

His eyes narrowed to slits as he looked at me. "Tonight? I thought that offer was off the table."

"No, I, uh…I think I need a couple of days to think about things."

Stuart pulled his car keys from his pocket and said, "Call me after you're done thinking, and maybe…"

"Sunday."

"Excuse me?"

"Let's have dinner Sunday."

He smiled. "Pasta Night? Only if you sing me the song."

And so I did.

Because if you can't be silly standing in a cold misty rain on the cracked asphalt of a municipal parking lot with the man you've just realized you never stopped loving, when can you?

TRUNK

Trebor Healey

Ending up in the trunk of a car headed for Houston was not what Bobby'd had in mind when he came to New Orleans. Of course, he hadn't counted on vomiting on the shoes of the Reverend Norman DuMay either, nor running into the likes of Old Croc and his creepy mojo medicine. In fact, Bobby'd come to New Orleans in order to avoid such things (an ironically interesting choice for such an escape), to lay low and get his life in order, to do the right thing. He'd come to volunteer, to help rebuild in the aftermath of Katrina, to turn over a new leaf for himself and his relationship to the world.

That's what he told himself anyway.

On a more visceral level, he'd been drawn like a magnet to the Crescent City out of an odd sort of identification. He wasn't so much appalled and horrified by Katrina as he was pruriently and subliminally intrigued with it. Perhaps it was a conviction that he was sinking fast and that what was happening on the flooded streets of New Orleans was a disturbingly apt metaphor for his own inundation—with booze, semen, crystal meth, and all manner of unbridled desire. What was that old line of Hamlet's? "'Tis better to take arms against a sea of troubles, and by opposing, end them?" Maybe he and this dear unfortunate city could help each other? Something like that. Bobby wasn't thinking too clearly. New Orleans as Yorick? Or was it all a fool's errand? Call it a sort of megalomaniacal codependence; call it a cry for a help; call it a cautionary tale for the neocon dream or any other twisted sort of messianic hogwash. Bobby was looking for an anchor, and what better place to look for it than the sea.

Glued as he'd been to his television set and his laptop through most of September, he'd witnessed the National Guard in their speedboats rescuing dogs and obese women off roofs; he'd seen the Superdome packed to bursting, the president smugly attempting a riff on "ich bin ein New Orleanian," though it came out "moron" or "asshole"—Bobby couldn't tell which. Neither he nor the leader of the free world could speak French.

Eight months later, channel surfing the TV, his laptop balanced on his knees, Bobby once again blazed to the nines on speed, with no fewer than nine IM boxes open with such names as 9inchbliss, Gutterthroat, and Gettheebehindmesatan, it dawned on him that no one was really doing anything much about the fate of New Orleans—least of all him (he'd been too broke buying drugs and booze to even send the meager twenty-five dollars in response to that letter from the Red Cross that came with the return address labels he'd been using for the past year), and that no one likely would. It had become a lousy reality TV show with no plot other than "the government doesn't care, it really doesn't." Katrina gave sink or swim a whole new meaning. Laissez-faire. Well, it was a French term and New Orleans was the Frenchest of cities, and America hates the French—even begrudges them their fries

now that the holy war is on. Meanwhile the vice president bela-
bors the country with the intricacies of flood insurance fraud
when he's not shooting his friends in the face with buckshot, and
the president is too busy feeding Christmas trees into a shredder
(wait those aren't trees, they're young men!) to be bothered with
such inconsequential things as chocolate cities—though he did
call his white friend "Brownie." Hey, let 'em eat brownies. But
who was George Bush, anyway—Willy Wonka? Did he look like
Johnny Depp? No. He was a godly man; he had people to kill
and nations to destroy. The Lord's work. He'd as likely rebuild
New Orleans as he would Iraq or the Tower of Babel.

Bobby snorted another line, muttering, "Man, this country
sucks."

Moments later, he nearly choked as he quaffed another Sierra
Nevada. Sink or swim. A jolt of guilt shook him, and he looked
around the room—clothes strewn about, scattered empty beer
bottles, and tiny cans of amyl nitrate; fast-food bags and wrap-
pers; a hole where his friend Kip had punctured the drywall
during a particularly out-of-hand sex scene. What on earth was
going on? How many beers had he drained while watching the
news reports of the devastation over those past nine months?
How many porn sites and Internet chat rooms had he barreled
into, ignoring the news stories of Katrina's wrath and aftermath
on the portal pages on his way in and out, while the tragedy
droned on at low volume from the TV across the room? How
many lines of speed had he snorted, brilliant white as a Katrina
trailer? How many boys had flooded him? Had he flooded?
All while the levees sat unrepaired. How many times had his
heart filled with horror and repulsion that he was comparing his
pathetic broken-down life—albeit one with a roof over his head,
a job, and three squares—to victims of a natural disaster? Was
his life really an ongoing hurricane? Was it that bad? Was he

that self-indulgent? He looked in the mirror, chipped the crusted scab of a speed bump off his cheek. Even FEMA wouldn't be able to help *him*. It was that bad. A line from back in the day when gay people had a political conscience flitted through his mind: The personal is political.

He thought of Father Robert, his Jesuit uncle. What had he always said? If things are really bad, and beyond help, go help someone else. Of course, that was easy for him to say. He had a vocation. What did Bobby have? A big dick? An AA degree? A habit?

There were lists of organizations on the *L.A. Times* website. He steered clear of the Christians, as he knew from experience that he'd always end up on the wrong end of a Bible quote with those geeks. He was a proud, out homo and that wasn't something he was willing to put aside. This was about helping other people, not sucking it up and taking abuse from selfish fucks whose only motivation was their own sanctimony and a low-point mortgage in the afterlife.

There was the Red Cross, the United Way, etc., but he didn't want to end up in some office in Baton Rouge. He wanted to be on the ground, knee-deep in it, just like he was in his own self-destruction. He chanced upon something called GUMBO (Greater United Metropolitan Betterment Organization), which looked sufficiently lefty and irreverent to be prohomo or at least laissez-faire about such things (one picture of its volunteers had a group of dreadlocked hippie boys playing hacky sack in a park, while nearby little girls in cornrows played ring-around-the-rosy). No-brainer. He immediately filled out the volunteer application form to join a crew gutting damaged houses for poor folks with no insurance in the Ninth Ward.

The minute he clicked to submit his application, he was ecstatic and felt newly self-empowered. He began cleaning up his room, the poppers and beer cans clanging together like the opening bars to some cheesy musical: *Poppers and beer cans and sweet apple strudel, faggots and rainbows and...* He felt—well—good, upbeat, upstanding, well-endowed, and attractive; a sure bet to get laid. He was full of himself, a narcissistic federal disaster area that Mr. Bush would be wise to do absolutely nothing for. *I'm an activist*, Bobby congratulated himself; *a do-gooder; part of the solution; a relief worker.* He felt so good, he threw a going-away party for himself, got shit-faced drunk, and blew his friend Ed in the bathroom.

Of course, what Bobby found in New Orleans was anything but relief.

It started on the airplane, where a comely flight attendant named Bo scribbled his hotel room number on a cocktail napkin after shamelessly flirting and feeding Bobby free gin and tonics between Phoenix and New Orleans.

Bobby made it a point to stop at three cocktails and took no speed breaks in the bathroom, telling himself he would simply make it a date and not do anything sexual.

He failed.

But he only had one bump, two beers, and he used a condom. Progress. And at least it gave him a place to sleep his first night in New Orleans.

He set out early next morning as the steward had an eight a.m. flight to Minneapolis and was clearly moving on to the next thing, showering and chattering on his cell phone while Bobby gathered his things together like a hobo, more or less ignored by his host.

He got a quick insincere smile and a small wave as the glorified waitress chortled on about the Denver-to-Dallas route with some queeny colleague, slamming the door behind Bobby as if he were putting the dog out, his gaze all but averted. In fact, Bobby barked, assuming of course that the joke would go unnoticed, as it did to all but himself.

He stumbled onto the streets of Metairie, which didn't look half bad, considering what had happened a year prior. He'd expected worse. He hailed a cab for downtown so he could stroll through the beloved historic district and assess the damage on his way to the GUMBO office out past the Marigny in the Gentilly District. He wanted to wallow in his heroism a bit, which was markedly different from what he usually wallowed in when he visited New Orleans for Southern Decadence each year. He purposely avoided Bourbon Street, strolling along Royal Street at first and then cutting up to Burgundy, threading his way around the "trouble spots" that might derail his "new leaf."

To his surprise, the French Quarter looked downright passable—in fact, he wouldn't have known there was a hurricane if he hadn't looked for the broken windows and damaged, tarped roofs, which were incidentally loaded with hot-looking Latin boys, hammering about and being masculine. Thank God they had work to do or he might have lingered.

Then things quickly deteriorated as Bobby headed out into the neighborhoods. Enormous trees upended, piles of refuse up and down the curbs, Katrina trailers parked here and there asserting their ugliness while the charming houses desolately frowned with abandonment, shamed at their high-water marks and concave porches like week-old diapers no one had bothered to change.

He checked in at the GUMBO office on Elysian Fields, a fairly undamaged area, if you ignored the blue tarps draped across every other roof, the boarded-up windows, and the ubiquitous red spray paint graffitied on every other house with dates and numerical renderings of how many dogs or people were left inside in need of rescue or food drops.

He thought briefly of Noah—his ex, not the biblical character. Noah had been a contractor. He'd also gone off the deep end with speed and vanished into the digital divide—he was either addicted to porn and Internet cruising or unable to pay his ISP bill, Bobby could never remember which. Regardless, the results were more or less the same. Man overboard.

The folks at GUMBO were smart, informed, and not fucking around. "We're here because the government isn't, and we aren't surprised about that." Bobby felt that old dread of self-righteous lesbianism that every circuit fool gayboy feels when his Peter Pandom is exposed under the glaring lights of women who have moved beyond taking care of and making excuses for boys.

"Uh, yeah, great…. Uh, me, too," he fumbled.

"Well, welcome Robert," the pretty mulatto girl answered.

"Call me Bobby?"

She gave a quick smile, as if he'd cracked a bad joke, and reached into a drawer for some materials he'd need to read.

His first order of business was to get settled in a house GUMBO'd recently lent to them. He and eight other volunteers would bunk there while he completed his three-week volunteer gig.

It was only a few blocks away, so he hoofed it over there, and sure enough it was rife with hippie boys in various states of undress. New Orleans is hot and humid, not a place for clothing. But the thrill soon paled after he listened to them talk for a bit. Hopelessly straight and conventional and moralistic, like most hippie boys, Bobby was soon annoyed by their unavailable prettiness, their reggae music, their guitars and bongo drums. He knew he'd likely be keeping more or less to himself, and that none of these boys would likely give it up for the visiting fag, no matter how hip and cool they thought themselves. "Yo bra, nice dreadlocks, chocolate city, yeah," and the ghetto fist-play greeting.

He grabbed an empty bunk in the last room down the hall and headed to the bathroom, where he deposited what proved to be a traveler's turd, challenging the plumbing with its size and girth. As the water swirled and rose, Bobby felt a sudden shame, thinking that what New Orleans, of all cities, really didn't need was another turd floating down the street. He felt guilty, Californian, a fuckup, a bad omen; he panicked. He searched the bathroom for a plunger. He flushed again. The toilet water rose on his own private Katrina moment, nearly cresting the rim before it began to retreat. *Thank God porcelain has integrity,* he thought as the water ebbed.

He went for help.

"No problem, dude, we all get traveler's turd on the road. There's a plunger on the back porch." Sheesh, what a frat house. He went to work with it, and as he plunged the third time, the plunger went inside out, and then quickly inverted itself, splattering shit across the walls, the toilet, and all over the front of Bobby's clothing. *Welcome to chocolate city,* he thought in disgust. An omen indeed. And then he heard the toilet drain, cough, and swallow. Praise Jesus.

Back at the GUMBO office, showered and decked out in cargo shorts and a polo shirt, Bobby mustered up the best attitude he could. The place was a zoo, and orientation was haphazard and fast. He was issued a white safety suit, as the dangers of toxic poisoning were substantial. He hadn't bargained for that. He'd heard of mold allergies and figured they couldn't kill him, but exposure to asbestos? Because what GUMBO did was gut and dismantle houses—something not covered by most insurance (and who had flood insurance anyway? Who could afford it?). And with a price tag of 7K, GUMBO was forced to beg donations and volunteers in order to make a dent in what was otherwise an almost insurmountable expense for most people. Admirably and against all odds, thanks to donations, sheer will, and an adopt-a-house program, they were getting people back into their homes, albeit slowly.

Bobby rushed home and modeled the white suit. It was made out of that weird sort of part plastic, part paper, part foil, part cloth stuff. The mask looked sexy at least—dangerous, sci-fi authoritarian—and like baggy jeans on a boy, the suit hung slack at the crotch and ass, so that if you could get beyond its clownish appearance, your imagination could conjure up tight butts and low-hanging balls, big uncut schlongs swinging pendulous and unimpeded like censors in search of a sanctuary. "My body is a temple," Bobby muttered. And he thought of Jared, Lars, Dylan, Josh, and Bennett in the next room, and how loose and naked their bodies floated inside those suits, like astronauts in space, the thick foliage where the hair stood out above their oversized cocks, like a fecund flower box on some resurrected shotgun shack of New Orleans. Bobby's fantasy soon tented the gossamer fibers of the suit's fabric—and it wouldn't be the last time—forcing him in the days following to repeatedly pretend that he needed to squat down to get at low chunks of insulation still clinging or scattered along the bottom of dismantled walls.

On one such occasion, the reverend showed up.

"I swear you look like children of the Rapture in those white suits. And so you are! Heh, heh. What you doing down there, son?"

Busted. Bobby looked up over his shoulder from his crouched position. "Uh, just doing what I came here to do, sir. To make these houses habitable again."

"Just in time for the next storm," the Reverend DuMay

chuckled, ducking under a scaffold and making his way through the little shotgun house Bobby had been assigned to work on his first week along with a one-week veteran, Tony, a Catholic boy from Boston—definitely not one of the hippie boys. Bobby did a double take on the reverend as he moved on.

"How you doin', son, welcome to God's country," DuMay beamed, greeting Tony.

Bobby stared, rapt. He'd never met a Southern preacher before.

"Has the Lord reached you, son, or are you lost still?" A grin crossed DuMay's face, and Bobby's jaw went slack as he awaited Tony's reply.

Tony didn't miss a beat. "Jesus is my Lord and savior, sir." And they high-fived. So much for avoiding Christians.

The reverend guffawed. "Oh, son, you are ripe. Ripe as a swollen peach. I could just pick you off the tree." And he laughed and pinched Tony's cheek as if he were a small child. Then he turned and winked at Bobby, before walking out the back and on to the next house.

"Who is *that*?" Bobby asked Tony, incredulous.

"Oh, that's the reverend. He's harmless."

"As in the crazy being harmless?"

"Oh, he's into Armageddon." And he shrugged his shoulders. "Takes all kinds."

Bobby scrunched his eyes. "Does it?"

"God works in strange ways. I mean all the reverend asks is if you've accepted Jesus Christ? Haven't you?"

"Sure, what the fuck, he's welcome along with everyone else. I don't play favorites."

"He's the only one."

Bobby glared at him. "Aren't you a *Catholic*?"

"Yeah," he said defensively, "we believe in Jesus, too."

Bobby arched his brows, but couldn't help smiling. Born of a long line of Marian heretics, Bobby thought it a dubious argument at best. But wasn't it just his luck that he got paired up with the religious one out of all the cute little humanist hippies, who were probably Wiccans or Buddhists. Then again, his chances of sex were probably higher with Tony, as a good fifty percent of Christian boys were major fence-sitters. *It's a fuckin' gay religion,* he thought, and he meant *gay* like a twelve-year-old meant it.

But Tony was kind of cute. In fact, he had a twinkle in his eye that Bobby was beginning to think was not the Holy Spirit. There's only one other kind of man who has such a twinkle in his eye. Well, twinkle or no, Tony also had a fat, homely fiancée named Emily whose picture was tucked in the frame of the Anglo Jesus portrait above his bed, right next to the palm frond from Palm Sunday. Damning evidence. Bobby saw him as several years shy of the self-discovery and reflection necessary to go down on a guy, but he also suspected that in time he would. Bobby didn't have that kind of time, and certainly didn't have that kind of patience—but then again, shouldn't he at least try to move things along for Emily's sake?

Lust springs eternal.

But how? He'd committed to three weeks. Oh, sure, one part of Bobby thought that was plenty of time. An hour was enough with a lot of men. But he'd need privacy and some downtime, a little booze—none of which were abundant, if available at all, in the bunkhouses of GUMBO.

They went back to work, lugging a stove out to the curb, hacking up some water-damaged furniture, and chipping away at more of the walls and ceilings. Quitting time came and they went out front to survey the Katrina pile they'd made, which they proudly compared to the other less towering ones up and down the street.

They unzipped their suits, and climbed out of them.

"Damn, it's hot," Tony whined, stripping off his T-shirt to reveal his excruciatingly perfect little chest. Ouch. Elvis Presley's "Don't Be Cruel" lullabyed through Bobby's code-red-alerted brain. Good God, but lust was merciless. And never one to pass up even a semblance of opportunity—or failing that, just some good old-fashioned interactive homoeroticism—Bobby did the same. They looked at each other. "Dude, you're ripped," Tony shared.

"You, too, man. You work out?"

"Nah, just lucky I guess."

"Lucky, eh?" *No, it's Emily who's lucky,* Bobby thought. Tony, he was about to go home and step in a pile of karmic shit called marriage that was far more substantial than any Katrina pile.

Just then the reverend came strolling by on his way back to wherever he came from before his visit. "Better keep those suits on, boys; the Lord comes like a thief in the night. Heh, heh, heh. Wouldn't wanna miss him." And he waved and hopped into a chauffeured blue Crown Royal parked two doors down.

"Can't they like get a restraining order for that guy?" Bobby thoughtlessly said into the middle distance.

Tony furrowed his brow. "It's a free country, dude. Jesus rocks." Bobby just looked at him and nodded slowly.

Unlike Tony and Bobby, the reverend wasn't part of GUMBO, though he took it upon himself to inspect their work often and "minister to them," as he called it. He ran his own outfit called BIO, which stood for "Bring It On," meaning the apocalypse. He was sure it was coming and thought the rebuilding effort foolish. But he was doing a lot of good in his own fashion, through his soup kitchens and revival flea markets where people could barter all manner of goods, and the faithful could come down from Kansas or Missouri and do big giveaways with whatever they had to offer: clothes mostly, canned goods, soap.

No, sir, he didn't see Katrina the same way the lefties did. He was elated with the nearness of Armageddon and thought GUMBO a bunch of ignorant, godless liberals, suffering under the sin of pride, thinking they could avert the wrath of God, offering false promise and material assistance to poor wayward lambs. He'd sort of stroll around the GUMBO houses, shaking hands, clearly struggling with his own pride issues, a gaggle of sycophants at his heels. Tacky as Jim Jones, he had a thick white mane of hair and wore purple-tinted oversized aviator glasses and beige leisure suits that swelled with his girth and shook when he laughed. "You're not that different from a bunch of communists really—and we know where they ended." And he'd burst out laughing. At times like that, Bobby wanted to snap back, "Yeah, well you ain't that different than Il Duce or Herman Goering, and they ended worse."

It was good he didn't though, because everyone laughed along with the reverend, and in fact, liked him. He had charisma, and a ready smile, a Southern congeniality that made him basically un-hateable. Besides, some of the hippie boys were in fact *wearing* Che shirts, and the word on the street was the levees were in no shape to hold back another Katrina, which would once again flood every single house GUMBO was repairing. So the reverend had a point, whether you wanted to reflect on it or not, or whether you espoused his biblical paradigm. And on top of all that, as everyone at GUMBO knew, the man had been there from the start feeding and sheltering people in tents, and his credibility in terms of relief work was unquestioned. On some level, they were all in it together, and he was just betting on a different horse than they were. The differences between

GUMBO and the Reverend DuMay was along the lines of the friendly banter between White Sox and Cubs fans, although with far more dire consequences for the winners and losers.

But couldn't the reverend put a cork in it? The hippie boys weren't proselytizing about Buddha or Leonard Peltier, after all. But DuMay just chattered on endlessly, full of the confident bludgeoning rhetoric of an unquestionably dominant religion, while he meandered about the houses, his booming voice echoing off what was the left of the walls. "The president loves New Orleans, like he loves Jesus. We're the chosen people, and the president is proud of our witnessing. There's no city he cares for more. Why we're like the troops. In harm's way—no holier place to be. The president knows that; he supports us as God supports the righteous. He's in awe of the grace of our crucifixion, and when the great hurricane Lucifer Katrina the Second comes, he knows we will be lifted up like buoys. Oh, ye of little faith, ye liberal devils, trying to drown us in your thirty pieces of silver. No, Lord, we don't want this cup to pass. We want to drink it down, drown in your righteousness. You oughta all go home and get your own houses in order, not ours."

"But, but…" Tony attempted a response. When conservative and liberal Christians collide.

"But nothing, son," and he guffawed.

Stern words, but the smile always spread across his face whenever he was most scolding, in effect emasculating and charming every audience that heard him. He was a preacher all right, the likes of which Bobby'd never seen. After all, Bobby had been raised Catholic, and Catholic priests were generally either white liberal wimps, corny yarn-spinning Irishmen, or besotted unimaginative English majors who churned out bad critical essays in place of sermons, outlining why the resurrection made things different than if he hadn't been resurrected, or why it's better to obey your mom then to tell her to fuck off. No duh. So Bobby had slept a lot during mass, when he wasn't fantasizing about the altar boys or other parishioners while the priest droned on.

But he listened when the reverend spoke. How he listened. The Reverend DuMay was an artist of the first order. He left people speechless, and Bobby found himself drawn to him.

"How you doing, Mr. Kennedy...Mr. Attorney General of thee You-nited States," he'd joke, "did you catch all the Mafiosi yet?! Heh, heh, heh. Mark my words, son, they'll shoot a proud man before they'll give him the keys to heaven. George Bush is a righteous man. It's written in the stars." And he'd gesture with his hand toward the sky.

Bobby would just laugh back, but he could detect the subtext, though he resisted the temptation to deconstruct the reverend's balderdash to preserve his own peace of mind. What was the point with these people? When all was said and done, Bobby found it simpler to just treat the reverend like a very good stand-up comic who he didn't always agree with, but who, he had to admit, was very entertaining. A guilty pleasure. He wondered if the reverend was aware that many people probably saw him this way—as a sort of clown. Bobby thought he was, and as if he were reading his mind, the reverend soon enough eerily quipped, "I'm but a fool, Bobby, an instrument. Oh, His glory is great." And he smiled ear to ear.

An answer for everything.

Well, try this on for size, Reverend. Bobby was jonesing for speed, and though he'd on several occasions shared a beer or two with the boys back at the house, in between hacky sack sessions, he was determined not to fall back into drunkenness and debauchery, sex in alleys, and most of all the ever-destructive crystal. He'd fought the good fight for two weeks. A new leaf. God, but he was horny as sin, and he'd fought too hard to be queer and proud to classify good sex as depraved along the lines of alcohol and speed. He'd vowed to have only healthy sex. But how does one find good, healthy sex? He didn't have the patience, and what's more, GUMBO was straight as the siding on a Katrina trailer. He was over outreach fantasies for the hippies, and Tony...oh, Tony. Tony was ruining him with desire. Lately, Tony had developed an annoying habit of looking over from his ladder like a bro and smiling. Bobby had tolerated it at first, when he was still busy collecting the requisite masturbation material for later, like a bird feathering its nest. But after a week, every smile felt like Eros pulling back his bow: One, two, three—all day long like Bobby was a hay bale or a sitting duck. He felt swollen and tenderized, sensitive to any touch. Tony just kept smiling and firing away, the heartless bastard. And then of course, there was the "Jesus rocks" answer to any and all good news or common sense truth shared with him—the Christian rocker's amen.

"Nice day."

"Jesus rocks."

"I like these crowbars."

"Jesus rocks."

And the hugs. Oh, the hugs. "Blessings, dude." At the end of every workday. But never when they'd taken their shirts off. Oh, no. Always once they'd put them back on. The cheap bastard. Bobby soon took to scowling at Tony's smiles and dodging his hugs. He knew it wasn't nice, but he couldn't stand the tease of it, even if Tony would never conceive of it as such. Tony was an idiot and a vacuous phony. But a hot one.

Tony eventually got the hint that Bobby wasn't into Jesus or his smiles—or was it more like he'd begun to feel that there was chemistry between them? That's when he'd start going on and on about his wedding to Emily, planned for when he got back to Boston.

"How old are you, Tony?"

"Twenty," he defensively answered.

"Isn't that kind of young to be getting married?"

"Better to marry than to burn."

I prefer fire, Bobby thought to say as a luscious bead of sweat rolled down Tony's cheek and onto his smiling upper lip. As Bobby gazed at the beautiful boy, their eyes locked in platonic love—or something—he knew what that night would bring. He'd had it. *Hell or high water.* Yeah, exactly. The water had receded, so he knew what part of that cliché was heading his way.

He'd stayed away for two weeks, but now he was dead set on Bourbon Street and the notorious Corner Pocket, where the dregs of the parish stripped for change, and the beer and speed breached the levee of whatever inhibitions remained in the poor lost lambs of the French Quarter.

It was Tony's fault, not his.

Tony did his bare-chested routine as usual at the end of the day, and this time Bobby just stared, quickly slurping up the drool that threatened to fall from his lower lip. Tony said, "What, dude?"

Bobby just shook his head. Tonight he'd clear the slate. He'd go down to Bourbon Street and clear the slate. He'd held out long enough. He'd avoided drunkenness, drugs, sex, and even fallen for a clean-living Christian and done the Lord's work. *But God, I miss that old leaf*, he sighed.

"You wanna go out tonight? Like down to Bourbon Street?" Bobby chanced.

"No."

"Great. See you tomorrow."

On went the shirt. "Blessings." The embrace. A stirring in

Bobby's crotch. They parted and Bobby waved, and it was all he could do to keep the digits surrounding his middle finger from dropping into a little fist.

Bobby didn't bother going home for a shower. He knew he looked enticingly blue-collar and was in no mood for anyone looking for a clean-cut soap-smelling boy anyway. He was looking for another beast.

He marched down Elysian Fields, sweat cresting his brow, the humidity so thick the clouds and the sky sort of merged into an amorphous bluish white-gray steam. He cut up Frenchmen, and, crossing Esplanade—one signal-light post stuck like a tiki torch in the grass at a forty-five degree angle (ah, the charms and grandeur of hurricanian ruination)—he had a laugh and thought of the River Styx. Whatever Eurydice he sought would be a sorry wreck of a slut indeed.

Sylvester was crooning at top volume when he entered the Bourbon Pub, and eyes swung about from the surrounding men as he entered from the street: some like babies toward shiny things, a handful like prowling cats, and still others like roused guard dogs who wanted a piece of his flesh or at least a good chase and tackle before moving on.

He glared back with his usual fuck-you-all visage, acquired among the clubs of L.A., and approached the bar. A sorry-looking go-go boy gyrated in a pair of boxer briefs, and Bobby momentarily wished the lad's pecs were as full of air as they looked so he could prick one with a pin and watch the boy fly around the room like a deflating balloon.

That's when he felt a distinctly reptilian presence at his side. He quickly glanced over out of a sort of animal watchfulness, and who did he see sitting on the stool next to him at the bar but the Reverend DuMay himself, a pack of Marlboros and a cocktail perched in front of him, like some flaming queen, his hair coiffed, and sporting a big oversized yellow-print Hawaiian shirt. He, too, looked at Bobby with the eyes of a hunter, but more like one with a long tongue that would strangle you in its embrace. Then he grinned, erasing all threat.

Figures the reverend would be queer. Bobby felt so tired suddenly.

"It's Saturday night, son, and the Sabbath is just around the corner. What are you doing in this den of iniquity?"

"Oh, just a little R&R, Father." Bobby was in no mood. He felt like he'd crossed over at Esplanade and was through with the provincial squeamishness of do-gooders and hypocritical Christians alike.

"I'm not a Father, son, I'm a reverend."

"Oh, sorry, I was raised Catholic."

"I suspected as much; you've always had the stink of popery about ya."

He clipped a quick smile. "And what exactly kind of stink is that, Reverend?" he shot back.

"Sorta like sulfur, like frankincense and myrrh, but cooked a spell too long. Heh, heh, heh." And then, "Can I buy you a drink, son?"

"Sure. Bud Light. Thanks." Why not use the reverend to get the buzz going, he figured.

"One Bud Light and one seven-and-seven." He turned to Bobby after ordering. "I drink seven-and-seven on account of the biblical references to the seven plagues, the seven angels, the seven days of creation, and the seven seals of revelation, not to mention how many times Jesus asked us to forgive one another: seventy times seven."

"Well, I drink Bud Light on account of it ain't Coors and they support the gay rags with advertising."

"I'll have to remember to boycott it. Heh, heh. Always preferred Coors myself. Heh, heh, heh."

"That's big of ya, Reverend."

"So you're a homosexual, eh, Bobby?"

"Yes, sir."

"Well, ain't you curious why I'm here?"

"You're one, too, I guess. Frankly, it doesn't surprise me."

"Heh, heh. Not quite, son." And he leaned over to whisper, "I'm undercover. Heh, heh." Then he sat back again. "I'm here to save souls. Do you know how disgusted our Lord would be to look down on this? I've started a new ministry because time is running out. The Rapture is gonna pass right over this place— and not Passover-style either, no sirree. These men here, they're all going straight to hell. And I aim to do something about it."

Just then "Stop! In the Name of Love" blasted out of the speakers. Bobby felt his political ire rising. He was taking a day off of his good behavior and besides, he was in his element. "Reverend, what makes you think that these guys here are interested in what you're selling?"

"I'm not selling anything, son; I'm revealing it. I'm offering it. For free. With a rebate. Money-back guarantee. The lottery itself." His smirk.

Bobby drained the beer and set it down, wondering if the preacher would offer to buy him a second, or whether he should drag the man off his barstool and to the door. The reverend looked heavy, though. A Herculean task. And didn't Hercules have *seven* labors or something? Maybe he should just start screaming, or blow a whistle ACT-UP style. But no one had whistles anymore.

"The Lord died once for your sins, son. Just once." And he pointed at the Bud bottle.

"What about the second coming?"

"You'll have to wait a spell, son. And better to be sober for it."

Bobby looked at him with disdain. "So how does this work, Reverend? You pick a guy up, take him home, tie him up, and convert him?"

"Whatever it takes, son."

"Let me tell you something, Reverend. Half the guys in here don't believe in your God, and the other half do and they figure Jesus is either queer like them or he just feels the love and supports all this." Bobby scanned the room. "You won't find any souls to save here, Reverend, but you might find a knuckle sandwich. My advice would be to skedaddle."

"Though I walk through…"

"Yeah, yeah…." Bobby walked away, resolved to keep an eye on the reverend, but also to get what he came for, which just then came stumbling down the stairs in a tattered wife beater, tattooed like Queequeg, with the kind of scruff that made Bobby's balls tighten and tingle.

The rest of the evening was more or less like most of Bobby's L.A. evenings of years past—a sort of time-suspended circus involving strange leering, smiling faces; a gloopy techno soundtrack; the perusal and exploration of numerous male orifices; the feeling of cold brick against his face, his hands; the hardness of cement on his knees; the burning in his nose, and the rising of frequent belches; the anxieties of, "Did he use a condom? I can't remember," and a chorus of, "Sure for a drink, I will. My name's Bobby," filling his head like a cacophony of advertising jingles. He rode the pinball night in the same way he always had.

It was as he was barreling out the door of the Corner Pocket, his head swimming, sure that the cute boy taking off the discolored, faded BVDs up on the bar was none other than his dear Tony—no doubt full of the gay-for-pay excuse that he needed money for the wedding—when he bumped into Old Croc on the sidewalk. Old Croc was dressed in heaps of rags, and his face shined with sweat. He had friendly, uncannily familiar eyes though, and when they met Bobby's they drilled right through Bobby's frontal lobe like an all-knowing mother's. "I been lookin' for ya," Old Croc smiled.

"What the fuck, leave me alone."

But Old Croc poked at him with his cane as Bobby reeled and leaned against the wall. "The mojo got you, and you'll be dead this time tomorrow if you don't take my mojo medicine."

All the superstitions of his Irish Catholic childhood were roused: black cats, ladders, broken mirrors, and cracks in the sidewalk. Old Croc held out what looked like huckleberries, and Bobby suspected they'd likely kill him on the spot. Not such a bad thing perhaps.

"You better take these or your mojo's gonna finish you off. This time tomorrow. No time to waste. The spirit told me."

Bobby looked at him. He was scared, but his reason told him this man was just a bum looking for a dollar and preying on scared tourists from places like L.A. where voodoo and juju nonsense only appeared in the movies. Bobby leaned down with his hands on his knees, muttering something unsuccessfully to send Old Croc on his way.

"Bobby!" he heard someone call.

Without lifting his hands or torso, he craned his neck and saw a yellow mass moving down the sidewalk. DuMay. "Shit," he muttered, and then he pulled himself up, reeled, and grabbing the huckleberries from Old Croc's open palm, slammed them back like a handful of peanuts.

"Beware of false prophets, son," Old Croc whispered. "Now gimme a little something, and ah promise you, the mojo will leave you be once and for all, and you'll find true love."

Bobby yanked a wad of bills out of his front pocket and proffered them to Old Croc, who quickly snapped the bundle up, turned, and limped off with his carved wooden cane around the corner and down Burgundy Street.

"Get thee behind me, Satan...or in front of me...or whatever," DuMay's voice trailed off as he hurried his girth up St. Louis Street. "Bobby, Bobby," DuMay called out like a lovelorn mother, "God bless you, my son, you are enveloped in the darkness, sick with the tree of knowledge and its foul fruit. But I'm here to deliver you...." And just as DuMay reached him, Bobby's hands went down on his knees again. As the reverend reached out to steady his shoulders, out came an explosive spew of vomit which the reverend was too slow to step aside from, his white loafers showered now in the orange and yellow regurgitated alcohol, Fritos, semen, beer nuts, and huckleberries of Bobby's dismal fall from grace.

Bobby woke up in the megachurch, propped up in a pew, huge metal rafters above him, and DuMay up there at the pulpit, fully wired, his voice echoing and resounding off the metallic walls of what appeared to be an enormous aluminum-sided trailer the size of an airplane hangar.

"I'm down in the trenches with ya, boys. The trench, that's what your kind of boy likes, ain't it? Heh, heh. Face up to it, boys! It's a trench, a foul gutter, an irrigation ditch full of crocs and snakes—all manner of disease, slime, and putridity. The Lord is gonna lift you up. These hands, my hands, will lift ya. And I ain't wearing gloves either. I ain't afraid of your filth. And I'll catch you when you fall, boys. I'll catch ya. I'm a catcher. Heh, heh. BIB, sons, that's what I call my ministry for you all. For the homo-sekshoo-all. BIB. Say it. BIB: Bringing It Back to the heterosexual fold. Bring It Back! Shout it out!"

There was a lame muttering of repetition among the sixty or so tortured homosexual congregants. "We're bringing it on and we're bringing it back! And you know what *IT* is, and where *IT* belongs. The Garden, boys. That's what a woman is. A garden. That's what the hoochie is—a garden! Not some toxic Superfund site like where you're puttin' it! And BIB's the way. Let me fasten that bib 'round your neck, like a bib of righteousness, and when that foul food of the devil drips from your mouth, the bib of the Lord will catch it and keep that pure white Sunday shirt of the second coming clean as mother's precious, holy milk." He pounded the lectern with his index finger. Bobby tried to follow along, but all he could think of were DuMay's fouled white shoes, his sore throat, and the ache in his rectum; his pounding head and burning septum; his parched mouth. "And the Lord, he'll recognize you at the apocalypse. And it's comin'. Mark my words. And there ain't no place at the table for the butt pirate. No, sirree! Now get that bib on! Get it on! Bring it on!"

Something in the reverend's words reached Bobby then, and feeling a surge of energy, he rose, watched the building spin for a few seconds, and once he'd secured his footing, bolted for the door.

Two no-necks stood with folded arms at the entrance, and as Bobby felt more vomit rising, he saw the horrified looks on their faces. They stepped aside and he proceeded to vomit into the cheap, aluminum-sided locked door, which snapped off its hinges and swung, collapsing like a space shuttle support platform, backward to reveal the plane of flooded Chalmette, Louisiana—its upended oak trees and ruined houses, a swath of destruction so immense Bobby could actually see all the way to Interstate 10 in the distance, and made straight for it.

"You can't run from Jesus, boys," he heard the microphone boom. "He's faster than vomit rising. You can't eat without a bib! The world is a trough of sin…You're pigs in it…."

It all faded to an echo as Bobby ran like an escaped convict, ran with all he had, his temples pounding with hangover, his ass aching, tears streaming down his face. My God, maybe he had been born again. But into what he couldn't tell.

He was sobbing by the time he reached the interstate and saw the gas station and the couple arguing. There was only one other customer, a local in a pickup, who soon disappeared into the restroom. He looked back at the couple, the car loaded down with luggage. They were definitely on their way somewhere else. Far from New Orleans—its trailers and mold; its hacky-sacking do-gooders and closeted straight boys; its traveler's turds and poorly-laundered BVDs sagging off the gay-for-pay strippers at the Corner Pocket; its fucking gumbo and jambalaya and beignets; its Christian preachers and old men like Croc; its omens and voodoo. It was true. Voodoo. Bobby was pierced full of holes. So what if a good number of the more recent needles were seven inches and made of flesh, or loaded with meth and Jack Daniels? He was poked so full of holes he had to escape or he'd sink like a little gay Titanic down into the swamp, never to re-emerge.

He was in deep trouble.

Old Croc had been right, and so perhaps was DuMay. Bobby had the sad realization then that when someone was as wrong as him, almost everyone else was right, no matter how harebrained or stupid they were.

The couple kept arguing, the man now back at the trunk, pulling something out and flinging it at the woman. A dildo. She tossed it in a nearby trashcan.

"You happy?!" he shouted.

"Oh, Jeremy," she sighed, and he marched toward her, leaving the trunk open as she burst into tears and he hugged her close.

Her head was buried in his chest and his back was to Bobby, who just then got a wickedly convenient idea. *I have to leave now,* a voice said inside his head. Why ask for a ride? Two quick steps and he let himself roll sideways like he'd done in wrestling in high school, and he was in the trunk. But how to close it, and wouldn't they wonder how it got closed? But before he could figure a way, it slammed shut and he heard the man's muffled voice. "It's fucking six hours to Houston; let's get going."

He was elated to be escaping, and escaping seriously, far, far away like so many others had done from New Orleans not a year ago. But six hours in a trunk?

Fortunately, he passed out almost immediately.

He awoke when the car thumped over a dead possum and the woman screamed, "You killed it!"

"He was already dead!" the man shouted back in a slightly high, queer voice.

Bobby had no idea how long he'd been trapped in there, but he wanted out. The trunk was humid, claustrophobic, and smelled like spare tire and Prestone. Within minutes of awaking, Bobby decided that it had been a very bad idea to climb into the trunk, and he resolved to get out as soon as possible.

The rest had done him good, and the hangover had progressed to the stage where a shot or two of whiskey would finish it off once and for all. But for that, he needed to get out. He searched for a latch. Not that he planned to bail out at seventy miles an hour, but just to see if there indeed was one that could be opened from the inside. Perhaps next time they pulled over, he could climb out? Of course, they'd likely just peed and filled the tank when he'd climbed in, so it could be hours. But how long had he slept? He did the math: 15 gallons at 25 mpg = 25 x 15 = ... close to 400 miles. At seventy miles per hour, that was five-plus hours. They might be driving straight through to Houston. He hoped they'd stocked up on sodas and water at the gas station. Shit. A wave of panic jolted through him before it turned to dread. On top of that, he realized that unlike his captors, he now needed to pee. He held it as long as he could. An hour later, the trunk had another pungent odor.

"Good God," Jeremy grimaced, turning his head, "this trunk stinks." Then he saw Bobby curled up in it. "And there's someone in it!"

"What are you talking about, Jeremy?"

"Come here, look!"

"I can explain everything," Bobby muttered. "Please, please, I mean you no harm."

Jeremy look at Jenny; Jenny back at Jeremy.

They helped Bobby out of the trunk, along with their bags, and they took him inside, where they bathed him. "I'll do it, Jeremy!" Jenny commanded him as he began setting out soap and towels, unable to hide the big grin animating his face. "You go watch TV or something."

"Jeez, Jenny, I'm healed, remember?" Jeremy suddenly turned serious.

"Healing, Jeremy," she corrected him, "heeeee-ling." And he stormed past her to watch the *700 Club*.

Bobby was still dazed from hunger, fatigue, and everything else, and he barely stayed conscious through the bath, remembering nothing but Jenny's beaming smile and somewhat disturbing over-vigilance with the sponge, especially in the nether regions. Eventually, she folded him in a towel, doused him with baby powder, and put him to bed, with a kiss on the forehead.

He woke up to their arguing in the kitchen, the sink running, and dishes clanging about.

"Are you gonna be okay here while I'm at work?"

"Yes, I'll be fine," Jeremy insistently and impatiently answered her.

"Can you handle this, Jeremy?"

"Yes, I can handle it!" he retorted.

"Don't get so snappy. I'm just trying to help."

"Well, have a little confidence in me," he relented.

"If I had confidence in you, I wouldn't have done the intervention. You need support, not confidence."

"I need both, Jeanette."

"Just...Remember what you learned. This is your Gethsemane. Your cup."

Jeremy thought of PE in junior high when he played goalie in soccer. "My what?"

"This cup shall not pass?"

"What are you saying?"

"I'm saying, this is it, your crucifixion. Do you have what it takes?"

"I'm getting crucified now?"

"Temptation, Jeremy! It's your turn on the cross. God is watching you." And the soft rock station droned on in the background as Bette Midler crooned: "God is watching us, God is watching us, God is watching us...from a distance."

"I'll be fine, Jeanette. You're treating him like he's a murderer or something. I'm strong, have a little faith."

"Him? He has a name! Hello!"

"Whatever."

"See that's the problem, you guys don't even bother remembering names." She audibly sighed. "I don't know. I don't like it. We shouldn't have had him stay."

"What?"

"I mean we don't even know him."

"Christian love? Hello?"

"Christian love? You're not Christ, you're a homosexual who's finding his way back to righteousness, Jeremy. You've got to be conscious of your fragile state. He might be Satan."

"Would you stop?"

"I'm trying to help you!"

"Then leave me be to sink or swim!"

"Sink or swim. Did you look at him? He's a torpedo is what he is. Or a major iceberg. Now I know what they mean by hand-some devil."

"I can handle it," Jeremy half-pleaded. "Now, what's his name?"

"I'm not telling. I feel like I'm leaving a drunk in the house with a case of beer in the fridge. It's insane." She paused. "I should wake him up and take him into town and drop him at the shelter."

"That is so cold."

"You like him, I can tell."

"Oh, please."

"Admit it; he's handsome."

"You clearly think so. How long did that bath run? An hour? Myself, I'm more focused on women and marriage right now. Reverend DuMay healed me, and I'm safe in my spiritual bib thank you very much." Then he added, "And you're gonna be late for work."

"Okay, well, that's the spirit. Keep that bib front and center, Jeremy. I love you." Bobby heard a kiss. "I have faith and confi-dence in you. Totally. God bless. I'll be home at six."

Bobby waited for the door to close behind Jenny before he emerged, disheveled, in a pair of boxer shorts.

Jeremy turned, blushed, and quickly went back to the dishes, barking, "There's coffee and cinnamon buns on the table. Help yourself."

Bobby fell into a chair.

"Excuse me," Jeremy called out over the din of the faucet, "uh... what is your name?"

"Bobby."

"As in Robert?"

"As in Bobby."

Jeremy turned the sink off and began sponging down the counter, his eyes locked on the sponge while he spoke. "Well, Bobby, um, this is a Christian home and we don't come to the table in our underwear. Do you think you could put something on?"

"Sure, but I don't have any clothes, and I don't know what your wife—"

"She's not my wife; she's my sister."

"Oh, uh, your sister. I don't know what she did with my stuff."

"You can wear some of my clothes. Let me get them for you." Their eyes met, both of them blushing now.

"Wow, you're cute," Bobby stated flatly.

"Please. I'm not gay."

Oh, yeah, sure thing, Bobby thought. Maybe he hadn't escaped after all. Bobby suddenly felt trapped again. "You know, I really think I need some clothes and that I just gotta go, like now. I'm kinda confused and uh, a little stressed, and uh...." Bobby couldn't help himself. He started to cry.

"Hey, hey, it's okay." Jeremy took a step toward the table, and then arrested himself. "Don't cry." But Bobby cried. Jeremy carefully sat down in the chair opposite, out of range of any physical contact. Until Bobby reached his hand across the table. Jeremy grabbed it immediately.

"I think I'm having some kind of breakdown," Bobby blubbered.

"It's okay," Jeremy offered, at a loss. Six was a long way off. "Why don't I call nine-one-one."

"I don't need nine-one-one. Just hold my hand."

But Jeremy's pants were full to bursting. "Uh, I can't do that."

"You can't hold my hand?" Bobby looked at him with a face of total heartbreak.

Jeremy blushed, felt a bolt of something rip through his chest, and looked down at the place mat in front of him. "No."

"Please," Bobby pleaded, blubbering, gripping Jeremy's hand more firmly as he began to cry some more. Their hands tangled together hungrily until both chairs went skidding back across the linoleum as they simultaneously lurched forward into a kiss. Bobby dragged Jeremy across the table and they careened onto the floor. Straddling him, Bobby stopped kissing Jeremy long enough to grab his cheeks, look into his eyes, and ask, "Who the fuck are you?"

"I have no idea," Jeremy answered. "Who are you?"

Bobby shrugged. And dove back in.

Pangs of guilt shot through Jeremy as Bobby once again smothered him, and throwing aside everything he'd just learned, he began lustily yanking back the boxer shorts Bobby was wearing. *They are my underwear after all; there can't be any sin in that,* Jeremy rationalized.

They muttered and wept as they communed together and didn't really stop crying completely until they'd betrayed the books of Leviticus and Deuteronomy, as well as Paul's letters to the Corinthians and Romans—and arguably Timothy.

Spent, splayed on the floor together, Bobby spoke first. "I fuckin' need help."

"You need help? If you only knew."

"Oh, I think I know." Bobby leaned up on one elbow. Jeremy looked back quizzically. "You were lost and wanted to be found—all that shit, right?"

"Something like that."

"Yeah, well, me, too."

"And so, what happened?"

"Well, until ten minutes ago, I was pretty sure it hadn't worked."

"What?"

"Well, you know, like, I'm not a religious guy or nothing. But like, you know the Lord works in strange ways? Or maybe voodoo does."

"Meaning?"

"Meaning I really like you. Like really, really, really."

"I'm not available."

"Uh, well, neither am I actually. I never am. That's what I mean."

"I'm not really following this."

"Well, you know, star-crossed lovers, all that shit?"

"Romeo and Juliet?"

"More like Romeo and Jude, or Jeff, or something."

"Romeo and Jeremy."

"Bobby and Jeremy?"

"I have a dog. He's pretty much my significant other."

"Well, I'm a speed freak."

"I'm a Christian."

"I can't stand Christians."

"I want to be straight."

"I want to move in with you and get clean."

"I want to do what we just did," Jeremy said, sitting up.

"Me, too."

"But I can't."

"But we will."

"No."

"Yes."

And they did.

DE ANIMA

Joel Derfner

It was the morning after my boyfriend told me he wanted to seek freedom from homosexuality through the power of Jesus Christ that I decided to knit the brain.

A few nights before, I had dreamt that I was Sydney Bristow from "Alias" and had to recover a microchip from an opera house during a production of *Turandot* before intermission and then all of a sudden I was sitting at a table with a bunch of people who thought I was a moron until I pulled out a knitted model of the human brain and named all its parts correctly, at which point they were forced to reconsider their opinion of me.

In fact I did not name all its parts correctly; some of them I was faking, but luckily for me nobody else at the table knew any better. The dream brain was not structured like an actual human brain, so I suppose I can be forgiven for not knowing all its parts, but then again, the dream brain had its own anatomy, which the dream me should have known, so that's really no excuse. The segment I dishonestly called the medulla oblongata, for example, was a strip of purl stitches running down the center of each side that had no analogue in real life, and even in the dream I knew I was confusing *medulla* with *middle.*

The real-life me had been on a sock kick lately, knitting socks in self-patterning yarn for my sister, in variegated purple yarn for my friend Kathy for her birthday, in thick nubbly ragg wool for my boyfriend. But I was getting tired of socks, and besides, they took forever, especially since Bill had size eleven feet.

So shortly after I woke up, I Googled *knitted brain,* not really expecting to find anything but hoping against hope that there might be an example somewhere since I can't do anything without a pattern—as a child I feared Tinkertoys because they didn't come with instructions—and the first thing that came up was the website for the Museum of Scientifically Accurate Fabric Brain Art.

"This website is dedicated to Daisy Gilford, our founder and chief archivist," read the museum's home page, "who passed away in 2005, tragically before she could begin work on a knitted brain, which would surely have been her *chef d'oeuvre.*"

I instantly felt crushed because I wanted to be Daisy Gilford's best friend and now she was dead. Sure, I could learn everything about her and write her biography or become her posthumous disciple or maybe just drop her name casually in conversation at cocktail parties and raise my eyebrows in surprise when people didn't know who she was, but it wouldn't be the same. She had been a shy woman, I was certain, uncomfortable in the limelight, but she had loved her three dogs (I decided) deeply and why the fuck hadn't the world mourned its loss when she died without having knitted a brain, goddamn it? How many people would have been made truly happy by a visit to the Museum of Scientifically Accurate Fabric Brain Art who now would never know real joy? I quit the Web browser and ate four bowls of Wild

Berry Cheerios in rapid succession (with skim milk, but still).

"So," said Bill as we finished dinner at his place a couple nights later (he had cooked some chicken concoction with nectarine sauce; I had no idea where he came up with these things but they were always delicious), "it turns out I have to leave town tomorrow."

"What," I asked, sucking nectarine sauce off my index finger, "is Morgan Stanley sending you to some last-minute conference in Hawaii? Make sure you bring back a hot cabin boy for me."

"No, they'll all be too exhausted by the time I'm done with them." He took my plate and put it in the sink; I considered lunging after it for more nectarine sauce but then decided it would be undignified. "Actually, it's not for work. I'm going to an ex-gay conference."

"So no hot cabin boy is what you're telling me."

"Noah, I'm serious."

"Then I should tell you I'm converting to Zoroastrianism," I said as I opened the freezer door and bent over to find the ice cream (no sugar added). "The Zoroastrians are dying out, and—"

"I was talking to my mother yesterday."

Oh, shit, I thought. This was very bad. Bill's mother spent an undisclosed amount of time every day praying that he might start dating Becki Cramer again (she had been his girlfriend for three weeks in eighth grade). Mrs. Roth was otherwise a nice lady and if I alienated her, I would never get her key lime pie recipe, so most of the time I held my tongue.

"She said, 'Honey, there's a conference in Asheville, North Carolina, that I think you should go to,' and then I—"

"You're seriously going to a gathering of people who think that Jesus will make you straight if you throw out all your porn and Barbra CDs?"

"Why do you have to turn everything into a joke?"

I slammed the freezer door shut. There was only butter pecan ice cream anyway, which I think is repulsive. "I do not turn everything into a joke. Genocide: not a joke. AIDS: not a joke. People pretending not to be gay but wearing this year's Marc Jacobs: a joke."

"I think they make them wear last year's Marc Jacobs." He opened the freezer again and pulled the repulsive butter pecan ice cream out. "Anyway, I'm leaving tomorrow afternoon. I'm taking the week off work."

"Why on *earth* would you do such a thing?"

"Gee, Noah," he said, throwing his spoon down on the counter, "maybe it's because not all of us were born wearing a feather boa."

"You came out when you were twenty-nine! Shouldn't you be over this by now?"

"You're not over Bette Midler's sitcom being canceled and that was six years ago."

"That's *completely* different." I picked up Bill's spoon; I needed ice cream to get through this and if butter pecan was what there was then it would have to do. "For one thing—"

"Please don't be like this. Please, just give me some room to examine my life."

"If you say the words 'right with God,' I'm going to pour cabernet all over your Armani sweater."

"Right with God right with God right with God."

There was no cabernet immediately accessible so instead I went into the living room, deleted the last episode of "Bleak House" from the TiVo so Bill would never know what happened to Esther and Lady Dedlock, and went home.

When the phone rang at 7:30 the next morning I knew it was Bill so of course I didn't answer it but of course, he knew I wouldn't answer it, so he just started talking into the answering machine.

"Noah, get out of bed and pick up. I don't care if you don't have your glasses on or if you drooled all over your pillow. If you're looking for the phone, it's in the living room. No, not next to the couch, on top of the TV. Pick up pick up pick up pick up pick up. Papa don't preach, I'm in trouble deep, papa don't preach, I've been losing sleep, but I've made up my—"

"*Okay, stop it!*" When all else failed, Bill knew that butchering Madonna was sure to enrage me. "What in God's name are you doing calling me at this hour?"

"I want to talk about this before I leave. I want you to understand what I'm doing here."

"I understand exactly what you're doing here. You're leaving me for Jesus. You're dumping me for a man who wears sandals in February and who's never used product in his life."

"Noah, don't be petty, I—"

"You know what? I don't think we have to talk about this. In fact, I don't think we have to talk about anything ever again. Have fun." I slammed the phone down so hard the receiver cracked (which was okay since I'd been wanting to get a new phone anyway), unplugged the cord, and put in the second season of "The Golden Girls." After the first episode was over (it was the one in which Blanche thinks she's pregnant but it's actually just menopause, and Dorothy, Rose, and Sophia start breeding minks), I called Kathy and told her Bill was crossing the Mason-Dixon line to become an ex-gay. She told me I should have drowned his mother in Lake Michigan when I'd had the chance, and then she said I was coming over to her place and we were going to bake chocolate chip cookies. Secretly I prefer the

Pillsbury chocolate chip cookies that you make with premade dough to every chocolate-chip-cookie-from-scratch recipe I've ever made, but every time I buy a tube I just end up eating all the dough in one sitting and gaining two pounds with no cookies to show for it. At least this way Kathy would be there to eat half of whatever we came up with.

"What are you going to do about this?" she asked as she measured flour over the electric stand mixer in her immaculate kitchen.

"What can I do? I called Orbitz.com and had them change his ticket to next week and charge the fee to his credit card, but he'll just change it back. Careful with the eggs."

"You should have canceled his credit cards. Give me the butter; you're cutting it totally wrong. You have to do something, if only for my sake. I'm not even halfway done interviewing him." Kathy was writing some article about gay Christians as her tryout assignment for Salon.com, a gig she'd wanted for years. "Go after him."

"I can't."

"Why not?"

I couldn't very well tell her that it was because Bill was the first person I'd ever dated who I didn't want to be when I grew up and the thought that we might not be together forever made me want to vomit up my spleen and therefore I was just going to act like this wasn't happening until it went away, so instead I said, "Because I'm going to be very busy for the foreseeable future knitting a scientifically accurate model of the human brain," and then I spilled granulated sugar all over the floor.

When I got back to my apartment there was a note on the door from Bill that I threw away without reading. (Okay, that's totally a lie; I read it and all it said was, "I'm bringing my cell—call me, sexy" and naturally there was no way I was going to call him, especially not after the P.S. that said "Nice try with 'Bleak House,' punk—they reran it late last night and I've already watched it—so there," so I decided to pretend I had thrown it away without reading it.) I started to watch another episode of "The Golden Girls" but it was the one in which George Bush visits Miami and I felt I didn't need to get any angrier than I already was, so I pulled out some paper and started Googling and making diagrams. I figured the thing to do was to knit all the cortices and lobes and structures separately and then stitch them together at the end.

I would start with the amygdala, I decided, the area of the brain that controls aggression and fear. (I know things like this because I once briefly dated a neuropsychiatrist. When he dumped me he said it was obvious that I had a hyperperfused locus ceruleus so I told him it was obvious he was an asshole.) The amygdala seemed an appropriate structure on which to take out my own aggression—it's not like I'm a moron, the metaphor was staring me right in the face—and the amygdala is also small, about the size of a walnut, so it was a less frightening first step than, say, the parietal lobe, which is huge and controls perception of touch, pressure, temperature, and pain. I looked through my yarn stash (I hate that term but that's what they call it), and after briefly considering a gorgeous soft green alpaca, went with a cheap purple polyester, as I suspected it was more appropriate for an ex-gay. I started knitting according to the diagram I had drawn up, yanking the yarn hard as I went. That fucker. Right with God, my ass. I yanked the yarn so hard, in fact, that my stitches were much tighter than usual and I ended up with an amygdala the size of a grape, which wouldn't do at all, so I had to rip out all the stitches and start over.

Then I got some sparkly red yarn and moved on to the cingulate gyrus, the strip on top of the brain in the middle that governs error detection. There were so many errors here I didn't know where to begin to detect them. For a while I focused on Bill's error in going to this stupid conference, and then as I knit, I moved on to his other errors, like not liking Bette and believing in God in the first place. Then it occurred to me that maybe the error was mine, in dating him for ten months. I mean, he hadn't come out until three years ago, and if that hadn't set off warning bells in my mind then it was my own damn fault. It wasn't quite as bad as when Kathy's ex-boyfriend dragged her with him to a Renaissance Faire held by the Society for Creative Anachronism—I tried my best to hide my dismay and be supportive but she could tell I was appalled, though the fact that she was going dressed as a thief mollified me slightly—but he was still obviously wrong for me and I should have seen it. My ex-boyfriend the neuropsychiatrist used to say that the cingulate gyrus was the root of all evil in the world. Privately I thought that my ex-boyfriend the neuropsychiatrist was the root of all evil in the world, but the right moment to tell him this somehow never came around, and with Bill's latest announcement I was beginning to wonder if maybe it wasn't the cingulate gyrus after all.

By now it was time for reruns of "Law & Order: SVU" to start. I've already seen all but one of the old episodes but I watch religiously, hoping that they'll show the one I haven't seen, in which Stephanie March is killed (though the surprise revelation about that had already been ruined for me by seeing the follow-up episode the next season). Unfortunately the episode on at the moment was neither that one nor one of the ones in which Christopher Meloni removes his shirt, so I turned off the TV and checked my email.

In addition to all the spam offering me good mortgage rates or asking me if I wanted a fuckfriend (actually I thought those ones were kind of touching, in a weird way), there was an email from Bill. "Hey, sexy," it started. "People here are very strange. No one is wearing Marc Jacobs at all—there's a lot of polyester. But they're talking about some interesting things. I don't agree with everything they're saying, but it seems worth listening to at least a little bit. I'm thinking about you, though, and—" *Hmph,* I thought. *I'd rather have a fuckfriend.* I hit Delete without reading any more.

By the time I fell asleep that night I had most of the limbic system arrayed in pieces before me but for the sake of variety I figured I'd take a break and skip to the parietal lobe. I started with the angular gyrus, which controls our understanding of metaphor. I wondered if it would be possible to have an angulotomy and remove my own ability to understand metaphor. I would probably find the modern world much easier to live in, not to mention reality TV's being a lot more entertaining. But as the angular gyrus took shape on the needles (yellow and orange striped cotton) it looked so cute that I decided I really couldn't do without it.

Bill called again the next morning and this time even though he did an entire verse and chorus of "La Isla Bonita" I still didn't pick up the phone. I called Kathy and asked her to come over and look at the brain I was knitting.

"That's really disgusting," she said. "If I were dating you I would make you throw it away."

"I would never date someone who would make me throw this away," I answered snippily.

"You're just going to let him go?"

"Kathy, he thinks Jesus can magically turn him straight. He belongs in a lunatic asylum."

"Yeah, but have you seen his abs?"

I said that wasn't funny and could she please leave because I had an occipital lobe to knit?

The occipital lobe is a large structure in the back of the head that deals with vision. I have no visual perception—well, not *none*, I mean, but I hate museums and art galleries because I never understand what I'm looking at, and back when I was driving I caused eleven car accidents—and when I learned about the occipital lobe I immediately understood that my problem processing visual information was the result of the trauma I suffered to the back of my head when I was two ("I *did* watch him!" my father apparently insisted to my mother; "I watched him climb up on the sink, I watched him fall down, I watched him start bleeding all over the floor."). As the knitted occipital lobe slowly grew—I decided, for variety, to use a cable stitch with this—I realized that museums and art galleries were all well and good but that my brain injury had given me true inner vision, which was much more valuable. I was knitting with a chenille yarn, which was irksome because it had no give and take, but it was shiny so I kept with it.

That night's first "Law & Order: SVU" was the one in which Christopher Meloni works out in his undershirt and then takes it off and puts it in his locker, so I took a break, though by knitting during commercials I had the occipital lobe almost done by the end of the show. Before "Designing Women" on Lifetime Television for Women and Gay Men, I got a good chunk of the parietal lobe done. (My hands were getting tired by this time, so I used size 15 needles, which I usually hate, and a chunky weight yarn. Dark blue.) I imagined that I was actually knitting a voodoo brain, and that once the parietal lobe was finished, I would have the power to control Bill's perception of touch, pressure, temperature, and pain, especially pain. I would stick needles into different parts of the knitted parietal lobe and he would all of a sudden get really cold or feel an unbearable agony in his right elbow. Then I figured, why stop at the parietal lobe? Fiddle with the hippocampus and erase his long-term memory, poke the hypothalamus and make him really horny. Let's see him try to be an ex-gay *then*. Then I deleted fourteen e-mails from him without reading them—I'm telling the truth this time—and made three cups of chocolate pudding and ate it all (I used Splenda, of course, but still).

"Noah, you *have* to call Bill."

It was unclear to me why Kathy should be standing over my bed yelling at me in the middle of the night. Obviously it was a bad dream, so I pulled the covers over my head, turned over, and shut my eyes again.

"I'm not kidding. My editor just called me and told me that he's moved my deadline up to Monday."

I stuck my head out of the covers and looked at the clock. "But it's five in the morning."

"My editor keeps weird hours."

"How did you get in here?"

"I still have your keys from when you went to Italy and I watered your plants. Now call Bill and get him back here."

"I can't do anything about it until I'm done with the brain."

"Then get out of bed and finish the fucking brain *right now.*" She pulled the covers off me and dragged me out of bed. "Where is it?" I pointed to the closet and she went over and started throwing pieces of brain at me. "You're ridiculous," she said as the cerebellum (which governs movement and balance) came hurtling through the air at my head. "Bill is the best thing that ever happened to you. Maybe he's a little weird sometimes with his mumbo jumbo Jesus crap, but I can't believe how immature you're being. And I don't have time for this"—here was the brain stem (alertness)—"because I have a dissertation about American natural history museums at the turn of the century to write, so would you just *grow up?*" I ducked to avoid the temporal lobe (auditory stimuli).

I'd never seen her so mad, not even the time her mother said, "Well, I'm sure that shirt looked good in the store." I was done with all the parts of the brain except for the orbitofrontal cortex (delayed gratification), the lateral prefrontal cortex (assessing alternatives to decide on a course of action), and the ventro-medial cortex (understanding emotion and meaning), and I didn't want Kathy to yell at me any more so I figured, okay, my knitted brain will have simply been partially lobotomized and Bill clearly doesn't understand emotion or meaning anyway, so I might as well start stitching it all together. But there was chocolate pudding all over my diagram so it was a little difficult to tell what was supposed to get attached to what (and my ex-boyfriend the neuropsychiatrist had dumped me before I learned where everything went) so I had to make it up. While the sun rose and Kathy watched TiVoed recordings of the "Barefoot Contessa" on the Food Network, I sewed the hippocampus (memory) to the occipital lobe (vision) and attached them both to the hypo-thalamus (sexual arousal) and then stuck the cingulate gyrus (error detection) on the side but then I realized I was sitting on the angular gyrus (understanding of metaphor) so I got that in as best I could and then I stuck the amygdala (aggression and fear) on top. "There, I'm done," I said. "Are you happy?"

Kathy looked at what I held in my hands. "That's not a brain."

I looked down at it. She was totally right. It was a mess of yarn of different materials and colors, uneven and graceless, bulging here and stretched thin there, with no discernable shape. "Hmm."

"I mean it's interesting. But it's not a knitted brain."

I looked at it some more. It was kind of compelling, in a gross and messy way. "Maybe it's a knitted soul."

"Whatever it is, you're done. Now would you call Bill?" She handed me the phone.

I dialed, and without waiting for any kind of response, spoke all in one breath (okay, maybe not all in one breath but nevertheless I didn't leave room for a word in edgewise). "Hey, Bill, it's me. Stop calling me. I haven't read any of your emails and I'm not going to return any of your messages and I will continue screening until one of us dies so you might as well give up. I hope you meet a nice girl and marry her and make Jesus and your mother very, very happy. If Becki Cramer calls I'll make sure to give her your number." Then I put the phone down.

Kathy looked at me, stricken. "That wasn't what you were supposed to say."

"I guess learning what a soul looks like has unexpected consequences, huh?"

We stared at each other for a while longer and then she left. I picked up the knitted soul and turned it over in my hands, trying to figure out which way was up. One way it looked like a chocolate cake, but a from-scratch chocolate cake, not from a box; another way it looked like my dog Fang from eighth grade (he was a Bichon Frisé). Then it looked like Christopher Meloni. Then it looked sort of like a giant version of Dick Cheney's nose. Then I turned it back so it looked like Christopher Meloni again. Then it didn't look like anything I could recognize. I went over to the computer and looked up two phone numbers.

When I dialed the first one, the phone rang and rang on the other end (hello, voice mail?) but somebody at the Museum of Scientifically Accurate Fabric Brain Art finally picked up and I said, "Um, I have something I wonder if you'd be interested in, maybe in memory of Daisy Gilford," and then I described the knitted soul as concisely as I could (which wasn't very) and before I was done she said yes they were very interested and I should send it for their metaphysical gallery, and I wrote down their address.

I dialed the second number. The finger I'd kept on the hang-up button when I'd pretended to call Bill before was trembling. I was subjected to the loathsome hold music forever (God, I need to get a speakerphone) but when an actual human Delta representative finally answered I told her, "I'd like a ticket on your next flight from LaGuardia to Asheville, North Carolina, please."

After I'd hung up, I put the knitted soul on top of the television, adjusted it until it looked comfortable, ate a bowl of Wild Berry Cheerios with 2% milk (I know, I know), went into my bedroom, and started to pack.

LIKE NO ONE'S WATCHING

Josh Helmin

Mark began with the torso. With smooth, careful lines, he formed the outline of the body, slowly adding detail and shape, sinew and flesh. He lay on his stomach, lounging across his bed, bare feet dangling off the side, sketching Jim Morrison from the poster of a famous Doors album cover that hung on his bedroom wall. He switched pencils and, gently using his fingertips, blended the shading around Morrison's nipples.

As Mark drew, he felt the familiar stirrings—fluttering, heaviness, and urgency—pressing inside his chest. Sometimes he had to finish drawings just to make the persistent, nagging ache go away. Often, when he finished a drawing, he would think about it after going to bed, his hands sliding beneath the covers in the dark.

The Doors blared from his nearby stereo. The music, combined with the kind of concentration that made Mark absentmindedly chew his tongue and draw for hours without looking up, kept him from hearing his sister's first loud, firm knocks on his bedroom door. The second set of knocks jerked him from his reverie, and he jumped up to turn down the volume on his stereo.

Brynn poked her head through the doorway. She noticed that the half-closed blinds in Mark's room cast long blocks of late afternoon sun onto the bedroom floor. She noted the assortment of pencils spread across his rumpled comforter, and spotted his sketchbook open on the bed. Brynn thought she saw a drawing of Jim Morrison's torso before Mark flipped the book shut and sat down on his bed. Brynn stepped over a skateboard flipped on its back, one wheel missing and awaiting repair, and sidestepped a massive heap of dirty, well-worn T-shirts, assorted sneakers, and rumpled jeans. A stack of homework lay untouched near the foot of the bed, alongside a pile of bulky college application packages.

"It kind of smells in here," Brynn said, taking in staccato whiffs of air. "Like pizza boxes and dirty socks."

Mark sighed and began drumming his pencil on the cover of his sketchpad. He pushed back a lock of hair from his face and looked up at his sister. "Okay, Brynn, lay it on me."

Brynn raised her eyebrows. "Lay what on you? Can't a little sister just come by and visit her brother?" It was Mark's turn to raise his eyebrows, and this time Brynn caved. "Okay, here's the deal. Tonight is opening night of the show and we're short an usher, and I was wondering if you could help out like you did that one time with *The Good Doctor.*" She said it briskly, half question and half challenge.

Mark sized her up, looking at Brynn's compact, scrappy frame in the oversized denim bib overalls she frequently wore, her straight hair hanging down her back in two buoyant auburn pigtails. Brynn, a sophomore at Washington High School, had quickly established a heady reputation for herself in the school's theater department by designing and building innovative, elaborate, and surprisingly cost-effective sets for the last two school plays. This would be her third and, rumor had it, finest work to date.

"Isn't this one a musical?" Mark asked, a grimace forming at the corners of his mouth and spreading to his eyes.

Brynn's free hand went to her other hip. "Well, are you doing anything else important this evening, Mr. Artiste, other than drawing naked men alone in your bedroom?"

Mark's face flushed a brilliant shade of crimson, and he turned his head away. He picked at a loose string on his comforter. "I wasn't drawing naked men. I was doing a rendering of a Doors album cover, if you must know." He looked at Brynn, hands still on her hips.

She arched an eyebrow and began tapping her fingers against her thigh. She watched her brother carefully, sure she was on the precipice of victory. He sighed.

"All right, I'll do the usher thing," Mark said. "But only for tonight. Got it?"

Brynn smiled and crossed her heart. "I promise," she said. "And, who knows, Marky? You might even end up having a good time."

Mark sincerely doubted it.

The parking lot of Washington High overflowed with midsize sedans, SUVs, and pickups. Every ticket for opening night had sold out a week earlier, thanks to Mrs. Calpern's clever casting of two popular football players in hammy supporting roles, combined with talented actors in the lead roles, and elaborate sets that set tongues wagging as soon as the curtain went up. Mobs of lip-glossed girls showed up early for the performance, jockeying for seats with proud parents, half of the Washington

Cougars football team, and a considerable contingent of gray-haired, denture-wearing members of the surrounding Denver community.

The theater's steeply sloped seating filled to capacity fifteen minutes before curtain. Mark, having dutifully executed his ushering responsibilities, squeezed into a seat near the back of the house before the lights dimmed. He hadn't planned on staying for the show—especially since he suspected it was a cheesy musical—but his curiosity about the sets Brynn had designed and built, along with the expectant Friday night buzz of the audience, lured him into one of the last available seats. He could always leave at intermission and pick up Brynn after the show.

There was an audible gasp when the curtain rose. Stage right was dominated by an elaborate castle set, complete with stone walls, furniture upholstered in crushed red velvet, and a heavy gilt painting hanging over a wide-mouthed stone fireplace. Center stage had become the common room of a poor peasant's cottage, and stage left was a provincial baker's kitchen.

As far as Mark could tell, the musical was a retelling of "Cinderella," "Jack and the Beanstalk," and "Rapunzel," with all the stories eventually intertwined and overlapping. As the play went on, Mark found that the characters' propensity to break into song during a scene wasn't as strange as he'd imagined.

From her perch backstage, Brynn peered at the audience and spotted her brother watching with rapt attention. She couldn't help smirking.

In a development that Mark found somewhat unnerving, his eyes were glued to the actor playing Jack every time he appeared on stage. Just the sight of Jack, played by Seth Stratton, a fellow senior with a mop of brown hair and a tall, lean frame, caused

Mark to hold his breath and his palms to sweat. Mark some-times stared at Seth even when he was supposed to be watching somebody else. In the first act, when Seth sang a song about his adventures up the beanstalk, Mark felt himself growing lightheaded. A low, dull ache began in his abdomen and moved downward.

Later, on the ride home, after the standing ovation and his embarrassment at nearly crying during the finale, Mark cleared his throat to speak.

"You know," he said, "I guess I'm not really doing anything tomorrow night."

"Okay," Brynn said slowly. "And?"

"And I was just thinking that, you know, if you guys still need ushers, maybe I could help you out. As a favor."

Brynn laughed and pointed a finger at her brother as he drove swiftly down Peters Boulevard. "Admit it! You had a good time!"

Mark shifted into fourth gear. "I will admit no such thing," he said, smiling into the darkness.

Mark arrived forty-five minutes early for the next night's perfor-mance. He brought his sketchbook along to calm his nerves, anxiously looking forward to the end of his ushering duties so he could slip into a seat and watch Seth Stratton onstage again. Mark's smooth, precise lines slowly formed into a reworking of the dense forest from Act One, including Jack and the albino cow that Jack traded for magic beans. He didn't look up until the first Washington High cheerleader arrived, snapping her gum, snatching at Mark's stack of programs, and brusquely asking where she could find seat 32C.

Mark sat closer to the stage for Saturday's performance, wiping his hands on his pants and catching his breath after each of Seth's songs. At intermission, he splashed cold water on his face in the blue-tiled boys' bathroom and gripped the sides of the porcelain sink, his heart thrumming inside his chest.

After curtain call, Brynn signaled to Mark, her pigtails bobbing as she waved her arms while the audience filed from the theater: zipping up jackets, turning on cell phones, and fishing for car keys in purses and pockets.

"Could you do me a big favor?" Brynn asked. "Our sound guy had to leave early, so could you get the microphone packs from the actors? One of the foam stones fell off the fireplace, and I have to fix it before we can leave."

"Yeah, okay," Mark said, sketchbook tucked under his arm, hands thrust in his pockets.

"Make sure you get the transmitter, microphone, and battery pack. They can't return it without the battery pack." Brynn shot down the stairs of the theater, clasps rattling on her bib overalls, and yelled for Megan, the perpetually frazzled stage manager.

Minutes later, Mark stood outside the men's changing room, listening to Chris Harper and Derek Bolling, the crowd-pleasing athletes, laughing about their Act One duet that had inspired two overzealous junior girls to throw lingerie onto the stage. Mark took a deep breath and knocked, relieved when Chris, not Seth, opened the door.

"I came for your microphone stuff," Mark said, gesturing toward the microphone hidden within a buttonhole of Chris's costume.

Chris ushered him into the room and began dismantling his microphone pack, handing each of the pieces to Mark. While Chris took off his microphone, Mark spotted Seth at the far end of the room, grinning as the others laughed and speculated about getting some action with the girls who threw the slinky lingerie.

Mark's arms were so filled with electronics by the time he got to Seth that he had to set his sketchbook on the counter to take Seth's microphone. Mark still hadn't figured out anything inspired to say to Seth, other than asking for his microphone. Seth was shirtless and looked tired but exhilarated. When Seth smiled at him, Mark dropped some battery packs.

"Whoa, you've got a lot of those things," Seth said, helping Mark scoop up the errant electronics. "Usually they have some sort of bag for them." Mark felt his face grow warm as he saw Seth eyeing his sketchbook on the makeup counter. "Do you draw?" Seth asked.

Mark's mouth was suddenly and inconveniently parched. Seth picked up the sketchbook and began slowly paging through it.

"Well, well, Mark Casey, it seems that you've got quite a talent," Seth said. He flipped to the sketch Mark had made of Jack and his cow in the forest. Seth looked up at Mark, his eyes a startling hue of green. "Seriously, Mark, these are amazing," Seth said, still flipping pages.

"I've got much better stuff than this at home," Mark said, surprised by his ability to speak with Seth's shirtless form and green eyes directly in front of him.

"You're over on Ridgewood, right?" Seth asked. "I've dropped off Brynn a couple times."

Mark nodded, pleased that Seth knew where he lived. He could smell the light mixture of sweat and soap from Seth's skin, and for a moment, he felt vaguely intoxicated.

"You doing anything tomorrow before the show?" Seth asked. "Because I wouldn't mind seeing your stuff. I could drive you to the school afterward. And Brynn, if she wants."

"Uh, sure," Mark said, his chest nearly exploding. "That's cool."

When Brynn drove home later, she looked at Mark sprawling

in the passenger seat and grinning at the suburban homes whiz-
zing by. Something was different about him. She momentarily
entertained the idea that he was high, but knew that wasn't
exactly Mark's scene. Could it be that he was crushing on
somebody from school? Maybe even somebody from the show?
Brynn, unable to imagine who, turned her attention back
to the road.

The next day, Mark flew around his bedroom, flinging open the
blinds, jamming clothes into the closet, throwing homework
into his backpack, and sticking the half-fallen Weezer poster
back up on the wall. He stood in front of his full-length mirror,
changing shirts four times before settling on a navy blue hooded
sweatshirt that he thought made him look rugged, yet handsome. He changed his socks after noticing that the first pair had
a hole in the big toe, and then sat on the edge of his bed, hands
folded in his lap, unable to think of anything to do before Seth
Stratton arrived.

Why was Seth coming over anyway? Was it just a friendly
visit, or could it possibly mean something else? Surely Seth
couldn't want anything more than to see his sketches. But—dear
God—what if Seth did want something more? Did Mark want
that, too?

Before he had another minute to think, the doorbell rang.
Mark grabbed a glossy college booklet that had come in the
mail and sprawled across his bed, feigning effortless calm, only
noticing that he was holding the booklet upside down seconds
before he heard knocking.

"Anybody home?" Seth asked, slowly opening Mark's
bedroom door.

"Oh, hey, Seth," Mark said. He was proud of how natural
he sounded.

Seth wore a leather jacket over a vintage concert T-shirt. His smile was easy and affable, his hands buried in his pockets. For a moment Mark thought maybe Seth was nervous, too, but he dismissed the idea. What would Seth have to be nervous about?

To distract himself from his nervousness, Mark started a conversation—which Seth seemed happy to join—that quickly turned to Mark's posters, CD collection, and then to the books that filled a tall shelf in the corner of the room. They discussed the artful lyricism of the new Bright Eyes album, their nostalgia for vintage Weezer, and their shared enjoyment of the book they were reading in English. ("Doesn't *Ordinary People* make you think of *Catcher in the Rye?*" Seth asked, almost causing Mark to kiss him.) They discussed college plans and expounded on the evils of AP and SAT exams.

Mark brought out a selection of his sketchbooks, and they sat cross-legged on his bed, examining each of the drawings. With the sketchpads open between them, Mark felt the ease of their conversation become almost palpable.

"You know," he said, looking down at his comforter, "I think you're really good in the show. You've got this great voice, and you make it all look so easy. I could never get up there and do that."

"Well, thanks," Seth said, laughing. For a moment, Mark thought he could see shyness surfacing. "I used to get really nervous and freaked out when I was onstage. Sometimes it got so bad that I thought I'd crap my pants or barf or something." Mark laughed. "But then, after a while, I figured out that the secret to the whole thing is kind of pretending like no one is watching. Then it gets much easier."

Without particularly meaning to do it, but suddenly wanting to desperately, Mark leaned toward Seth. He closed his eyes and gently placed his lips on Seth's. The kiss lasted several seconds. Then, breathing heavily, Mark opened his eyes and watched Seth open his.

Without saying anything, Seth heaved himself off the bed, grabbed the doorknob, and was out of the house before Mark's bedroom door shut. Mark fell back on his bed and closed his eyes. He punched his headboard twice, the second hit breaking the skin on his knuckles.

That night, when Mark refused to come out of his bedroom when it was time to leave for the show, Brynn stood outside his door for almost fifteen minutes, trying to piece everything together. She closed her eyes and rested her head against the doorframe. What was going on with Mark, anyway? Why had Seth left in such a huff?

After Brynn finally left for the theater, Mark stayed in his bedroom and stared at his drawing of Jack in the forest. With a few quick rips, he shredded the page to confetti. Then, as he hadn't done during the finale of the opening night performance, Mark cried.

Mark slept fitfully, waking in a tangle of sweaty sheets. Monday morning seemed particularly cruel as he stepped into the shower. At breakfast, Mark avoided Brynn's questioning glares.

Brynn knew she wasn't just imagining the vacant look on Mark's face as he walked through the halls of Washington High. Something was definitely wrong.

Mark had to be called on twice during third-period calculus before he responded. He skipped fifth period, opting for an unauthorized study session in the library, which turned into endless circular doodling in his organic chemistry notebook.

Seth hadn't come to school that day. Mark was sure of it. He'd looked for Seth's face in the hallways, and listened for the voice that had made his palms sweat when he first watched Seth onstage.

Mark didn't see Seth for three days. Then, on Thursday after lunch, Mark found a note slipped through the air vent of his locker.

Can we talk? Seth.

It was written in careful, rounded script. Mark read the note two more times before he crumpled it in his hand and dropped it in a nearby garbage can.

On Friday, Mark skipped school altogether.

"Mark, we really need you tonight," Brynn said, standing in the doorway of Mark's bedroom. Mark lay on his back, staring at the ceiling. "We've got enough ushers, but Mike Thompson, who usually does spotlights, broke his arm skateboarding, so I was hoping—"

Mark turned his head toward his sister and narrowed his eyes. "Brynn, I'm so sick of playing backup for your precious little theater department. Contrary to what you may believe, I have a life, too. Have you ever considered that maybe I don't want to waste another night playing Brynn's obedient helper for the stupid school musical?"

Brynn folded her arms, and her mouth became a narrow line. "I thought you enjoyed helping out. It's not like you don't have the time to do it, Mark. You're here in this room, drawing away on a Saturday night, and we need the help. Okay? We need the help, and I thought we could count on you."

"Yeah, well, you can't tonight," Mark said, his eyes again fixed on the ceiling.

An icy, lingering silence filled the room. Then, without

knowing why it came to her, something clicked in Brynn's mind. She looked at Mark.

She knew. She didn't know how, but she was certain. She slowly turned and treaded down the hall.

Minutes later, Mark heard Brynn's car squeal into the night after she backed out of the driveway.

Brynn barged into the men's changing room without knocking, which didn't seem to faze anyone. The sight of Brynn Casey rushing around the theater department, usually putting some last-minute details together, was common enough. Seth slowly pulled his Act One costume over his head, looking pale and drawn, the bags under his eyes visible under his stage makeup.

Brynn walked up behind Seth. "I need you for a sound check," she said, her voice stern.

"But we already did a sound check," Seth said. "I've got the channel on six and the green light is on and—"

"We need to do another one," Brynn said, taking Seth by the wrist and leading him out of the room. She walked him down the narrow corridor, past the women's changing room and the bathrooms, and into a cavernous choir rehearsal room. She opened the door, shoved aside a rack of green and gold choir robes, and pushed Seth into the room. The rack squeaked across the room, the choir robes swinging on their hangers.

"Brynn, what's—"

"Listen to me carefully, Seth Stratton." The sight of Brynn with her brow furrowed, pigtails quivering, and voice stern, silenced Seth. "I don't know what's going on with you and my brother, and maybe I'm reading this whole thing wrong, but I don't think I am."

She watched Seth's surprised face as he registered what she was saying.

"Mark won't say a thing to me, but I know *something* is going on between you two." She began pacing back and forth. "I don't know if you guys had some stupid argument, or if this is a lovers' spat, and I don't know if you're the one who needs to say sorry, or if he is."

Brynn planted her feet and looked Seth in the eye before she went on.

"If you're the one who needs to say sorry, say it. And if he's the one who needs to say it, *make* him say it. I'm sick of him moping around the house, and sick of watching you two stumble around the halls of this school like miserable zombies." Brynn poked Seth's chest with her finger. "So, Seth, be a man and *take care of it*, huh?"

Suddenly aware of how loud she'd become, Brynn smoothed the front of her overalls, readjusted her pigtails, and took a deep breath.

"I mean, take care of it, *please*." She patted Seth on the shoulder, like a coach would a player after a pep talk. "Besides," she said, looking up into Seth's eyes, "I think he really likes you. A lot."

Brynn turned and left, the heavy door clattering shut behind her. Seth stood alone, the choir robes swaying back and forth on the rack across the room.

Mark's cell phone vibrated at half past eleven. He picked up the phone and saw that he had a text message from an unknown number.

Help me with something at the theater? Brynn.

Mark sighed and snapped the phone shut. He felt guilty for being an ass earlier that night. He'd never admit it—at least not without significant prodding—but he did, in fact, enjoy helping out at the theater. It was nice to be needed, to be part of something. Secretly, he was proud to be the brother of the girl who made heads turn with her fantastic sets and her ability to single-handedly keep the theater department from falling apart.

The parking lot was almost empty when Mark pulled up to the school. He entered through the theater's backstage entrance and fumbled through the darkness toward the stage. Onstage, the lights still shown dimly, and Mark guessed that Brynn was in the lighting booth.

He was climbing the stairs to the booth when he heard someone behind him say his name. Mark turned and froze, seeing Seth, still in costume, standing in the elaborate forest set from Act Two.

"I can't talk right now," Mark said evenly. "I have to help Brynn with something."

"Brynn's already on her way to the cast party at Chris Harper's house. I sent you the message."

Mark turned, pulled his car keys from his pocket, and headed for the exit.

"Mark, wait!" Seth yelled, running halfway up the exit stairs. "Could you please come down here? Just for a minute?"

Mark sighed and slowly turned around. He descended the stairs and followed Seth into the woods.

"I've been stupid," Seth said. "It's just that, you know, I'm not even sure what to say. I've never done any of this before."

Mark folded his arms. "Me either."

"I'm terrified of being 'the gay theater kid,' just one more cliché in this stupid cliché high school. It scares the shit out of me. But then I start thinking about what we talked about when I came over to your house—everything I said about being onstage and acting like no one's watching—and I feel like the biggest hypocrite." Seth stepped closer to Mark, and Mark let his arms drop to his sides. "I guess what I'm saying is that I don't know what I'm doing, and I'm scared as hell. But I was thinking that maybe I should put my money where my mouth is and see if we can figure this thing out."

Seth stepped closer to Mark and reached for Mark's hand. When Mark didn't pull away, Seth raised up on his toes and, in the middle of the enchanted forest, kissed Mark Casey. Their fingers intertwined, and Mark wrapped his arm around Seth's waist, pulling Seth firmly toward him.

"Now that," Mark said, "is a lot more like it."

Seth laughed, and Mark kissed him again.

At the cast party at Chris Harper's sprawling house on the edge of town, everyone sat on logs around a bonfire. Chris's mother had brought out a pile of old blankets, and the cast and crew huddled under them in groups, drinking lightly spiked apple cider and singing favorite numbers from the show. Brynn saw Seth and Mark appear at the bonfire, stepping out of the darkness like ghosts. She smiled and gave them a small wave, which they sheepishly returned.

"I'll get us drinks," Seth said.

Mark nodded and went to grab a blanket. He approached the pile of quilted covers near his sister.

"Anything you want to tell me, Mark, dear?" Brynn asked with a mischievous grin.

"Nothing you haven't already figured out," Mark said. He tugged gently at one of her pigtails, and she smacked him on the shoulder. He laughed as he walked away and sat down next to Seth on one of the logs.

"Let's give them something to talk about all week at school,"

Seth whispered into Mark's ear. He pulled the blanket around their shoulders.

"Please," Mark whispered back, "this will give them something to talk about all semester."

Seth laughed and scooted closer, resting his head on Mark's shoulder. They felt the heat of the fire on their faces, the warmth from the cider blooming in their chests. They listened as the fire crackled and snapped, and watched it send a spray of brilliant orange, red, and yellow sparks into the starless night sky.

AT THE END OF THE LEASH

Jeffrey Ricker

B rian had a soft spot for the big dogs. It seemed the larger the breed, the gentler the demeanor. Some of his favorite clients were Great Danes with their regal profiles, mastiffs with their sturdy dependability, Newfoundlands with their gentle stoicism. Every so often he would walk a dachshund or a Pekingese who would prove to be an exception to the rule, but in general, the bigger the better.

Casey, one of his favorites, was kind of in between. Not huge, but not small. Brian had been walking Casey, a Weimaraner, for three weeks, every Monday through Wednesday at three p.m., long enough for Casey to steal a bit of Brian's heart. With his ice gray eyes and smooth silver-gray coat, he had an otherworldly look that made people stop and take notice. Then he'd lick your face and break the spell.

Brian had never met Casey's owner. The agency had supplied Brian with a key to the tenth-floor apartment overlooking the park and instructions to feed Casey and take him for a brisk walk, at least half an hour, Monday through Wednesday. His owner commuted to Chicago three days a week, and the house-keeper took Casey out briefly in the morning, while a friend in the building took him out before bedtime. That left just the afternoon, which Brian covered.

Although Brian had never met Casey's owner—C. Jacobs, according to the agency—there were photos on the console table in the front hall, next to Casey's leash. Vacation snapshots mostly, they showed a dark-haired man who apparently liked sunny places and sunny blonds. There were photos of beaches, waterfalls, and a couple of cruise ships. In most of them the dark-haired man stood next to a blond man, who sometimes had his arm slung over the dark-haired man's shoulders. Brian assumed the dark-haired man was C. Jacobs since he was in most of the pictures, and perhaps because of a little wishful thinking. In one, C. Jacobs was shirtless and wearing a Speedo. Brian knelt by the table to get a better look—picking up the framed picture would have been a violation of the service's rules—and noted that, even though he didn't particularly care for Speedos, C. Jacobs had the sort of body that could get away with wearing one.

Suddenly, Brian found himself knocked to the floor with a lapful of Casey. The dog must have taken Brian's kneeling on the floor as an open invitation to play and had leaped on him, bumping the table and sending the pictures scattering.

"Shit," Brian muttered and quickly began gathering up the photos, and then wondered if he should leave them where they lay and let Casey take the blame. It was mostly his fault anyway. For his part, Casey sat at a distance, looking cowed and waiting patiently while Brian rearranged the pictures. Since he had to touch them anyway, he took a closer look at the Speedo picture—the man really was gorgeous. The blond man was undeniably handsome, too, but—Brian didn't know whether he was imagining it or not—had a fake look about him. His tan, his hair color, his smile seemed fake.

And his chest was obviously shaved.

Eventually, Brian returned the photo to the table. Casey wagged his tail when Brian looked his way. How long had he been lost in that photo? He really needed to start dating again, or at least forget about the last failed attempt.

Of course, there were a lot of those to forget, and none of them lately. The last ten months had been a drought of unprecedented duration for him. The time of year reminded him of it. It was the end of February, the Christmas holidays seemed so long ago that he couldn't even remember what he'd been given, and there were no other holidays to color the gray monotony until Easter. There was nothing to do but duck his head, hunch his shoulders, and look forward to sunlight again.

He treated his dating drought similarly. He wasn't really doing anything about it, so much as waiting for the cloud cover to lift.

The weather outside matched his mood. It was chilly and overcast, but the clouds held no promise of rain. Casey, oblivious to the weather, led Brian down the sidewalk.

Brian's client list consisted of a handful of regulars he'd had for years, in some cases, as well as a certain percentage of turnover. Some were short-timers to begin with—temporary business travel, a huge project at work that meant late nights before they could get home to the dog, or a newborn taking all their time and energy. Some ended with no explanation, a situation that roughly paralleled Brian's dating life. In the case of dogs, though, if he ran into them again, he greeted them like old friends, and indeed that was what they were to him. Also, unlike his dating life, when one client moved on, there were always plenty more waiting for attention. So when he stopped walking Casey a couple of weeks later, Brian was disappointed and missed the dog for a little while, but soon had a Siberian husky named Odin to take his place.

Another of Brian's regulars was Waldo, a mastiff he walked every weekday at one p.m. His owners had a seven-year-old daughter named Hildie, whose dark, somber expression matched her flat black hair. When he and Waldo returned to the house, Hildie had usually arrived home from school and was reading on the sofa or having her after-school snack at the dining room table. As soon as Brian removed the leash, Waldo trotted to Hildie's side and sat down, and Hildie placed her small hand on top of his head. He would remain there until she lifted her hand or got up: Lancelot to her Guinevere.

The Friday before Easter, Brian walked up to the front door of Waldo's owners' house and turned to find Hildie coming up the walk behind him.

"You're home early," he said.

"Half day," she replied, skirted around him, and inserted her key in the lock.

When they opened the door, Waldo, at the sight of Hildie, batted his front paws on the slate floor of the entryway, one then the other, just hard enough to hear his toenails clack. Brian had never seen him so demonstrative before. Hildie, who stood just above the dog's eye level, placed her hands on either side of his face and rubbed with just enough vigor to make Waldo's ears flap.

Then she walked in, parked her rolling bag, took out a book, and perched on the couch. Waldo glanced at her for a moment, and then looked up at Brian, waiting for the leash.

"We'll be back in a little while," Brian said.

As he opened the door, Hildie called out, "Marcella, may I go with Waldo and Brian?"

The voice of Marcella, the housekeeper, drifted out to them from some other room. "Do you have homework?"

Hildie looked at the book spread open on her lap, and then closed it. "Not today."

"Well, wear your coat, dear."

Out the front door, Brian and Waldo usually turned right and followed a long circuit around the block that took exactly half an hour and was long enough for Waldo to take care of all his business. Hildie turned left and walked down the block without looking to see if Brian was following. Waldo looked after her and with a whimper big enough to sound like worn-out brakes, trotted off in pursuit, leaving Brian with no choice but to follow.

"We usually go that way," Brian said when they caught up with her.

Hildie didn't look up at him, just kept marching resolutely forward, the hood of her jacket bouncing against her back. "There's a park down here. Waldo likes the park." She managed to make it sound like any other destination was simply unthinkable. Given that the 230-pound mastiff seemed to agree, they went to the park.

Hildie pushed open the wrought-iron gate and waited for Brian and Waldo. Once the gate was shut, it was like they were closing the door on the city. Yews taller than Brian lined the perimeter and muffled the traffic noise. The branches of elms were bare of leaves but still made a canopy over the meandering paths, which were bordered by still-empty flowerbeds.

There were few people in the park—a couple of women with strollers, an elderly man being gently led around by a Chihuahua, and a man with a Weimaraner.

Brian recognized the dog before the owner. It was Casey, his old three p.m. Monday-through-Wednesday, and holding the leash was C. Jacobs.

For a while Brian stood there trying to reconcile the images and the apartment with the person who was waiting for his dog to finish sniffing a pile of decaying leaves. He was taller than Brian thought he would be, a good four inches taller than Brian. Finally, someone he would have to look up to. But he was getting ahead of himself, as usual. The photos in the apartment must have been from a few years ago because, as he and Casey walked up the path toward them, Brian thought C. Jacobs looked a little older, though not in a bad way. And his hair was shorter, with a few flecks of gray.

As he stared, Brian's curiosity turned to alarm. C. Jacobs was coming toward them. Brian would have to talk to him. He looked around, trying to think of a way they could go without looking like they were running away, but the only option was right back out the way they came.

"Are we going to just stand here, or are we going to walk around?" Hildie asked. She followed Brian's gaze to C. Jacobs and the dog, taking more note of the dog than the man. "Don't worry; Waldo's really good with other dogs."

Brian could think of nothing to say to the man, who was almost right in front of them now. It vexed him that he knew him, in a way, but didn't know his name, not really. C. Jacobs. What did the C stand for? It was undefined. Solve for C, like an algebra equation. Craig, Christopher, Charles, Corin, Cole. If you knew the name of a dog breed, you knew something about the dog. A pit bull and a boxer might sometimes bear a resemblance, but if you knew which was which, you knew to expect markedly different temperaments. Knowing C.'s name, Brian thought, would give him some insight that the apartment and the photos and the Speedo and the sweet, otherworldly dog had not yet revealed.

"Is he friendly?" C. Jacobs asked, gesturing at Waldo with Casey's leash.

"Yes," Hildie said before Brian had a chance, and soon the two dogs were circling each other, sniffing and generally making a tangle of their leashes.

"What's his name?" Hildie asked.

Brian almost said it before C. Jacobs could. "Casey. What's your dog's name?"

"Waldo," Brian said.

"He's gorgeous," C. Jacobs said.

"Thanks," Brian said. Hildie gave him a glare, and Brian added, "Actually, he's not mine. I just walk him for his owners. This is Hildie, their daughter." If he had to know that Waldo wasn't his, Brian wanted to make sure he knew the kid wasn't, either.

"Dog walking must be a good business. Someone comes in to walk Casey during the week while I'm out of town."

Brian felt like there was a hot wire strung through his heart that was vibrating as if struck by a piano key. He felt like if he opened his mouth, all that would come out was the noise of that note. So he just nodded and went, "Mmm."

"Too bad I didn't meet you sooner. I had to fire my last walker, and you could have had the job."

Suddenly, the note caught in Brian's throat went flat. He'd been fired? The agency hadn't said anything about being fired.

"Fired, huh?" Brian asked, trying not to sound too defensive—or too interested. "What'd he do, try and steal your dog?"

C. Jacobs shook his head. "Nothing that extreme, but in that case I'd have had him arrested, I guess, not fired." He stuck out his hand. "My name's Carl."

Carl. Carl Jacobs. That was a nice, sturdy name.

"I'm Brian." *The guy who's going to sue you for wrongful termination,* he thought, and then squelched that line of thinking. "And this is Hildie, and that's Waldo."

Carl grinned. "You already told me that."

"Oh, yeah." Brian grinned, too, while his mind chased itself in circles trying to figure out what on earth he could have done to get himself fired by a client. He kept coming up with nothing. He'd been doing this for five years, and damn it, he knew he was good. He could remember only two clients he'd lost before this, and in each case he'd asked to be reassigned. How come the agency hadn't said anything about this?

"Would you like me to take the leash?" Hildie asked, jarring Brian from his self-interrogation. He'd also been staring at Carl, who looked puzzled but was still smiling. Brian looked down at Hildie's outstretched hand. Waldo had played out the length of the leash and was sniffing at the side of the path along with Casey. They seemed to have become fast friends. Again, Waldo looked up at Brian, and then at Hildie. Brian was getting a good idea of where he fell in Waldo's hierarchy of authority figures. He handed over the leash. "Just don't go too far."

She took the leash, gave him a look that was the equivalent of rolling her eyes at him without actually doing so, and went to Waldo's side.

Brian turned back to Carl.

"Talk about Little Miss Take Charge," Carl said.

"No kidding. Maybe I should split my fee with her."

"Listen, this may sound a little forward, but would you like to have dinner sometime?"

"Dinner," Brian said, while thinking, *You are reading my mind and know exactly what I want you to do and are willing to do it.*

Carl turned a bright crimson that started at his ears and spread like wildfire across his cheeks. "I have this theory that people who own dogs are automatically in a different category. You can't hide things from dogs, you know? They follow their hunch when it comes to people because it's all they've got. So if someone has a dog or if my dog likes someone, I figure they're good people."

Your dog liked me, and you still fired me anyway. Did you bother to check with him on that first? Brian felt like kicking himself, both because he didn't like this defensiveness that Carl had managed to inspire in him—which also made it that much harder to be charming—and because Brian knew that, against his better judgment, he was going to say yes.

Carl must have sensed Brian's hesitation, because he added, "I'm sorry, I didn't mean to put you on the spot. Well, no, I did mean to, but I don't even know if you're single. Or gay, for that matter."

"Yes on both counts, and it's not that, it's just"—*Make a joke, Brian, make a joke; you used to be good at being charming*—"if you date everyone who has a dog, you must be pretty busy."

Carl laughed out loud, bigger than the joke deserved, but Brian warmed at that half-nervous, half-unconscious sound. "Well, not *everyone*. Just the cute ones." He blushed again.

"Of course, I don't actually own Waldo. Or any dog, for that matter, so does that negate your theory?"

Carl considered it for a moment, and then shook his head. "Proxy owner, so in your case, it's like you own dozens of dogs."

"Great, I'm a dog slut."

Carl laughed again. It was so maddening to Brian. He felt like this all should have been his idea, and yet here was the guy from the pictures saying and doing everything right as if following a script Brian might have written in his head if he could write a coherent sentence. And yet outshining all of Carl's charm and good looks and enchanting dog, flashing in capital letters in Brian's mind were the words HE FIRED YOU.

Maybe, though, that was the more interesting equation. Brian didn't need to solve for C. He needed to solve for why.

If he was lucky, maybe he'd be able to solve both.

"Okay, dinner. When?"

"How about tonight?"

Brian paused. He didn't want to seem too eager, or too desperate, but the truth was, he had nothing planned, and if he wasn't desperate, he was at least eager.

"Sure, why not?"

They agreed on a time and a place, and then Hildie called out, "Did you bring a baggie? Waldo went number two."

"Duty calls, but I'll see you at seven," Brian said.

"Call if anything comes up," Carl said.

"Will do."

Brian headed toward Waldo and Hildie, searching in his jacket pockets for the plastic shopping bags he carried with him all the time, when Carl called after him, "Hey, don't you need my phone number?"

Ricardo's was a small Italian place in Lafayette Square. It was quiet but romantic: muted lighting, exposed brick, and a mantelpiece in the bar that held what looked like family photos. The hostess led Brian to the table where Carl was already waiting and stood to greet him, the grin on his face making things stir in Brian's gut besides hunger.

"So," Carl said after they'd ordered a bottle of wine, "how did you get into the fast-paced and exciting world of dog walking?"

Brian laughed. "It's only fast-paced if they're not neutered and get a whiff of a bitch in heat." Out of nervousness and desperation for something to do with his hands, he grabbed a slice of bread from the basket on the table, tore it in half, and began to nibble. "It was flexible enough so that it let me have time off for auditions."

"You're an actor?"

Brian shook his head. "Was. I spent a couple of years in New York after college going to every audition I could finagle my way into, which ended up not being very many. Since I needed to eat and pay rent, I started walking dogs."

He'd realized he liked walking dogs a lot more than running from one audition to another, especially after so many with so few callbacks. He couldn't read the casting directors, or they couldn't read him, but he could always read dogs. And once he decided the title "struggling actor" wasn't worth the struggle, there wasn't much point in staying in New York either.

"Sounds kind of like you did it in reverse: pursued the dream job, and then realized the day job was more fulfilling." Carl took a piece of bread, too, and then asked, "It *is* fulfilling, right?"

Brian nodded and hoped his smile didn't look forced. It was the same sort of question his parents and fellow former acting students had asked when he'd stopped going to auditions, though they'd worded it much less diplomatically: *Are you serious? Are you out of your fucking mind? Are you really throwing your acting career to the dogs?*

To which he'd responded, *What acting career?*

"In ways that acting never could be. Dogs are the most real people there are."

Carl smiled. "That's pretty much how I feel about Casey."

"Yeah, he's a great dog—at least, he sure seems like it. So what do you do?" Brian asked, anxious to steer the conversation away from himself and not dwell too long on his near-miss about Casey. For a while, Carl explained distribution channels, retail marketing, and shirt manufacturing, along with frequent single-day roundtrip flights and how he'd accrued so many travel points from hotels and rental cars that he was able to take a free international flight every year—if only he had the time. Even listening to it exhausted Brian.

"Wow, and you really enjoy that?"

"You really enjoy walking dogs?"

"Point taken." The waitress brought their bottle of wine, and Brian was glad for the pause in their conversation. The truth was Brian *did* enjoy his work, even if it had been something he'd just fallen into, something that hadn't been part of the plan. Much like Carl hadn't been part of the plan. He wondered about Carl's own plan, and the blond in the pictures and what had happened to that plan.

"Must make dating kind of tough," Brian said.

Carl nodded and picked up his glass. "Sometimes." A sip. "But not always." He smiled and held out his glass. Brian picked his up and clinked it against Carl's.

"I wish I was there more often for Casey, though," Carl continued. "It's hard to leave him for half a week and let friends and strangers take care of him for me. It makes me feel like a bad parent."

Brian shook his head. "Trust me, I've seen bad pet parents, and you don't strike me as one of them."

Even in the dim light, Brian could see Carl blush. "Thanks. I guess you've seen all kinds. I bet you inspire a lot of trust from your clients. I mean, they let you come into their homes when they're not there and leave their pets in your hands."

"Yeah, I guess they do," Brian said, feeling himself tense a bit when he thought, *All of them but you, apparently.* "Was that the problem you had? With your dog walker, I mean."

Carl nodded. "At first it didn't seem like a big deal—some things were moved around. I figured the housekeeper might have done that when she was cleaning, but I've employed her for years and she's practically my fairy godmother. But then things started to go missing, and…"

Carl trailed off, and Brian felt like he had to grip his own chair to keep from standing up and shouting, "I'm not a thief!" It was so maddening that he knew the truth but couldn't say a word to clear himself.

Even then he couldn't completely absolve himself of blame, could he? He *had* touched some items in Carl's home, even if it had been unintentional. But there was no way he would have taken *anything*, not if he wanted to keep his job.

It was already dark by the time they stepped outside. Brian hadn't been able to keep his mind from wandering while they ate, and at one point Carl had paused, fork hovering over his plate of linguini, and asked, "You okay? You seem a little distracted." Brian had assured him it was nothing—and he wanted it to be nothing. Despite his misgivings, Carl was a nice guy. Maybe they'd get past it.

Maybe Carl would never even have to know about it.

Brian looked down the sidewalk. There was a coffeehouse a few doors down and next door to that a bar that specialized in chocolate desserts. "I don't suppose you'd be interested in some dessert, or maybe some coffee?" Brian asked.

"I'd love to," Carl said, and Brian could almost hear the "but" before Carl had a chance to utter it, "but I'll have a lot of work to do tomorrow before I go out of town on Sunday."

"They're making you travel on Easter?" Brian asked.

Carl shrugged. "Beats getting up at four on Monday morning." He smiled. "I'm back in town Wednesday. Can I call you?"

Brian smiled, too. "I'd like that."

For a moment, Brian thought Carl might lean closer for a goodnight kiss, but instead he just smiled wider, grasped Brian's hand and gave it a quick, strong squeeze, and then turned and headed down the sidewalk. As Brian watched him get into his car, he tried to feel neither too disappointed nor too relieved. In the long run—if there was a long run where Carl was concerned—it was probably just as well that their date ended early. Now Brian could do his obsessing at leisure, without an audience.

On Monday he called the agency to try and learn more about the firing. Ellen, the scheduling manager, sounded harried, as usual. Brian heard her shuffling papers on her desk as they spoke.

"Good lord," she said, "how did you find out about that?"

"Long story," Brian said. "How come no one told me about it?"

Ellen sighed. "We weren't even going to bring it up because it just wasn't worth the trouble. It's the only complaint you've had in five years, and the guy didn't have any evidence to support it. Plus, everyone else loves you, and we figured it was more his problem than yours, so why should we make it our problem? We gave him a different walker, and it's not going in your file. End of story."

Brian could hear her still flipping and shuffling papers. "You're sure everything's okay then?"

"Honey, don't worry about it." Flip, flip, shuffle. "If you ask me, I'm guessing he's just high maintenance. Or paranoid. Be glad he's not your problem anymore."

The problem was Brian wanted Carl to be a completely different kind of problem, which wasn't necessarily a sure thing at this point anyway. Still, he didn't want the previous problem to interfere with anything that might happen.

It occupied his thoughts over the next two days. He came up with no answers but all sorts of questions, like whether he should just tell Carl, or tell the agency, or just let the whole thing slide. He knew so little about Carl—which was to be expected, after all. They'd only had one date, and maybe the smartest thing to do now would be to head off the complication before it developed.

Right. And head back into the drought? No.

So when Carl called on Wednesday, Brian found himself feeling more relieved than anxious. They made plans for Friday. Then another Friday. As Brian got to know Carl better, he saw no signs of the high-strung, high-maintenance neurotic he assumed had fired him and worried might appear. Instead, he was pleasantly surprised to find that Carl was someone who was driven, intense but also surprisingly gentle natured, and devoted to his dog almost to the extreme.

And yet...despite all that, Brian found himself holding back over the following weeks. Carl still hadn't mentioned anything about the blond man in the pictures—or really, about any prior relationships beyond generalities. But for Carl to keep so many photos of the man on display, the relationship must have been important, or at least very recent, if not both. And Brian hadn't been back to Carl's apartment to ask.

As much as it frustrated him to have so many pieces of information without knowing the whole story, Brian was grateful for one thing: that he wasn't Carl's dog walker anymore. As much as he loved Casey, had that been the case, there was no way he could carry on the masquerade, and it would have been far too tempting to snoop—and that could cost him his job.

If Carl noticed any of Brian's ongoing reticence, he didn't let on. Maybe he figured Brian wanted to take things slowly, or was just nervous, or maybe old-fashioned. The shyness that Brian found so endearing abated as time went on, and Brian didn't mind that at all. Still, he figured that intensity had to boil over at some point.

He only slightly underestimated by how much.

It was a Saturday night, and they'd just met for dinner at a little Brazilian place. The weather was nice enough that the restaurant opened up its patio and they ate outside. The enclosure was festooned with strands of hanging lanterns, which along with the candles on the table was all the light they had. Between that, the breeze, and the food, Brian felt pleasantly drowsy.

After dinner, Brian paused outside, taking a deep breath of the cool spring evening. They had planned to go to a movie, but Brian felt like a darkened theater would put him to sleep. He stepped to the curb and asked, "What if we just grab some coffee and call it a night?"

He turned back to find Carl standing closer than he'd realized, his typically shy smile now less shy, more mischievous.

"I've got coffee at home, actually."

Brian smiled, the flush of warmth racing through his abdomen and settling further south. He raised his arm and pointed toward his car just to keep himself from grabbing Carl right then and there. "Want me to drive?"

Once they were in the car, though, Carl placed one hand on Brian's chest, pushed him back against the seat, and kissed him, his other hand cupping the back of Brian's neck. After he got over the surprise, Brian let himself be carried along by Carl's momentum. And Carl had momentum. He kissed Brian like a suffocating man gasping for oxygen. It was as if the shy man had stepped back and let the intense, driven businessman take the lead. Carl raised himself out of the passenger seat and knelt with one knee on the armrest to get closer to Brian. If there'd been room behind the wheel, Brian was certain Carl would have crawled into his lap.

"At this rate, we're never going to get to your place," Brian said, still a little breathless when they finally came up for air.

With that, Carl eased back into the passenger seat and buckled his seatbelt. "Better drive then, chief." He rested his hand on Brian's thigh as Brian backed the car out and headed west.

"So," Carl said after a few moments, "you need me to give you directions?"

"Huh?" For a moment, Brian felt a rush of panic. He knew the way to Carl's place, but of course Carl didn't know that. Thankfully, his brain restarted without too much of a delay. He brushed off Carl's question by saying, "I'm sorry, did you say something? I couldn't hear anything on account of I'm concentrating on your hand down there."

"Am I distracting you?" Carl slid his hand up Brian's thigh and Brian felt like he might lose control soon.

Eventually, Carl gave him directions, Brian pretended he needed them, and by the time they pulled up in front of Carl's building, he'd almost completely undone Brian's pants. As Brian rearranged his clothing after they got out, Carl said, "We'd better get inside before I rip off the rest of your clothes right here."

"Probably not the best impression to make on your neighbors," Brian said.

He made a point of playing dumb when they entered the building, letting Carl lead the way to the elevator, press the button for the tenth floor, and guide Brian down the hallway to his front door. They didn't make the trip in a straight line. They leaned against the elevator buttons and ended up stopping on the fourth, sixth, and ninth floors, nearly setting off the alarm in the process. In the hallway on the tenth floor, Brian figured turnabout was fair play, pinned Carl against the wall, and managed to unzip his pants and get a hand inside. Carl moaned loudly enough that Brian worried the neighbors would hear them. They half stumbled, half ran down the hall to Carl's door.

Inside, they nearly tripped over Casey, who was curled up on the floor just beyond the door. Carl fumbled for the light switch on the wall and Casey, mistaking their clumsy embrace for an invitation to roughhouse, rose up on his hind legs and placed his forepaws on Brian's arm.

"Down, boy," Brian said.

"Me or the dog?" Carl asked, trying to put his keys on the hall table and missing. They clattered to the floor and sent Casey skittering away, but not before he banged into the table and sent the photos tumbling to the floor.

"Shit," Brian said. The sense of déjà vu threw him for a moment, and then he knelt down to start picking things up.

"Don't worry about those," Carl said, kneeling beside him and pulling Brian closer, knocking him off balance. They both fell over. When Brian moved to get up, Carl wrapped an arm around his waist and kept him there.

Brian had noticed, when he'd tried to straighten up the pictures, that the ones with the blond were no longer there. He glanced toward them, just to make sure. Some of them were lying on their faces, others turned right side up, and on none of those was the blond man visible. Yet in the absence of any evidence of him, he loomed even larger in Brian's thoughts.

"What's wrong?"

Brian realized he wasn't looking at Carl, and turned his face back to him. "Wrong?"

"I don't know. You suddenly tensed up. Is everything okay? You're okay with this, right?"

Brian pushed himself into a kneeling position, and Carl propped himself up on his elbows. They still had their jackets on, but they'd managed to make a mess of everything else they were wearing. The tongue of Carl's belt dangled where Brian had unbuckled and yanked it out of a couple of belt loops, his pants were undone and pushed down over his hips, his shirt was untucked, and it looked like it had lost a button. Brian's belt was still buckled, but his pants were unzipped again. And behind them, Casey was curled up by the door. What could possibly be wrong with this?

They stood and Brian grabbed Carl's belt, pulling him closer. "This is more than okay."

Brian was greeted with a lick across his nose when he woke up the next morning. He sat up, petted Casey behind his ears, which he knew Casey liked, and looked out the window. Carl's bedroom overlooked the vast spread of Forest Park to the east. Morning sunlight streamed through the window and gave the air in the room a yellow frost, almost like fog. It wasn't just the haze in the air or his head that made the moment feel dreamlike.

Brian swung his feet over the edge of the bed and stood up. The bedroom door was open, and Casey trotted out. There was rustling coming from somewhere else in the apartment, which Brian identified as kitchen noise. Breakfast in bed? The morning was getting started on a high note.

"Good morning, sleepyhead." Carl didn't look up from the omelet he was sliding onto a plate when he heard Brian walk in. He set the frying pan down, looked up, and smiled wider. "*Really* good morning."

Brian looked down, suddenly self-conscious about walking around naked. "Sorry, breakfast has that effect on me."

"Gee, if only I'd known it was that easy."

"Do you have anything I could wear for now?"

Again the wicked grin. "Oh, no, I don't think so."

Carl was insistent Brian not get dressed for breakfast. They settled onto the couch facing the balcony and ate while the room warmed up. Daybreak lengthened into midmorning, breakfast gave way to sex, and the couch gave way to the window, with Carl kneeling with his back against the balcony's glass door and Brian standing before him. Every time he raised his face from the man at his feet, the view with its expanse of sky sent a wave of dizziness washing over him. He braced his hands against the window and let the wave carry him, half fearful he would pass out and half not caring. By lunchtime, they were exhausted and hungry again, and Casey needed to go for a walk.

"And really, I need to get going," Brian said, pulling on his jeans. Carl was still leaning against the window, his own clothing scattered around him. He grinned—not wicked or dirty, but simply basking naked in the afternoon and Brian's attention. Brian leaned over and kissed him.

"I had a really good time," Carl said.

"Me, too." Brian was surprised how difficult it was to pull himself away. "Back on Wednesday?"

Carl nodded. "I'll call you as soon as I get in."

Brian was barely out the front door of Carl's building when his phone rang. It was Ellen from the agency.

"I need a big favor," she said. "Joan just went into labor this morning, and I need you to cover for her clients. There's one this afternoon and two during the week."

"That doesn't sound like a big deal."

"Hopefully you'll still feel that way when I tell you that one of the weekday clients is the guy who fired you."

Brian nearly tripped down the steps. He regained his footing and then said, "What the hell, Ellen? You can't just do that."

"Brian, I'm in a bind here. Everyone else is booked up

solid or has a conflict. The regular walker is about to pop out twins, and you're not. It's just for this once, please? He's out of town, so it's not like he's even going to find out. If you do it on Monday, I'll try to get someone else lined up for Tuesday and Wednesday."

Brian knew it was a bad idea, but he agreed to it anyway.

As he unlocked Carl's door Monday afternoon, Brian felt this time he truly was an interloper, even though—or perhaps because—he'd been invited in just a couple of days ago. Now here he was, scratching Casey behind the ears, fetching the leash, and Carl would have no clue about the intrusion.

And because he was there, he had to bend down and look a little closer at the photos on the hall table, though this time he kept a firm grip on Casey's leash so he wouldn't jump up on him. The same vacation photos were there, the same beaches, the same cruise ships. The only thing missing was the blond. All the photos of him were gone.

He spent the half-hour walk with Casey wondering what other evidence of the blond had been expunged in the meantime. Then, much to his own surprise, he suddenly dismissed that question. What did it matter? Clearly, the man was no longer part of Carl's life, so why should Brian worry about it? So Carl hadn't mentioned him yet. So what? Had Brian given Carl the laundry list of his own past failures? Okay, perhaps he'd sketched out the broad outlines for him, but he'd done it in what he was sure was a humorous and gently self-deprecating fashion. There was nothing here to worry about.

Until Tuesday.

Ellen hadn't been able to find anyone to take over for Brian, of course. She begged, she sounded as harried as possible, and finally offered up extra money if Brian kept covering for the regular walker, who was now a new mother and wasn't going to be back to work for a while.

All right, he'd told her. This week, but no more.

It had started raining gently when Brian entered the building just before three, and it turned into a full-on downpour by the time they got back down to the street. Casey, undeterred, waited patiently under the awning outside while Brian struggled with his umbrella and tried not to drop the leash. When he'd finally accomplished the task, he gave Casey's leash a tug and out they marched into the rain—and almost right into Carl.

For a moment, neither of them spoke, the percussion of the rain and the slush of traffic providing a chorus to their silence. Casey, apparently concluding that they weren't going anywhere for a while, sat down.

"So," Carl finally said, "are you kidnapping my dog?"

"No." Brian knew he had to say more than that, but he hardly dared to breathe.

Carl raised an eyebrow, still waiting, no doubt, for Brian to explain. "So?"

"You're home early," Brian blurted.

"My meeting got rescheduled. I don't remember giving you a key to my place yet."

Brian shook his head, still not sure what to say but equally unable to silence the chorus of recriminations in his mind: He would lose his job. He'd never get to see Waldo again, or Casey, or any of the other clients he'd come to look forward to walking, these friends of his who never said a word to him and yet gave him everything they had. Carl would break up with him, would never speak to him, to say nothing of giving him head, again, and good lord, he was so good at that. And what if—as he'd been starting to wonder— what if Carl was the guy who didn't just bring an end to his dry spell but ensured there'd never be a dry spell again?

When someone finally found the voice to speak, it was neither Brian nor Carl. It was a woman walking toward them with Waldo on a leash and Hildie by her side. Hildie was holding an umbrella. The woman, who Brian knew was Hildie's mom though he couldn't remember her name, was drenched, as was Waldo.

"Brian!" Brian and Carl both turned to see her waving from half a block away.

"Hey," Carl said, "isn't that—"

"Yep," Brian said before Carl could finish, and waved back at her. Finally remembering her name, he added, "Hi, Rebecca."

"I didn't think it was fair that you got to take Waldo out on all his walks, so we decided to take him out a little early as an extra treat."

Hildie held out her free hand to Casey and said, "I think he remembers me. He probably remembers Waldo, too. What's his name again?"

"Casey," Brian and Carl replied, almost simultaneously. Hildie frowned at them.

Rebecca smiled and said to Carl, "Isn't Brian the best dog walker? I don't know what we'd do if we had to switch. He's the most reliable and trustworthy one we've had." She looked down and smiled at Hildie, who didn't smile back. "I'd even trust him with Hildie here."

"Yeah," Carl said. "Brian's really good with doggies."

"I'm not a dog," Hildie said, glowering. Rebecca and Carl laughed, and then chatted about the relative merits of Waldo's and Casey's breeds while Brian quietly wished for the rain to turn into a hailstorm and pelt him into unconsciousness.

Mercifully, Rebecca finally said, "Well, I'd better get Waldo back home and take Hildie to violin practice." She held out her hand to Carl. "Very nice to meet you. I suppose we'll see you tomorrow, Brian."

"Sure thing," he said, though he figured it was probably far from a sure thing. At that point, he was just glad that she and Hildie and Waldo were walking away.

As Brian watched them leave, the rain finally petered out to a lackluster drizzle. It was hard to believe that it was May and fifty degrees and rainy, when it had so recently been April and unseasonably eighty on the weekend and sunny. Brian and Carl had taken Casey to the park along with a blanket and a couple of sandwiches, spread themselves out in a little spot on the hill down from the art museum, and watched people in paddle boats on the canal, joggers along the paths, and a couple of kite fliers. It was at that point that Brian had thought how nice the summer was going to be, spending weekends doing nothing more than this.

Now, it might as well have been winter again.

As soon as Waldo's entourage turned a corner, Brian turned back to Carl and said, "I'm so sorry I didn't tell you this sooner, but I'm the dog walker you fired in February."

Carl cocked an eyebrow. "I kind of guessed that. Obviously, you're not my pregnant-with-twins dog walker."

Brian shook his head. "She had them this weekend. That's why they asked me to sub for her. There wasn't anyone else."

"She did? I'll have to send her some flowers or something." Carl looked down at Casey, still sitting at their feet. "Shouldn't we at least take him around the block?"

Brian shrugged, and they started walking. He shouldn't have felt so indifferent—what if it were the last time he got to see Casey? Truthfully, though, he was more concerned that it might be the last time he got to see Carl. At that prospect, his whole explanation of what happened just poured out of him—the photos on the hall table, how Casey had knocked them over, his curiosity about the blond man, everything.

That's when Carl began to laugh. He was trying to keep it to himself, but when Brian looked over, Carl's grin spread out into total glee. And Brian suddenly felt offended.

"What the hell's so funny?"

"You mean besides the look on your face?" Carl's laughter was like a dam breaking. When he noticed Brian didn't join him in the levity, he tried to control himself. "Oh, come on, this is pretty hilarious, isn't it?"

Brian stopped and crossed his arms. "I don't see how."

Carl regained his composure and then said, "This whole time I was so pleased that Casey liked you so much. It never occurred to me that you already knew him better than me."

"He's an easy dog to like," Brian said, "but you already knew that. You know how you said you can tell a lot about people from whether or not Casey likes them? I kind of think the reverse is true as well. You can tell a lot about people from their dogs. It's not an exact science, but more often than not, if I like the dogs I walk, I know I'd like their owners."

That seemed to sober Carl, and he said, "I think I owe you an apology. I figured out my dog walker wasn't the one taking things, but I never bothered to inform the agency." He put his hand to his forehead. "Jeez, you could have been fired and it would have been all my fault."

Brian shrugged. "Luckily, everyone else loves my work. So who was behind the disappearing things?"

"My ex-boyfriend, James."

"The blond in the pictures?"

"Pictures?" Carl asked, and then, as realization dawned, added, "Oh, pictures. Yeah, that was him."

"Bad breakup?"

"You could say that if you were prone to understatement."
Carl jammed his hands into his coat pockets and hunched his
shoulders. "He moved out around the same time I signed up
with the dog walking service. He used to walk Casey when I was
out of town. His schedule was more consistent than mine. I can't
say the same about his affection." He pulled a hand from his
coat and ran it across his forehead. "Anyway, there was some
confusion after he moved out about what was mine and what
was his, so I changed the locks. If you're worried about him
coming back into my life, you don't need to. He moved out of
town, and even if he hadn't, I wouldn't ask him."

Brian nodded and looked down at the leash in his hand. Casey
had grown tired of standing and waiting for them to move and
was now sitting and shifting his gaze between Carl and Brian.

"I should have said something sooner, but the longer I didn't,
I figured it might weird you out to know I'd already been in your
apartment when we met."

"Only if you were going through my drawers and sniffing
my dirty underwear." He gave Brian a sidelong glance. "You
weren't, were you?"

"No!"

"You're sure?"

Brian narrowed his eyes. This glimpse of Carl's wicked sense
of humor was a different side of him. It threw Brian off a little,
which was exciting in itself. "You're just having fun at my
expense, aren't you?"

Carl shrugged. "Maybe a little."

"It's just…"

Carl put a hand on Brian's forearm. "Come on. What?"

"Look, things with you have been going better than they
have for me with anyone else in a long time. I didn't want to
jinx things before we'd even had a chance to get started."

"It's been a while since things have gone this well for me, too."

"So," Brian asked, "am I your rebound guy? Is this going to last longer than a walk around the block?"

Carl threw his hands in the air. "Who knows at the start if anything's going to last at all? I didn't exactly plan any of this. It just happened. That's the way these things always go, isn't it?"

"True." Brian looked at his watch. "I've got a three forty-five that I'm going to be late for." He held out Casey's leash. "Since you're on your way home, do you mind?"

"Okay, just this once." Carl took the leash. "So, I'm dating you, and the other one's a new mommy. Does this mean I have to get a new dog walker?"

"I don't know. Do you want a different one?"

"No. But does the agency have any rules about dog walkers sleeping with their clients?"

"I think there are laws against sleeping with dogs, and besides, that's not my kink."

Carl blushed, and Brian was glad to see that he could still make him do that. It didn't last long, though.

"But you can probably think of lots of interesting things to do with a leash," Carl said.

Brian grinned. "That'll cost you extra."

TWO TALES

Paul Lisicky

1. Bear Week

I'm going to hate the way this sounds, but let's get it out of the way: An ugly man sits down beside me on the bench while I'm talking on the phone to Mark. And while I know you're probably shaking your head at *ugly* (not to mention, where is the compassion?), I'll just say that he leans into me with a boozy smile and reaches up into my shorts for the prize. Get it? It doesn't help that this transaction happens while I'm describing the action on the street to Mark, and how do you say, "there's a half-naked man squeezing my dick in public" while tourists are walking by with their ice cream, as if we're just another part of the show? Mark is sounding a little jealous, or more precisely, like he wants some of what I have for himself, and I want to say no, it's not what you think it is, but how can I tell him that the man resembles Uncle Fester, or one of the extraterrestrials from *Close Encounters* minus the charm, without hurting someone?

In truth, I don't think the man would be all that bad if he got himself a T-shirt or a personality; if I were a different sort, I'd sit with him until he recovered himself and maybe find out that he, like me, is a Joni Mitchell fan. But who has time for speculation when his hand's all too happy to have found its home, and he's resting his head near the top of my chest like a demented baby about to nurse? Sweet Jesus. Luckily, there's Adam, big Adam, walking down the street, with an unmistakable expression of concern and suppressed horror on his face. Without pause, he summons me over. I put my arm around his shoulder, as if our connection has been long and intimate, and we walk on into the throng, leaving the man to fall sideways into the space where I'd been.

Of course, none of the above would have happened without the handy device of the cell phone, which left me defenseless, although I'd believed it was giving me power, even as it enabled me to put my arm around a man I've somewhat known for years but had always been a little bit afraid of. But this is not the lesson that you think it is, and my story's not yet coming to a close though it might feel that way, as I'm still talking to Mark, to tell him Adam's come to the rescue. Adam? he says. Adam who? Big Adam. *Big* Adam? he says. And Adam, hearing himself referred to in terms that must flatter him, shifts his arm atop my shoulder to show me how many hours he's been putting in at the gym. And you know what? I kind of like it. No doubt Mark must hear the lifting inside my voice, and Adam must wonder what it feels like to be in Mark's skin right now, itchy and three hundred and sixty-five miles from the tumult and fire of Gay Tourist Town, with your partner under the wing of someone you vaguely know, and the thinnest quaver passes between Adam and me, as if it originated through the phone signal itself, and that's our cue to break apart, and I nod thanks to Adam, say a firm good-bye to

Mark, and I'm on my way back to the White Horse Inn.

I'm entertaining myself, telling this sequence of events to myself. One piece in front of the next and back again and back—and isn't it a beautiful night for stories? The sky so scrubbed with stars it hurts. Then a familiar face moving toward me, lit up by the lights outside the pharmacy. Mike, whom I've always liked but don't know so well. What? he says, looking at what must be the goofy grin on my face. *What?* And how can I not tell him the story all over again: the boozy smile, the rough wet hand, big bad Adam, and we both crack up and redden, not because it's new to me anymore, but—*what?* Beards and dicks and big daddies careening around us like trucks through waves of water. And isn't Mike's face looking different than it's ever looked? His screwy smile, barely concealing his secret animal? And just as I lean in closer, to tell him I'm going to write this story and put him in it, I get ahold of myself, cough, and say "so long," with a promise to see each other at the reading Saturday night.

And in this way, the ugly man seems to have tied four unlikely men together by giving us a rope we wouldn't have known we'd wanted. And made a better thing of the word *ugly* for one evening. And made us laugh.

Or almost. Ahead—how has he gotten ahead?—he's leaning into another man on another bench in front of Town Hall. So much for thinking I was singled out. Up goes the hand into the shorts. Down goes the corner of the good man's mouth. Where's Adam when we need him? Where? *There,* in my in-box, twenty-eight days later, as I'm sitting down to write this story: *I remember that night. I was happy to have helped.*

2. Friend

There once was a Paul. Not me, but another Paul whose left

ear stuck out more than his right. Not that you'd notice, but
Paul certainly noticed. So much so that he wore caps inside and
outside, which gave him the air of an aging Italian gentleman,
even when he was a teenager. If you really want to disparage
yourself, I'd think, you might want to consider your slouch, that
mustard-green cardigan, your already fuzzy hairline—my *God*.
Of course, I could say those things because I loved him and he
didn't love me back. Wait—that's probably shorthand, but what
could be done about two seventeen-year-old boys, and one whose
need was so ferocious that his gaze sent the other backing out
the door? When I think about Paul now, I think about the time
he confessed, with pants down after awkward sex, to driving
his head into the side of his parents' bathtub. Not just once but
again and again. And he said it with the smiling resignation that
suggested his performance was no way to escape the body, even
though he finally did escape the body, though not in the way
you're thinking.

When the barber pointed out the bump on the back of my
head, I didn't lift a finger. Oh, no. I didn't work or wobble it; I
didn't stand in front of every three-way mirror I passed looking
for signs of growth. And when it was clear that it was meant
to last a while longer, I didn't tape it with duct tape, nor did I
pour apple cider vinegar onto a cotton ball, which I'd learned
could burn the finish off the finest chair. Though I actually did
consider the words of the farm boy who sprung open his pocket
knife on the second meeting of the writing class: "Do you want
me to cut that tick off the back of your head?"

"Let's poke fun at the wounded," said my friend Michael
sometime later, and I'm still trying to figure out why the whole
band of us laughed, and it didn't come off as mean.

Once I read a novel in which a man walked into a remote
woods only to find a hermit, quite calm and dignified, who

performed plastic surgery on his face with a mirror. The new face wasn't exactly handsome, nor were his stitches remotely transparent, but that was beside the point. Purity, perfection: neither had their place here. We were up to something better. The hermit led the character to a house he'd built with scraps found by the road. He sat the character down in a chair, dropped a teabag into a teacup. Quietly, he walked across the room. He lifted his violin from the lid of his piano, drew his bow, and began to play the most spontaneous notes that had ever been played. The character closed his eyes; if it wasn't music as he knew it, it was something richer, stranger. Song sparrows? Marsh wrens?

"Friend," said the man from the novel.

"Friend," said the hermit, swallowing back tears.

Wait. I'm mixing up two stories here, *The Bride of Frankenstein* and who knows what else. And the woods are black, my flashlight's dead, and why is that deer chirruping up ahead?

"Wait," says the hermit, playing up an octave.

"Listen," says the man from the novel, reaching for a plate.

"Yes?" say I.

And for some years, the two live happily together in the woods.

HEART

'Nathan Burgoine

I met Jeremiah Carey at a bar. Now, before you think I'm a typical raver freak, club kid, or something even less savory, I didn't want to be there. Every now and then, Tony, my ex, shows up on my doorstep, demands I be social, and drags me out somewhere loud and bright and obnoxious.

Thus, the bar.

It was some DJ from Toronto who had Tony's attention, and the music was pulsing so loudly that I figured half the glasses behind the bar would be chipped by last call. I didn't recognize the music, which meant I wasn't likely to endure the night for very long.

It didn't take Tony long to get to the center of the dance floor and show off. He's good at that; in fact, his ability to capture a room's attention was one of the things that first attracted me to him. That, and he just sort of grabs life by the neck and hangs on for the ride. He's a good guy, but he's also really self-absorbed and has the attention span of a goldfish.

Thus, the ex.

Still, shirtless, sweaty Tony doing the groove on a speaker was something to spark memory lane, and I couldn't help but smile from my vantage point at the bar, where I was perched on a stool, nursing a Canadian after enjoying dancing to the first—and only—song I'd recognized all night.

The DJ stopped the music and started "shouting out" to guests and sponsors, or I wouldn't have heard the voice beside me.

"He's good," he said.

I nodded, not looking over at him, still watching Tony, who'd leaned in close to talk with a blond guy in a blue tank top. "He loves music. Loves to dance," I said. Tony saw me watching and blew me a kiss. Blue Tank Top turned to scope out potential competition.

"Mary Higgins Clark," the guy beside me said.

I turned and looked at him for the first time, blinking. "What?"

He was a little guy, though he looked about my age, really slim. He wore a red T-shirt and a pair of plain jeans, and had very fair skin that, matched with his sandy hair and soft gray eyes, gave him this aw-shucks look that was sort of refreshing, in a country-bumpkin way. He smelled like soap. No cologne, just soap.

"Mary Higgins Clark," he repeated "She wrote a novel called *Loves Music, Loves to Dance*. It wasn't bad."

"You read a lot?" I asked, speaking louder as the next song began thumping from the DJ booth.

"Occupational hazard." He grinned. "I work in a used book-store, down in the Market." He turned back to watch Tony dance some more, now nearly chest-to-chest with Blue Tank Top, and then sighed, flashing me a slightly gamy grin. "I don't suppose he's a big reader?"

I laughed. "Nope. Tony never understood why I could spend a whole night reading instead of heading to some rave or something." I had to lean in close to his ear for him to hear me.

The guy's gray eyes turned back to me, and he seemed a little surprised. I'm over six feet tall and a solid one-ninety, and I hit the gym every workday, given it's what I do for a living. I get mistaken for a dumb jock a lot. Other than having brown hair, unlike Archie's buddy, there's a reason my nickname is Moose.

Okay, two reasons, but I won't brag.

Either way, when someone is surprised that I have a library, and it's not all back issues of *Men's Health,* I don't take it personally.

Much.

"Who's your favorite author?" he asked, warming to the subject. It was the strangest conversation I've ever yelled back and forth in a busy bar.

"Lately? Christopher Moore," I said, and a delighted smile crossed his face. Suddenly his eyes weren't gray at all, they were blue.

"I loved *Lamb!*" he shouted. "Have you read that one?"

I nodded and put my beer down. "Aiden." I offered a hand.

"Jeremiah," he shouted, and took it. "But call me Miah."

It was the first time I've ever stayed at a bar longer than Tony.

When he finds me sitting outside the hospital, Tony takes my hand, something he has never done in public, even when we were dating.

"Moose, I'm so sorry." He's wearing a tight black T-shirt and the necklace he says is lucky. He's been at a bar. His hair is messed up from a night out, interrupted by my call.

"Tony, I just...I need to be alone for a minute, okay?"

Tony squeezes my hand, and then rises. "I'll be right inside, okay?" He sounds a little hurt, but like he's okay with it. I'm not even looking at him.

It's not until Tony leaves that I first see the flickering yellow-white at the other end of the hospital parking lot. I stand and start toward my dead lover, trailing angry, impotent fire behind me.

It's a pity nothing burns.

The first time he spent the night, Miah walked around my bedroom, his eyes lighting on everything. He walked slowly, like he did everything, deliberately touching nothing but noting the photos, observing my plants, and stopping at the pictures I had hung over my bed. He liked the one of the lightning bolt striking the ocean.

"Wow," he said, voice hushed, "that's powerful." Then he turned to the bookcase in the bedroom, which made my bookcase tally rise to four so far on his tour of my apartment. He grinned. "More books," he said.

I smiled. "Not just a dumb jock, eh?"

"I dunno," he teased nervously. "You're a trainer at the Y. For all I know, the books are for show. Maybe you use them as weights." He smiled up at me.

I stood in my bedroom doorway, watching him. Since that first conversation three weeks ago, I'd been entranced. His beautiful sometimes-gray, sometimes-blue eyes devoured the world. He wasn't aggressive, or even hyper, like Tony, but the way he *watched*...It was insatiable. His body was sedate, but his *eyes*...

He glanced at me when I didn't reply, and smiled. "What are you thinking about?" he asked. It was one of his more common questions, I'd learned.

"Kissing you," I said truthfully.

"That's straight out of the *Big Book of Boyfriend Things to*

Say." He blushed. "Where you hiding your copy?"

"Are we boyfriends?" I asked.

Miah stopped and sat awkwardly on the bed. Perched on the edge, he looked around the room and fixed on a pair of my socks on the floor.

"Are you okay?" I asked, and sat beside him.

"There's something I have to tell you," Miah said, and his eyes were very gray.

Afterward, he slept with his cheek on my chest, and I did something I hadn't done since my grandmother died. I tried to touch the source of the thing she said made me special. I let the font rise inside me, the hot, liquid-gold sensation filling my pores. It was hard—harder than when I was a child—but there seemed like so much more of it inside me that for a moment I was ashamed.

All that gift, I could nearly hear my grandmother say, *and you keep it for yourself.*

And then all I could hear was the rush of it in my ears, painful, a thundering heartbeat.

Heartbeats...

Miah had taken off his shirt slowly, shyly, and showed me the long scar where they had cut him open and fixed the worst parts of his faulty heart. He told me how he took a pill every morning, and how that was probably enough to keep him going for as long as anyone usually goes. He told me that, unlike Tony, although he loved music, he sure couldn't dance. There was a reason he kept himself so sedate, I realized, why he tired easily and moved so gently. It was frightening to think of a heart as something so fragile.

Then, very quietly, he'd added a request.

"So, being as it's already sort of cracked, try not to break it, okay?"

I kissed him. I wanted to wrap him up in my arms and make him warm all over.

So I did.

But now, with the gold fire filling me so close to my skin that I was crying from the heat of it, I could see the life in him, and it flickered every now and then, his cracked heart skipping a beat.

Gently, I curled against him, slowly rolled him onto his back, and straightened his head on the pillow. I kissed him again, and let a little of the fire pass between my lips. In his sleep, he stirred a little but didn't wake.

The flickers died down. His frail glow grew steadier for a while.

I smiled, kissed his forehead, and went to sleep holding him against me, my thumb rubbing slowly up and down the scar that bisected his chest.

You're a good boy, I heard my grandmother say.

Or maybe it was just a dream.

At the end of the parking lot, the echo of Miah is gazing at me with eyes more golden than gray. The echo of him, the memory, looks at me with a vaguely pained expression, and then reaches up and touches his own chest.

I nod, and my vision blurs with tears.

Miah's echo puts his arms down and looks around. It's a cold night, but he's wearing a plain red T-shirt and blue jeans, exactly as the day I met him, except now I can see the parked cars right through him, and somewhere near his calves, he fades away into flickering bits of pale yellow light.

He opens his mouth, but then a confused and frustrated look covers his face. He cannot speak, or can't remember speech, or doesn't have enough...life...in him to do it.

I draw my font up and exhale a fiery stream. It settles into him, and his edges tighten, his eyes grow brighter, and he smiles.

"What are you thinking about?" Miah's echo asks me. Like warm breath on a winter's night, clouds form at his words, but they are gold and yellow and orange.

"Kissing you," I say truthfully, and the tears come.

"We need another bookcase." Miah grinned from where he was sitting on the floor, putting his paperbacks in between mine on the bottom shelf. He turned to look at me as I came in from the cold. He had all his books unpacked now, his entire library, and it was piled up—alphabetically, by author—all across the apartment floor.

"Then we need another wall, too. You've been at that all day?" I asked, tugging off my jacket.

Miah grinned and lay down on his back, putting his hands behind his head. "Reading is to the mind what exercise is to the body." Then, in segue, "How was work?"

"Clever." I smiled and crouched down beside him. I kissed his forehead, and he reached up and took the back of my head and dragged me down for a lip-lock. I sat down, and he shuffled and put his head in my lap, looking sleepy and pale.

I brought a sliver of the font to heat my vision, and saw that he was pale in more ways than one.

"Are you feeling okay?" I asked.

He glanced up at me and smiled wryly. His eyes were impish blue. "You're as bad as Ian."

I raised an eyebrow in mock jealousy, and was a little disturbed to find I really was jealous. "Who?"

"Ian. He runs the bookstore. Haven't you met him yet?" He seemed surprised at that, and I realized I'd never really gone to his bookstore, beyond picking him up after work. I decided

I needed to visit the store soon, especially when this Ian was working.

"No," I said. "And if he cares when you look tired, I like him already."

"I'm always tired," Miah said, without heat.

I stole another kiss. "So long as that's all he cares about."

Miah laughed. "He's a nice guy, and he has a boyfriend of his very own." He reached up and touched my chin. "He's really sharp, though. Like you—he takes one look at me and says," Miah's voice dropped a little, "'Miah, you need a break. Did you take your pill this morning?'"

I smiled, mostly at the news of Ian's happy relationship. "*Did you take your pill this morning?*"

He nods. "I've been feeling so good lately I'm tempted to skip, but I take them anyway."

"Don't skip them, okay?" I was a little scared.

"Cross my heart." He winked and did so with his finger. I took it in my hand and kissed the fingertip.

"Clever," I said again.

He frowned. "I really do feel better."

I took a deep breath. "There's something I should tell you."

The echo of Miah reaches toward me, and his flickering fingertips touch my lips. They have pressure, presence, and he blinks in surprise.

"I'm sorry," I say, crying still. "I'm so sorry."

He pulls his fingers back and touches his chest. "Nothing," he says, and already his voice is less distinct.

I was staring at the ceiling when he spoke, not yet sleeping.

"How did you...I mean, when did it start?"

I turned on my side, moving the covers and sheets, and took

his shoulder to turn him toward me. In the darkness, his eyes shone slightly in the faint glow from the streetlights through the bedroom window. He smelled of soap.

"My Grandmother Nan told me I could do it. She could tell it was in me."

"Just like that?" he asked.

I thought back to it. One afternoon, playing at her house, before my grandfather was sick, my grandmother had taken me aside.

"She asked me if I saw lights inside people," I smiled at the memory, "and taught me to look for it. She said I was different from her, that I saw suns where she saw oceans, but that font poured out of us pretty much the same."

"Font?" Miah snuggled under my chin, and I wrapped my arms around him.

"She called it her font, like a fountain. To her, every life was like this wonderful, cool river, and she—" My voice caught, and I had to stop for a second.

Miah shifted on my chest. "What happened to her?" he asked quietly.

"My grandfather had a stroke when I was eleven," I said. "She...did something, with her font. He got better, really quickly, but I could tell it wasn't good for her. Her own fire—you have to understand, I was watching everyone at that point, figuring out what I could see, what I could do—it got so low, so unsteady." I sighed. "It was awful. It was like he got better a little bit and she got worse a whole lot, day by day."

I gripped him tighter for a moment.

"Then, when he started to talk again, and could walk, she went to sleep one night and didn't wake up. The doctor said she had an embolism, but I think that was just the side effect of emptying herself out into him."

Miah went quiet. He kissed my chest.

"So I stopped," I said, a little defensively. "I mean, I saw what happened if you gave too much, and I didn't want to die."

Miah kissed my chest again. "I think you're wonderful," he said. "But I don't want you to hurt yourself over me. The pills are good. I know how to live like this, I really do. I'm used to it."

I kissed him on the forehead.

Miah lifted onto his elbow. "I'm serious. I don't want you to do it anymore..."

"I'm not doing what she did," I protested. "It really is like a spring. It fills up again a little every day. I'm just giving you the extra, the stuff I get back just sitting in the sun for a while."

"But—" he started.

"No." I shook my head. "Miah, please. I'm not...I'm not hurting myself. There's a lot inside me, enough to share with other people. It's what—"

I broke off, and heard my Grandmother Nan's voice.

You, me, we are springs for other people. We're here to give them a little extra. Our font is to be shared, not kept, or all that extra life, it just seeps away. Don't waste it.

"It's what I'm supposed to do," I said, feeling guilty. Maybe even ashamed.

He shifted and kissed me, full on the lips, slow and lingering.

"What's it like?" he asked. "What do people look like to you?"

I smiled into the darkness and lit the fire behind my eyes. It was getting easier with practice, though it still felt like stretching an old muscle. Miah's outline, a soft golden aura with that guttering dark place over his heart, burst into being in front of me.

"It's like seeing souls." I smiled. "And yours is the handsomest."

He laughed. "More from the *Big Book of Boyfriend Things to Say.* You're just trying to get me to put out."

I let my hands wander. "Is it working?"

When it happened, I finally got to meet Ian. He was in the emergency room, standing to one side, and the name tag clipped to the pocket of his black polo shirt was the only reason I knew who he was. He had mismatched eyes, one green, one blue, and that's all I seemed to be able to focus on when I looked at him.

"What happened?" I asked.

"He just fell down," Ian said, stepping back from me. That was when I realized I'd almost yelled my question, and that I was angry. "He was stacking some books, and then he sort of slid down the wall." Ian shook his head and swiped at his eyes with the back of one hand. "He started laughing, at first, he...he said he had a head rush. And then..." Ian shivered.

"Where is he?" I asked. Ian blinked at me, and I left him, went to the desk, and found the nurse. I gave Miah's name. She asked who I was; I lied.

I was already calling the font to my skin.

"Miah," I say. *This is not really him. He is gone. This is what remains of my lover.*

Echo is too cold a word, and I can hear my grandmother's voice in my head: *People don't always go right away, baby.*

Miah's eyes, as golden as sunlight, close. He is still touching his chest, but it's easier to see through him now. The faintest smile touches his lips, and he opens his eyes and tries to speak again. But the words don't come.

Sometimes, they need a little help in moving along, something they gotta say or do first, and I give 'em a bit of my font to keep going.

The font fades fast without a cup.

Sometimes you can see them for a bit, after they die, before they go on. My grandmother's eyes were hard. *But only a bit, baby.*

Miah should be going. He is—*was*, damn it!—a beautiful, wonderful, special man and he should already be gone. I have stoked him with my own font, and I do not know if it was the right thing to do.

But I have done it.

I open my mouth, and kiss my dead lover, and flame pours into what is left of his soul.

In his room, there were wires, and under his nose, a little tube with two nubs aimed at his nostrils. He looked like he was merely sleeping, his eyes shadowed deeply, his lips a terrible color that I told myself wasn't blue. Machines blipped, and a nurse was writing something on a clipboard. I stepped inside, and the nurse frowned at me.

"I'm sorry; he can't have visitors right now." I looked at her, and she softened. "Are you family?" she asked.

I'd just finished this dance at the front desk, and I wasn't about to try it again. I hated lying, saying Miah was my brother, when we looked nothing alike, when we had different last names, when it was obvious I was lying.

"He's my—" My voice was hoarse, and I cleared my throat, thinking that at any minute I was going to lose it completely. His skin was so pale. "He's mine," I said.

The nurse got it and touched my arm as she passed me. "You can't stay for very long, okay? He should sleep if there's any way he's going to—" She stopped and swallowed. "He should sleep."

I nodded. I think I thanked her. As the door closed, I let the fire boil inside me, the font rise until it felt like it would sear my tongue.

He's getting better, Nan, I can tell.

To my own eyes, brimming with gold, the room swam with yellow light.

Yes, he is.

I brought the flames to my lips.

Are you okay, Nan?

I pulled the only chair over and sat beside him. I took Miah's hand and leaned over his exhausted face to kiss him.

I'm just tired, Aidan.

Pale gray eyes opened.

"No," he said.

Miah slips his arms around my waist and puts his head on my chest.

"I'm so sorry," I repeat, and tears are streaking my face now. "I should have…"

Miah pulls back and looks at me, golden eyes shining. "It doesn't hurt," he says, wisps of gold flickering from the edges of his lips. He slides one hand up onto my chest, taps a heartbeat with his fingers, and then lets his hand fall.

"I'm not tired," he says, and he holds out his free hand. I take it with my own, and he smiles up at me. I am nearly blubbering now. My chest is shaking with each breath, and my tears hurt my eyes. And my heart…

"Can we dance?" Miah asks, voice nearly a whisper now. I can see through him again.

We dance in the parking lot, and I close my eyes. He presses against my chest, and I spin him. We step and turn and rock back and forth gently, without music. He grows lighter in my arms, and for a while, my tears gather in his hair. I can even smell his soap.

My heart.

There is wetness on my arm, and when I open my eyes, he is gone. Another tear falls off the end of my nose. I take a long, shaky breath, alone in the cool night.

And my heart keeps beating.

PARTY PLANNING

Rob Williams

We were on our way to set up for Linda Simon's sweet sixteen birthday party when my mother, who was driving, slammed on the brakes of our burnt-red station wagon, causing the entire contents of the back seat, including tablecloths, multi-colored disposable plastic cups, streamers, rolls of butcher paper, and Mrs. Kingston to come hurtling to the front of the car. Mrs. Kingston, our neighbor and my mother's new party planning assistant, was fine, if a little disheveled and shaken, but the tiny black pillbox hat she had attached to her head with an elastic band had slid further forward so that it was just below her forehead.

"Cocktail napkins!" my mother screamed at her. "For God's sake, how hard is it to get simple cocktail napkins!"

Poor Mrs. Kingston. She was a novice. She'd only been assisting my mother for a few days after begging for years to let her tag along, to help out. ("I'll just watch from the sidelines. I won't be in the way.") My mother said she just didn't have the knack for parties. Her taste in streamers was appalling. But her husband had left her three months ago and my mother took her under her wing. A new project. My mother was famous for her projects.

And now Mrs. Kingston had made a mistake. She'd bought rectangle-shaped paper dinner napkins, and not the square, thin, cocktail napkins with the shell embossing that my mother had asked for.

"You can't *fan* a dinner napkin!" she screamed again.

"Maybe we can cut them in half?" asked Mrs. Kingston, her voice cracking. She had straightened her hat and was now picking up the plastic cups that had fallen between her legs and onto the floor of the car.

"Don't be an idiot," my mother said. "You can't even do a simple thing like buy cocktail napkins. We're going to have to stop at the five-and-dime, which is going to put us seriously behind schedule."

"I'm sorry."

Party planning was never something my mother got paid for—she worked part-time in the credit union where my father was manager—but it was her hobby, and from the time I was old enough to hold a glue gun or know the difference between a sequin and a spangle, I was her assistant, her right-hand man.

A Tupperware party, as hosted by my mother, would become a Tupperware luau. We'd drink frothy, fruity drinks out of coconut shells. She would light citronella tiki torches and place them around the backyard, and then put Tupperware products on tiny rafts and float them out into the middle of our pool. In order to inspect the goods, guests had to take a dip. For that party I made two dozen multicolored crepe paper leis and draped our backyard fence with fish netting and glitter-encrusted seashells.

My mother also made her own clothes, not in the traditional

sense—not with tissue paper patterns—though she had a sewing machine. Instead she would buy her clothes, jeans with elastic waistbands, plain sweatshirts in soft pastel colors, at Gemco or Mervyns and then she would *alter* them, as she called it. She would accessorize them. She would BeDazzle the sweatshirt or a pair of jeans with beads, sequins, puffy wash-proof glitter paint, and remnants and leftovers from her projects. Because she never threw anything away.

Party planning kept her extremely busy. My dad was free to have his poker nights and his football Sundays while she whipped up theme parties for the community. The neighbors "hired" her to plan their events. The elementary and high schools consulted her for their dances and parties. She was never paid for it; she would have a budget to work with, but she never charged for her services. She was having too much fun. Sometimes she would be treated to lunch or receive bouquets of flowers, fruit baskets, or gift certificates. Mostly, though, my mother's reward came from being completely in control of someone else's celebration, someone else's happiness.

She pulled the car into the store parking lot, and I decided to save Mrs. Kingston any more embarrassment by getting the napkins myself. I knew exactly which kind to buy, but really I just wanted to get away from my mother, who'd been growing more and more irritable since my decision a few weeks earlier to keep my party planning assistance to a minimum. I was, after all, a sophomore in high school, and I was beginning to realize that my constant creative collaborations were hindering my social life. I wanted to go to parties, I told her, not plan them.

The other problem was that we were becoming a familiar sight in our community, too familiar: mother and son in the station wagon, the back seat crammed with foam rubber, yarn, old costumes, ratted wigs, and odd pieces of furniture. Hardly a holiday or friend's birthday party went by without us playing some part in the planning of potential merriment.

There was a time when I thought I had the most inventive mother in the world. What was more, she seemed to understand me. Unlike my father, who was frustrated at my failed attempts at helping him change the oil in the station wagon, my mother marveled at my craftsmanship. She respected and often sought my opinion for color schemes and flower arrangements. She helped cultivate my artistic inclinations while offering up excuses to my father for my athletic and automotive shortcomings.

I had decided that Linda Simon's sweet sixteen party was going to be my swan song—the last party where I would be my mother's sidekick. Sure, I would be available for consultations or questions about color schemes and party themes. But no longer would I assist my mother *at* the parties, donning embarrassing homemade outfits: a court jester in satin knickers, a butler in white gloves with an oversized bow tie and tails. I had finally gathered up enough nerve to tell her a couple of weeks earlier, much to her dismay, as we were setting up for my sisters' high school Valentines Day dance. It was a fifties theme—a sock hop—and as usual, my mother and I spent several evenings in her sewing room going over the preliminaries.

While she silently sewed my sisters' poodle skirts, I put on a K-Tel record that she'd ordered off the television. It was a two-record set of 1950s girl singers who chirped about love and loss, boyfriends and bobby sox.

"Heatwave" by Martha and the Vandellas came on the record player while I kept myself busy with the party decorations. I glued shiny chunks of confetti onto old 45s we found at a garage sale. I also covered several hula-hoops with glitter, and then started going through a stack of glossy black-and-white photos of 1950s celebrities: Connie Francis, Tab Hunter, Troy Donahue, Annette Funicello, and Frankie Avalon—signing their names in thick black marker.

Then I sprinkled these with glitter.

Tension hung in the room like too much V05 hairspray, as my mother let it sink in that I would no longer be her party planning assistant. But how else did you break up with your mother than by being completely honest and straightforward?

"It's just...It's time for me to move on," I told her, sounding like one of the soap operas my grandmother watched. "We've had a good run."

"Forgive me if I'm a little shocked that you've never said anything to me before about this. But if that's what you want to do, break up the partnership."

She continued working, pretending that she was fine, that she could get along without me, but I could tell by the way she hurled the spool of thread into her sewing box that she was upset. She held up several colors and styles of felt poodles, comparing them to the skirts, and let out a series of dramatic sighs. Every few minutes she'd look over at me as I was painting the malt shop signs she'd sketched. Several times she started to say something but stopped and shook her head. It was clear she wanted my approval or opinion on something, but because of my recent proclamation she was forcing herself not to ask. She hemmed and hawed over two poodles, one covered in fake rhinestones and the other trimmed in fake fur, until I was about to scream.

"Mother," I finally blurted, "why don't you just try the brown poodle with the little puffs of fur on it?"

"Yes. I guess the brown poodle is better. But what about the leash?" She languidly held out a thin black ribbon.

"You could go with that. But the whole ensemble would be

sort of boring. I mean, the skirt and the brown poodle are both pretty tame. Why don't you use the multicolored sequin leash—the silver and gold thing we used as a necklace last year for the flapper costumes?"

"I don't know." She wrinkled her forehead. "I just don't know."

"Mom, what are you talking about? The sequined leash would go great with the brown poodle. Look." I picked up the strap and held it next to the poodle—its fake black onyx gemstone eye caught the light and sparkled like a lone star in the night sky—then I realized what she was doing. My mother was trying to prove to me how vital my involvement in all of this was; how she just *couldn't* do it without me, trying to entice me into staying on with her.

She smiled at me with a skirt in her lap, arms crossed over her chest, a needle poking out of her mouth.

"It's not going to work," I said and handed the poodle back to her.

"What's not going to work?"

"You know what. This game of I'm-so-helpless-without-you."

"I don't know what you're talking about," she said and picked up her puffy tomato pincushion covered with pins with the plastic colored balls on the end.

"Yes, you do. You're trying to get me to stay on with you, working as your assistant, but I told you I'm done."

"Done? You mean completely?"

"Mom. I said I would offer my advice if you need it but yes, done. I'm not going to any more parties with you. No more late nights sprinkling glitter onto records, or cutting out snowflakes, or shellacking fruit."

"But what about Linda Simon's sweet sixteen party in two

weeks? You practically planned the entire thing—it was your idea to make it like a film premiere." She began pinning the poodle to the skirt.

"Okay. I'll help you with Linda's party, but that's it. Really, Mom. You have to let me go."

We sat, not talking to each other for a few minutes as I finished up the last of the photos and she pinned the second skirt. Then I watched her try to thread a needle. She dabbed the tip of the thread on her tongue and held the needle close to her face. She attempted to push the end of the thread through the tiny hole but missed. She tried it four more times.

"Let me do that." I took the needle and thread from her.

"Seems I can't do anything right anymore," she said, pouting. "Aren't you going to miss our little projects together, sweetie?"

"Mom."

I threaded the needle and handed it back to her.

"We're good together, you and I," she said, stabbing the needle into the felt. "It'll be hard to find someone out there who appreciates you like I do. I'm just worried that you're going to be all alone without something to do with yourself this year."

I didn't say anything. But in my mind I pictured myself five, ten years from then, never having gone to college, still living at home, still accompanying my mother to parties. Me, in a Hawaiian shirt, with a ukulele. Or me as a harlequin in diamond-patterned tights. Me, alone.

I set the stack of glossy photos down on our workbench and looked at the list to see what to work on next.

"I'm going to start drawing the sign for the kissing booth," I told her. As I grabbed a few thick magic markers and a piece of poster board, the first few bars of "Who's Sorry Now?" began to play on the record player.

My mother and I had truly outdone ourselves with Linda Simon's sweet sixteen. Because Linda was a budding actress, and her family liked to pretend they were from money, we'd turned her party into an old-fashioned movie premiere. Her mom wore a mink stole and, it was rumored, rented diamond jewelry, and her dad hired limos to pick up Linda's close friends and family members and bring them to the house.

Party guests, who were mostly Linda's snotty drama club and homecoming court friends, had to walk up a red carpet that was rolled out and down the Simon's driveway (actually butcher paper painted red with tempera paint—my mother was creative *and* thrifty). Strobe lights attached to the roof of the house clicked on and off like reporters' flashbulbs. The neighbors, playing the part of movie fans, lined the driveway, instructed by my mother to *ooh* and *ahh* and to thrust slips of paper and autograph books at partygoers in their dresses and suits and ties. There was even a movie screening: a video of the first sixteen years of Linda's life played on the Simon's wide-screen television. My mother had connections at our local video production company who put together the movie from the various family snapshots and 8 mm films. Small bags of popcorn were served to the audience. Card tables with crisp black tablecloths dotted the room, and, per my suggestion, fragrant gardenias and votive candles floated in small round fishbowls on the tables. My inspiration was the Coconut Grove and Club Babalu from "I Love Lucy."

During the spectacle, my father drove by the Simon's house in his Ford Pinto on the way to his poker game. I watched from the porch as he carefully slowed down to let more partygoers, in feather boas and top hats, cross the street in front of him. The familiar look of blank reticence, or maybe relief that it was me and not him suffering through this, was on his ruddy face.

I'd refused to wear the turtleneck that matched my mother's terra-cotta-colored silk pantsuit, opting instead for tennis shoes, a white T-shirt, and gray pullover V-neck sweater. Mrs. Kingston looked ridiculous in her black bow tie and tiny pillbox hat, frantically running back and forth for my mother, helping with crowd control and keeping the gawking, hammy neighbors at bay as the procession of Linda and her friends walked down the red carpet. I'd reluctantly agreed to usher people inside to tables and seats for the movie, after which Mrs. Kingston and I were supposed to serve hors d'oeuvres and slices of birthday cake off of round metal trays.

The strobe lights were still blinking as my mother barked at her new assistant, who looked like a lumpy bellboy, to carry a huge floral wreath inside. "And don't smash the flowers! Please!" she yelled as she pinned one of the extra gardenias to her lapel.

I wanted another chance to escape while the movie was playing, so I told Mrs. Kingston to go on in and that I would get the wreath. Outside, the sky was just beginning to darken and the streetlights were starting to pop on. On the Simon's curtained front window, I saw the silhouettes of partygoers as they laughed and mingled.

In front of the house, slips of autograph paper had been carelessly tossed, littering the lawn and sidewalk. I picked one up, and on it were the words, *Love Linda, Sweet Sixteen 1985.* I recognized my mother's handwriting and noted that she'd gotten pretty creative with her new calligraphy pen. I was about to crinkle the paper in my hand when I heard footsteps shuffling behind me.

"You collecting souvenirs?"

It was Linda's eighteen-year-old brother, Kurt, in some seriously scuffed black Dr. Martens boots. I was surprised he'd come down for the birthday. Kurt had dropped out of high school the year before and last I'd heard he was living in Berkeley. His breath smelled metallic. *Probably alcohol,* I thought. He swayed in front of me.

"No," I said. "I have enough of these at home."

"Oh. That's who you are? I thought you looked familiar." He put his face closer to mine. I could see his nose hairs. A shiver passed through me, but one of those good shivers. "So it's your mom who's responsible for the debauchery," he slurred.

When he pointed at his house, the black bracelets he was wearing moved from his wrist to the bottom of his palm. From the way he was squinting at "the debauchery," I took it that he wasn't crazy about the party in his house, and decided not to mention that I'd created the 3-D star centerpieces on the tables inside, or that I had BeDazzled Linda's name onto a director's chair.

Kurt looked different to me. Older. I think we used to consider him somewhat hardcore. Possibly one of my sisters had even referred to him as a punker. But in those days, my sisters called Duran Duran punkers. Kurt was the first guy in our neighborhood that we knew, or had heard of, who had *both* his ears pierced. He wore shirts and pants that had a lot of snaps and zippers on them. He used to break-dance and do strange moves, like the Robot, on a flattened cardboard box in his garage. Kurt went "both ways," as one of my sisters' friends put it. They said that after a school dance his freshman year, he'd been caught having a three-way with a guy and a girl in a van in the school parking lot. The term *finger fucked* was bandied about...though whose finger fucked whom was still a mystery.

"You're the kid who had the wild Halloween costumes every year, aren't you?" His brown hair had the remnants of faded blond-orange streaks in it. *Sexy,* I thought. He wore a frayed denim jacket with a small blue button that said *English Beat* on it.

"Yeah." I tried to sound disinterested. "I used to do stupid stuff like that." But it was true—with the help of my mother, my costumes had won first place in the Halloween Carnival five years in a row. I was everything from a walking fish tank to the Jolly Green Giant.

"You used to be a queenie little squirt. But you've grown up, I see."

"Gee, thanks," I muttered, irritated.

He gave me a suspicious once-over, and shook his head as if he were trying hard to stay awake. Something about the way he said, *I see*, the way he let the words linger, made me forgive him for the part about me being queenie. I didn't want to look in his eyes, which were bloodshot, so instead I focused on the rip in the knee of his acid-washed jeans.

"What grade are you in?" He fumbled a lighter out of his jacket pocket.

"I'm in tenth."

"Oh, yeah? Sophomore, huh? You have Mr. Dimatillo yet?" He flicked at the lighter.

"Not until next quarter."

"Yeah?" said Kurt, and then he licked the thumb he'd been using to flick the lighter. "Mr. Dimatillo rocks. You tell Mr. D that Kurt says hello. And he owes me a pack of Camels."

"Okay. I'll tell him."

"Uh huh." He tried to burn the fray on the front pocket of his denim jacket.

"Did you use a cheese grater to give your jacket that look?" I asked.

He didn't look up. "No, I used a razor."

"I tie-dyed a denim jacket for my sister," I blurted. "Which isn't easy, getting the little rubber bands around bunched denim..." My hands were bouncing as I spoke.

Kurt looked up and smiled, but then quickly stopped himself. I was still holding the slip of autograph paper.

"Let me see that," he said. He pulled the wrinkled pink paper from my hand and tried to smooth it out in his palm and read it. "Jesus Christ," he muttered. He held it up. "Want to play with fire?" he asked, but didn't wait for my response. He lit the autograph paper with his lighter, and we watched as Linda's name, in my mother's handwriting, hissed and glowed and then browned and began to disappear into ash. When the flame almost reached his hand, he dropped it on the red butcher paper still rolled out over the driveway.

We watched the bit of flame make a brown, smoky circle on the red butcher paper, and then a tiny jab of orange fire shot up an inch or two before it sputtered out.

"Let's try this again," said Kurt, as he bit his lip and picked up a few of the scattered squares of autograph paper. He handed one to me, and then flicked his lighter below the three he had in his own hand. He touched his flame to my square of paper, and I watched as the corner slowly curled and felt the heat spread closer to my fingers.

"Let's burn this whole damn thing," he said. Then he tossed his flames onto the red butcher paper. I tossed mine, too. We followed the four small flames as they began to spread over the red carpet, but either the paper was still wet or it was fire resistant, because soon the flames dwindled down to four perfect streams of black and red smoke.

"That sucks," said Kurt.

"Let's try to burn it again," I said. For a moment I thought maybe my voice had squeaked, or that I had sounded queenie, because Kurt stopped and looked at me. But I wanted to finish what we had started.

"Well, all right," said Kurt, and he handed me his lighter.

I knelt down to set the edge of the butcher paper on fire. I flicked the lighter several times, but it wouldn't catch. My thumb was starting to hurt.

"Hey, hold on," said Kurt. He knelt beside me and grabbed the lighter from my hand. The crotch of his jeans was ripped away and I could see he wasn't wearing underwear. I couldn't see his dick, but I saw his balls, fuzzy and pink, dangling just below the zipper and torn seam. I heard him click the lighter several times, but I didn't look up from his jeans.

"Now we're doing some damage," he said, and then he caught me staring. I turned my head quickly to the butcher paper, which was smoking and beginning to curl in several places, the flames a little more than an inch high. Bits of red-edged ash were starting to lift up from the driveway.

"What were you looking at?" Kurt asked. His words were slow and teasing, not angry. I didn't think he was looking for an answer.

Nervous, I sputtered, "Nothing."

The smoke seemed to be getting thicker, and there was a burnt, chemical smell, like when my mother cleaned the oven. I tried to rise from my knees. My throat was tight, my eyes watered, and I imagined that we were being consumed by the heat and smoke. As if the roll of butcher paper was engulfed in flame and curling around us. Kurt started to get up also and grabbed my elbow to lift me.

"It's okay," he said. But I wasn't sure what he was talking about. What was okay? That I was staring at his crotch? That we were setting fire to his driveway? I was confused and excited, and my eyes were burning.

"Yeah, I know," I said. "But I've got to go. My mom's inside and she's probably wondering where I am. I'm supposed to be helping with the party."

I thought that maybe I should leave, try to walk down the street away from the party and my mother and Kurt and toward my neighborhood. But not too fast. I needed to act cool, like yes, everything was all right, though I couldn't get my knees to stop shaking. Kurt was right in front of me, his crotch at my eye level, and I felt another shiver of pleasure run through my body.

There was a buzzing in my ears that soon began to sound familiar. It was my mother's voice calling me, coming from the front kitchen window of the Simons' house. Probably wanting me to change a record or to pick up plates and cups.

But I didn't want to join the party. I was where I wanted to stay.

I heard my name again, louder.

I needed to get up.

"Can you help me?" I said to Kurt, who was still gripping my elbow.

"Sure," he said.

"Where's that wreath? Go get the wreath and tell my son to get in here."

"Straighten up," he said as he pulled harder on my elbow and put his other hand on my back to lift me up off the sidewalk.

Kurt pulled me up so quickly that it threw me off balance. I rose up and felt like I could have flown over him. Instead, I was falling into him, and as I did he tried to catch my body to stop the momentum. His hand on the small of my back reached down lower.

My mother stepped through the Simons' open door and onto the porch, followed by Mrs. Kingston, just as Kurt's hand was cupping the left cheek of my ass, our bodies close, our knees just touching, as if, even by accident, we might have been falling into an embrace. Kurt's hand was holding my ass like someone would hold a cantaloupe, or throw a softball underhand, and in his grip, which couldn't have lasted more than a second or two, I found myself lost in a flurry of images. Like the flash of film and photos playing on the television in the Simons' house, I saw myself and Kurt, and then it was the face of another man, and then several others, in an embrace. Whiskers brushing my face. A strong, heavy arm over my shoulder. The clicking of our belt buckles. Warm breath in my ear.

I let go of Kurt as the two women walked across the driveway to us.

"I thought you were going to bring the flowers in," said my mother, standing between me and Kurt. Mrs. Kingston poured a small fishbowl of water onto the still smoking butcher paper.

"I was," I said numbly. "I just...I got distracted."

"I can see that." She kept her eyes on me, not turning to look at Kurt, who stepped off of the curb and pulled a pack of cigarettes from his jacket pocket.

"I'll take it in now."

"That's all right," said my mother, her hand on her hip, as she turned to Mrs. Kingston who was standing right behind her. "She'll take care of it." She ushered Mrs. Kingston closer to us. "Rita, will you take the flowers inside and place them next to the birthday cake? Please?"

Mrs. Kingston, whose confused grimace shifted quickly to an urgent smile, handed me the empty fishbowl she'd used to douse the butcher paper. "Certainly." She straightened her pillbox hat, carefully lifted the wreath with both hands, and looked back at me once before carrying it into the house.

I started to follow her when my mother grabbed my arm and then slipped the fishbowl out of my hands.

"That's all right, dear. Mrs. Kingston can take over from here."

"But I was going to help with the cake and setting up the

dance floor," I said. An enthusiastic round of applause came from inside the house. The movie was over. Next on the schedule was the lighting of the candles and then the cutting of the cake. My mother had perfected her technique of dipping the cake knife into a pitcher of hot water after each slice in order to ensure a perfectly cut piece of cake. Her cake cutting was legendary. Each piece was exactly the same width; no frosting roses were ever damaged; no one was ever left without a slice. She'd only recently taught me to do this, and tonight was to be the first and last time I would get to perform the task. To be honest, I'd sort of been looking forward to it.

"Don't worry about it. We've got it under control." She bent over and picked up a piece of autograph paper smeared with ash. "Why don't you clean up the paper in the front yard here and then…and then why don't you head home," she said, with a slight nod toward the street. Then she let the paper fall to the ground and walked back up the driveway and into the Simons' house.

Kurt was already halfway down the block, a trail of cigarette smoke wafting behind him. I began to roll up the butcher paper, with its shoe prints and burn holes. The strobe lights blinked on and off, casting quick, elusive shadows over the driveway that disappeared before I had time to memorize them. Inside the house, I could hear my mother's voice introducing Linda to the partygoers. She spoke slowly, no longer yelling, but now high and light, like a wind chime. I wondered if Kurt would keep walking or would he wait for me at the end of the block. Or would there be someone, someone else. Soon. Waiting for me.

TWO KINDS OF RAPTURE

Andrew Holleran

He was standing in a trance on the corner of P and 15th Streets, wondering if he had chosen the right bottle of wine, when the others came up behind him. Someone made a wisecrack and he turned and saw them. Under the streetlight they looked forlorn—men of a certain age—sheepish at discovering they'd all been invited. *So it's to be the four of us*, he thought. *We're like four men courting the same woman*—which wasn't far from the truth, he reflected, as the light changed and they crossed the street. He swung his brown paper bag in the direction of Bob's brown paper bag, and, he saw an instant later, the paper bags Dirk and Kevin were carrying, too, and smiled. They were all bringing a bottle of wine. Moments later they rang the bell of the tall brick house on Swann Street, and embraced their hosts in the hallway, and passed through the long narrow Victorian rooms to the garden out back, and sat down beside the flickering torches from Pottery Barn set in the flowerbeds beneath the ivy-coated walls.

Their hosts—Paul and Tim—took drink requests, as he sat there thinking: *We're like a quartet of maiden aunts who have crossed town to see a favorite nephew, recently married, in his new home.*

Of the aunts he was the oldest at fifty-five; Kevin was fifty-four, Bob fifty-two, and Dirk—Dirk announced, as their hosts left the garden to get their drinks, that his fiftieth birthday would occur next month. Dirk's news gave him pause: to think that five years separated him from Dirk! *There really isn't much time left,* he thought, looking up at the sliver of a moon in the blue sky, *not much left at all.* When their hosts came out with the tray of Cosmos, he felt even older—because, he realized, as he took his first sip, this was the first time he'd ever had a Cosmo. His contempt for trends simply meant that he adopted them when they were on their way out.

Fifty, he thought—*Dirk is just turning fifty! And still so good-looking.*

To look at Dirk in the torches' light—the thick silver hair, the big masculine body—was to see one of those men who were only going to get more attractive as they age. Not only that, he had the sardonic confidence that made it count. *Maybe the butt's a bit big,* he thought—there had been a reference to twenty pounds lost as they walked through the kitchen—but this was a small drawback on what was essentially a type that would never have trouble attracting younger men—which was what Dirk was, conveniently, interested in.

Men our age are like cats, he thought, as he took another sip, *who ignore each other when put in the room together. You must have someone young to show them a good time.*

That would be their hosts: Paul and Tim. He could no longer hear as well as he should, though he refused to do anything about it, so when Paul sat down on the steps across the patio, he turned toward him to make sure he could read his lips. Making an effort to listen, the way you strained to complete an exercise at the gym, was new to him, but that's what it had come down to: One had to concentrate now to hear.

There was no one he would rather listen to than Paul, however. *Paul's so ahead of the curve,* he thought as he looked at his host across the patio. *Already coupled, owner of a house, a house they bought for far less than it's worth now, both of them bright, handsome, ambitious, funny.* In only their mid-thirties, their hosts were in several significant ways more successful than the guests. About the guests he thought there was something indubitably sad. Perhaps it was his own distaste for growing old that had diminished them in his eyes, condemned them for a victimless crime, though it wasn't quite victimless—the victim was the person growing old. Whatever the reason, he could not help seeing them all critically. Kevin taught physics at a local boarding school; he even looked like Albert Einstein, with his frazzled hair, bushy eyebrows, and rumpled air. Yet talking to the knockouts at the gym while they waited for the machines was what he lived for. "Are they nice to you?" he'd asked Kevin once. "Some of them," Kevin had said. "The ones who talk to me."

"But why *do* they talk to you?" he'd asked.

"No reason," Kevin said, "except that they're nice. Because there's no reason otherwise to talk to me."

There was none, indeed: He looked like Einstein. He was also extremely bright, good-natured, and funny, but at the gym Kevin went to it was all about body parts. It would have been entirely understandable if Kevin were boiling with resentment, he had always thought, but this didn't seem to be the case. Kevin was as content to chat with the stars at the gym as he was to sit here in the garden listening to Dirk tell them about the boys he had met in Montreal.

"The boys in Montreal," Dirk was saying, "think I'm a professional hockey player!" Everybody laughed. In reality the big bruiser produced baroque operas in a restored colonial mansion in Virginia, where he held candlelight dinners for his backers and talked about rare opera recordings; but Dirk looked like a professional hockey player, and that was what mattered. Homosexuals were like texts, he thought, in the current literary theory: the reader's subjectivity was required to complete the work of art.

Bob, on the other hand, looked just like what he was—an editor in the publications department at the Museum of Natural History. If Kevin showed no results whatsoever for all the hours he spent at the gym (no doubt because he spent all his time there talking to handsome men), Bob did not even work out. With his white hair and beard, he was one of those gay men one saw around Washington who seemed to be making a public state-ment by looking as much like Walt Whitman as possible. But Whitman had had Peter Doyle, while Bob was forever lamenting his lack of a boyfriend. There was no way to tell whether the latter deprivation had more to do with Bob's appearance or his opinion that homosexual relationships were inherently doomed—even though he was sitting in the garden this evening with living proof of the opposite proposition: their hosts.

Of their hosts Tim was considered the handsome one; deep-set dark eyes; perfect, chiseled features; and dark brown hair made him look like the template for every good-looking intern on Capitol Hill. Saturnine in appearance, sardonic in speech, he lay now on a lawn chair in the center of his guests in khaki shorts and a Hawaiian shirt, receiving his due as an object of beauty while Paul ran back and forth replenishing drinks and canapés—a division of labor so habitual that once, halfway through another dinner, a guest had turned to Tim, after Tim suggested they move to the living room, and said, "Oh, do you live here, too?" He did; but Paul did all the work. Tim's looks were his reason for being—another feature of the dwelling everyone was allowed to enjoy, like the carved walnut mantelpiece in the dining room, or the old portrait of Paul's grandfather above the fireplace. Of course, Tim was also intelligent and this sometimes left newcomers nonplussed; as if someone that good-looking could not be witty, too.

This did not stop Dirk from leaning forward to examine Tim now, however, as if he were a chair he wanted to acquire, and saying, "Am I wrong, or am I seeing the beginnings of a receding hairline?"

"I beg your pardon," said Tim.

"Oh, no," Kevin said passionately, "that hairline will never recede!"

It was Paul, in fact, who had the receding hairline—and a face that looked like a prosperous squire in one of those eighteenth-century colonial portraits. But Paul was his favorite—his blue eyes had seduced many more people than Tim's perfect face, because Paul was superior in kindness and tact. Paul was thoughtful beyond the ordinary run of manners, Paul the one whose company he loved, Paul whose voice made him smile and sit up when he heard him call out now, "I'd like to make an announcement!"

Everyone in the garden fell silent.

"As of today," Paul said, raising his glass, "we are the proud owners—of a new garage!"

The guests applauded, and then Paul explained that a man living in a condominium two doors down with a garage in the back had sold them his space, which meant that now, whether or not they kept a car, the value of their own house had increased by at least a hundred thousand dollars.

The news somehow made him ashamed of himself; perhaps because he was renting a mere studio apartment a block from the YMCA where he and Paul played racquetball every Wednesday. The game was the high point of his week. They had discovered they both played the sport at the dinner where they'd met the previous year and become instant friends. In fact, after their first match, Paul had suggested they have lunch, and, moments after settling into their booth in the restaurant, Paul had leaned forward and said, as if to someone he'd known for years, "I'm in trouble and I need your advice."

"What is it?" he'd said.

"I've fallen in love with someone in Boston," Paul said.

"Fallen in love! But what about Tim?"

"The problem is I don't really love Tim anymore—or rather, I love Tim, but I'm not *in love* with him. Though I have to admit the guy in Boston is being a prick."

He didn't know what to say; surprised by the intimacy offered so soon after meeting, he couldn't tell if he was just expected to listen, or if he was supposed to offer advice because he was older and presumably wiser. The problem with the latter assumption was that he had never been good at finding a boyfriend even when young, and now that he was in his mid-fifties he had given up on having one altogether, though every time he stepped out of his building he hoped that Mister Right would be walking down the street.

"Not *in* love with him?" he'd finally said. "But aren't you always left with someone you're not in love with? Isn't that the normal evolution of a marriage—infatuation gives way to something deeper, more domestic?"

Then, before Paul could reply, he attempted to ascertain more precisely, like a doctor, the nature of his new friend's malaise. "Is this just the seven year itch?" he said. Paul shook his head.

Then was he simply bored with domesticity, he asked. Or, since the man in Boston didn't return his feelings, was Paul attracted to him only because he was playing hard to get? Or was Paul merely rebelling against the fact that he had bought a house with Tim? Surely he wasn't just discovering that domestic and romantic love are two different things, and that the former is less rapturous than the second?

Paul tried carefully to answer all these questions, but the answers weren't very coherent. In fact, nothing was sure or settled when they parted—except the distinct annoyance he felt on having heard Paul's confession. To a single gay man, he thought, couples were like someone from a poor neighborhood who becomes rich and successful: proof that it can be done. Couples were needed, as symbol and reality: symbols of requited love, actual owners of a home to which their single friends could come. *Otherwise I would not be in this garden tonight*, he thought, as Paul came over and asked him if he wanted another drink. Otherwise Paul would not be sitting down on the chair next to his and speaking of a deadline he had to meet—the sort of concern that made him think Paul's life (as a chef) was manageable again, order had been restored, the house, both literally and figuratively, still stood.

"But how are *you*?" said Paul, with his customary courtesy. "How's your class?"

"Not bad," he said.

"And personal stuff?" Paul said. "Are you dating anyone?"

"Dating anyone?" he said. *I've been sitting in the sauna at the Y fingering my nipples*, he thought, *waiting to see what comes in the door.*

"Not at the moment," he said.

"Well, we'll fix you up!" said Paul. "Did you see the article in the *Blade* yesterday? It said Washington has the highest number of same-sex couples per capita of any city in the country."

"What city has the most?" said Dirk in his deep, impossibly rich voice.

"Los Angeles," said Paul, "or New York. I forget. But both of them have a much greater population. In percentage, we're higher. I'm not surprised. Washington is *such* a married town."

"That's because everyone here, including gay men, is so conventional," said Kevin.

"Then why can't I get married?" said Bob.

"Because you're too old!" said Kevin.

"Thanks a lot," said Bob.

"That's why you should start looking for an Asian," said Kevin. "Asians like older men. But you won't find Asians in Halo. In Halo you have to be right out of the Abercrombie & Fitch catalogue. You have to start going to Omega."

"Or Montreal," said Dirk. "In Montreal they appreciate a mature gentleman. In Montreal they think I'm a goalie!"

Everyone laughed.

"Only your goal is to sell that broken harpsichord you tried to unload on George Reed last spring," said Tim, which got another round.

The old men laughing at what the young man in the garden had said were all in modern dress, but the flickering torches made him think of a scene from the Bible: Susanna and the Elders— the way everyone seemed to be hovering over Tim, in his khaki shorts, his black-and-white Hawaiian shirt, stretched out on the chaise longue as he now proceeded to tell them what satisfaction he had felt laying this brick patio with his own hands. He was surprised to learn that Tim had done work around the house, so surprised it took him a moment to lean forward and tell Tim that he had a wonderful opportunity, in the empty flowerbeds bordering the patio, to make a really beautiful garden.

He started suggesting things Tim might plant, until he realized Tim had no interest in horticulture whatsoever, an impression confirmed when Tim returned to the topic of the Fundamentalist Christian who had sold him the bricks—a man, Tim said, who had told him he believed in the Rapture: the moment when the elect would all be taken up into Heaven to be joined with Christ.

"I experienced the Rapture a week ago, in my hotel in Montreal," Dirk said. Then, before the laughter faded, Kevin asked, "What exactly is the Rapture?"

"It's supposed to happen just before the world comes to an end," Tim said. He leaned forward. "It's like being picked for baseball in grade school. The people who are saved are plucked from earth and taken directly up into Heaven. Everyone else is left behind."

"Plucked? In what way?" said Kevin.

"I don't know," said Tim. "Maybe they levitate."

"I think they disappear," said Bob.

"You mean you'll be going up in an elevator with five other people," said Kevin, "and three of them will suddenly become invisible?"

"Yes," said Bob. "And the rest of us will know—we missed the cut."

Let's face it, he thought, *Paul and Tim are not the usual gay couple in their thirties. They like older men.* Paul had once told him that every gay man should sleep with someone older twice a year so that when he turned old someone would return the favor—a sort of sexual socialism; and Tim had his own mentors. Once Paul had talked about the coaches he'd had in Little League, and he assumed that's where Paul's affection for older gentlemen had begun. For Tim, it involved an aspiration to learn—one of his best friends was an eighty-seven-year-old activist whose name was legendary in gay politics. Whatever the motivation, both his hosts seemed to value their elders: so rare in gay men. He presumed they had friends their own age who served another function. No doubt they had sex with them—or perhaps didn't, to keep their own marriage intact. He couldn't say. The only sure thing was that all the guests this evening were the beneficiaries of an unusual respect for age. He turned to Tim to press on him again the fact that he now had an opportunity, with the flowerbeds bordering the patio, to make this a rare garden; but Tim was still not done with the Rapture.

"The brick salesman told me something else," said Tim. "Apparently the Fundies have a seating plan for Heaven. Did you know that? They already know just where everyone will be placed—whereas *we've* decided to let you sit where you want," he said, standing up. "Dinner's served, gentlemen!"

In the dining room there was a momentary hush as the beauty of the candles, the dark wood of the wainscoting, the flickering fire, the pale peonies just starting to come apart, the china and silver bequeathed Paul by his grandmother, were appreciated by the guests. He sat down, sipped his wine, and the room began to glow; the more he sipped the more it glowed, and the more he was touched by how much effort his hosts had gone to, to make them feel welcome. *This is it*, he thought, *the rapture that is not religious—exactly what everyone else was striving for: the house, the table, the handsome couple! Poor Dirk, going to Montreal to be admired by French Canadians. Poor Kevin, waiting patiently at the lat machine to speak to whatever thirty-five-year-old he considered the best-looking man in Washington. Poor Bob, going to the bars. Poor me, walking back and forth from apartment to gym, gym to museum, museum to bookstore, bookstore to apartment, alone on Saturday night, which really is the loneliest night of the week, especially when nobody calls.* That was why he trudged back and forth between museum and gymnasium, cathedral and movie house, searching for a distraction from what he believed could really be located only in the embrace of another body. But it was all too late, too late, he thought as he listened to the rest of them talking about some basketball tournament in which he had no interest. *What's really odd about this group,* he thought, *is that they actually follow professional sports.* So to change the subject, he turned to Kevin at his side and asked if some of the people at his gym were not annoyed when he tried to talk to them.

"Of course!" Kevin said. "Some of them can be quite cold, in fact, and some days I go home feeling very depressed. But then some of them are really nice." In fact, Kevin said, he had finally divided the clientele into people who would talk to him and people he should never even say hello to, especially because there were, even among the beauties, two cliques who would not speak to each other, one of them composed of people in their twenties, whom he left alone, because he felt that people in their twenties had the right to ignore old men; the other group made up of men in their thirties who already felt *they* were too old. But this was no cause for quitting, he said.

He settled back into the bliss of the candlelight, the wine, and the faces of friends as the hours at the dinner table melted like wax on the candles—so gently that it was only the sight of Tim yawning, and Paul looking at the clock, that made him realize they both were ready to have the evening end. He pushed his chair back.

"You can't leave yet!" Tim said.

"I must," he said. "In fact, I'm shocked that I stayed this long."

He often felt that having a good time only occurred when

someone else made an effort; pleasure did not just happen, he knew, it was the result of work.

So, even though he assumed everyone else knew better than he what Tim and Paul really wanted at that moment, having been their friends for so much longer, he didn't want to risk overstaying his welcome, and he found himself at eleven o'clock in the entrance hall, alone with Paul, thanking him for the evening. "By the way," Paul said in a low voice, as he handed him his coat, "I'm sorry I dumped all that on you about the guy in Boston."

"Don't be silly," he said. "Why would you feel sorry?"

"I don't know. It just seems self-centered."

"Not at all," he said. "Did you decide what you're going to do?"

"Yes. I decided," Paul said, "that the guy in Boston is totally commitment-phobic. In fact, a sort of lunatic. And Tim is the best thing that ever happened to me, and I love him a lot."

He smiled at Paul as he put his hand on the doorknob.

"Though I still can't stop feeling there's something more," Paul said. "I mean I just hate to think that this is it!"

"That *what* is it?"

"This house. Tim. The garage."

"Well...how does Tim feel about it?"

"He's totally content," said Paul. "He could go on like this forever. I'm just not sure *I* can."

"But you have a house!" he said.

"So? Nothing is permanent," Paul said. "Certainly not a house."

"If a house isn't permanent, what is?"

"I don't know." Paul shrugged. "Maybe nothing."

He sighed. "Does Tim know you feel this way?"

"Of course. We talk about everything."

"You're such an advanced, modern couple," he said.

Paul laughed. "Are you crazy?" he said. "We're a mess!"

"No, you're not. I think you're extraordinary. And I think this is just the classic dilemma of every couple—one is domestic, the other a wanderer."

"But I'm almost forty!" Paul said. "I want something—*more* in my life!"

"Everybody does," he said. "Except Dirk. Dirk seems to have it all."

"Dirk?" Paul said. "Dirk is the most miserable person I know! Dirk *sets* himself up for unhappiness—because of the sort of person he's attracted to. I have a friend who's twenty-five. He and Dirk went on a couple of dates. He told me that Dirk sees his ass, sees his face, sees his basket, but doesn't see *him*! Dirk is a mess."

"Oh, my," he said. Then he opened the door, stepped outside, and stood for a moment at the top of the stairs looking down at the street. The street was so narrow, the dark red brick houses so high, that the gingko trees planted in front of them had tilted forward in their attempt to get at the sunlight, which made a sort of arch. Everything, houses and trees, seemed to be leaning in, on the verge of a collapse. Down below, the cobblestones gleamed gray and silver in the lamp light. No one was out, it had just rained, and the sidewalk and street were plastered with yellow leaves. The leaves were heaped in the gutters, pasted to the bricks, in a solid golden swath, all the way down to the end of the block; it looked as if the street was paved with gold. It was one of the most beautiful things he had ever seen.

"Well," he said, turning back to Paul. "Everything's a trade-off."

"I know," said Paul. "Thanks for listening. And thanks for coming!"

The dark green door closed, and he went down the steps. *Here I am*, he thought, *out on the sidewalk at ten after eleven.* It had been after all just a visit—to the house of two young men who had cooked a dinner. That was all it could be, he thought. It couldn't be any more than that. He thought of what Tim had said about the Rapture as he walked down to P Street. *What happened to Dirk in a hotel room in Montreal was certainly rapture,* he thought, *even if it did not last, even if you were still on earth when it was over. And that's the only rapture most people will ever know—the kind that occurs on earth. Rapture,* he thought, as he walked past the people coming out of Whole Foods with their bags of prosciutto and bottled water and organic raspberries. *Rapture,* he thought as he turned onto 17th Street. *Paul's complaint is that he can no longer find rapture with Tim.* He came to a stop, halfway down the stairs at the side entrance of his building on 17th Street, and saw, through the window of the superintendent's basement apartment, that the family had already put up their Christmas decorations, though it was still only October. But there in the light of their television was a small Christmas tree on the mantelpiece, its tinsel and ornaments rose, green, and blue in the light of the program flickering on the screen. *Paul wants rapture with the man from Boston,* he thought, *Bob wants rapture with an Asian boyfriend, Kevin wants rapture talking to someone good-looking at the gym. I found rapture in a street of yellow leaves, and the super from Guatemala, or his wife and daughter, have located it in a miniature Christmas tree. But better than all these is love,* he thought as he went into the building. *Oh, how I wish I were in love.*

EVERYONE SAYS I'LL FORGET IN TIME

Greg Herren

The bed still seems empty every morning when I wake up.

It's been almost two years since he died. We were together for almost fifteen years, and the disease took us by surprise. Then again, you never see things like that coming. I suppose on some level we knew we weren't immortal, but it was something we never talked about, never planned for. Sure, we had powers of attorney paperwork and wills and all of that in place, but we never thought we would ever need them. We loved each other and had a wonderful life, and thought it would go on forever. But cancer doesn't care about love when it starts rotting you from the inside out.

When it finally took him, my life didn't end. I didn't go into the grave with him, no matter how much I wanted to, no matter how much I just wanted to curl up and cry. I still had my horror novels for teenagers with deadlines looming, a cat to take care of, bills to pay, a life to somehow keep living. The world didn't stop turning, even though I thought it should.

I had to get used to all the changes, the little ones that you don't think about so they blindside you and make your eyes unexpectedly fill with tears and your lower lip quiver. I had to get used to cooking for one, shopping for one, dealing with those sudden moments in department stores when I'd see a shirt he'd love and pick it up, carry it to the cash register, and have credit card in hand before I'd remember, and then somehow manage to hold myself together while smiling at the clerk and saying, "Um, I don't think I want this after all," before returning it to the display table and fleeing the store. I had to find ways to fill those hours that used to be our time together, flipping idly through the many channels on the television, looking for any distraction to take my mind somewhere else. I had to get used to sleeping alone, to not having something warm and cuddly next to me every night and every morning. There were no more pancakes on a tray with a glass of milk to surprise him awake in the mornings. I accepted that I would never again see the sleepy smile of childish delight he always displayed when he smelled the maple syrup. He was so cute, just like a little boy on those mornings when I'd decide to give him his favorite treat.

I got through it all; I survived; I went on. I went through the closet and the dresser and took his clothes to Goodwill. I did all the things you're supposed to do, and I got through it all.

But the bed still seems empty every morning when I wake up. The house seems quieter, no matter how loudly I play the stereo. The world seems different, somehow—the sun a little less bright, the sky a little less blue, the grass a little less green.

Everyone says I'll forget in time.

He wanted me to find someone else, but in a rather perverse way, I've found I like the solitude. My best friend David is constantly pushing me to go out to the bars, cruise the Internet, get out and meet someone, anyone. I know it comes from a really good place of love and kindness and concern, but I don't want to meet someone else. No one can fill that empty place inside of me. How do you replace someone who was the perfect one for you? I guess that's the part people don't really understand. I would rather be alone than make do with someone just for companionship. If I ever feel like getting laid, I can head down to the bars or go into a chat room or even wander the dimly lit hallways of the bath house. But even that is somehow unsatisfying. I can't find solace in a stranger's arms, only instant gratification—and even though I can remember a time before I met him when that was enough, it isn't now. Sex came to mean something to me when I was with him, and sex just for release doesn't cut it anymore. After it's over, the house is still quiet when I come home, the bed is still empty when I turn out the lights, and I still miss him.

I go through my usual morning ritual. It's raining, and I try not to think about how much we loved staying in bed on rainy weekend mornings, cuddling and tickling each other and laughing. Those were the mornings when I'd usually gone into the kitchen and made his pancakes and brought the tray in to him.

I make coffee; I brush my teeth; I shower and shave and get dressed. I bring the paper in from the porch; I read through it, go through the sale papers, and then put it all in the recycle bin. I drink my coffee and feed the cat. I straighten things up. I putter around the house; do a load of laundry; try to fill the day. I'm at loose ends, having finally finished my latest manuscript and mailed it to my editor on Friday. The day stretches out in front of me, an endless rainy day full of empty hours. I debate going to the video store, maybe shopping for things I don't need, but can't seem to make up my mind until the phone rings around eleven.

"Have you eaten?" David asks.

"No."

"Why don't you come over for lunch?"

I sigh. I've heard this before. David's partner, Russ, is kind of a mother hen. After the first year, he decided I needed to find someone else, and since I wasn't making an effort, he was going to make the effort for me. "You can't go on being the widow; it's just not who you are," he declared to me one night over a bottle of wine. It was almost always under the guise of a meal: a lunch on a Sunday or a dinner on a Friday night. I would walk down the block and be introduced to someone Russ thought was perfect for me, and we would make stilted conversation over a few glasses of wine and a good meal. Nothing ever came of these things—Russ, bless his heart, wasn't really sure who would be right for me, so I never knew what to expect when I went over there. I didn't mind so much, really. I enjoyed Russ's cooking and spending time with him and David, even if some-times it reminded me of what I'd lost, seeing them speak the secret language of couples that I once spoke. And the guys Russ tried to set me up with were always nice. But the spark I'd had once wasn't there with any of them, and it was hard to explain why.

I wasn't really sure I knew myself.

"What's his name this time?" I ask with a good-natured groan.

David laughs. "His name is Jeff. I think you might actually like this one."

"What time?"

"Come on over now; we're having mimosas."

I hang up the phone and look out the window. The rain has let up some, and the sun is breaking through clouds. I can even see patches of blue sky. I grab an umbrella just in case, and head down the block to their house. A car full of laughing teenagers blaring the latest rap hit goes past, its tires throwing up a bit of the water puddled in the street. They are so young it almost hurts to look at them, young and carefree with their whole lives in front of them, and I smile. The air smells moist from the rain, and everything is dripping—the trees, the bushes, the massive elephant ferns. I think again that maybe the answer is to sell the house, maybe get something different somewhere, make a fresh start, but I love my house. Even with its memories, even as empty as it seems now. And it's nice having Russ and David down the street.

I open their gate and walk up the sloping sidewalk to their front steps. I ring the doorbell and the dogs start to bark. I stand there for a minute, thinking about just opening the door and walking in, when I hear footsteps and the door opens.

My jaw drops but I say nothing.

"Hey, Terry," he says shyly. "Do you remember me?"

I search the recesses of my mind for his name. Even though David told me on the phone, it's gone, but *I know this guy.* I remember him. Seven years earlier when we went through a bad patch, thought about separating and breaking up, I struck up a conversation online one day with a guy who sent me his picture. He was shirtless in the photo, with the kind of body I always associated with Olympic swimmers—broad shoulders, muscles everywhere, a thick chest with big nipples, and an amazingly flat stomach. His face was narrow, the buzz cut of his dark hair emphasizing the prominent cheekbones, the strong chin, the dark round eyes on opposite sides of a rather handsome nose. We'd met for coffee, and despite the overwhelming attraction I felt for him, I hadn't given in to the temptation to go back home with him, or to offer to bring him back to my place. He'd been a sweet guy with a good sense of humor, but after that day I'd never given him another thought, or even seen him again anywhere.

"Yes," I finally say when I realize I've been staring at him for much longer than manners permit, "but I'm sorry, I don't remember your name."

"Jeff." He opens the screen door and sticks out his hand. It's big and strong, and I can see the veins in his defined forearms. He's wearing a yellow polo shirt, which shows off his tan, and khaki shorts that reveal muscled and hairy calves. He stands aside to let me in the house, and he's still smiling. "It's nice to see you again."

"Yes, yes it is," I babble like an idiot. Just in time, David comes out of the kitchen with a tall glass filled with orange juice and champagne.

"So you two have met." He smiles. He's wearing a black tank top and jean shorts. David is handsome but very fair; he burns easily and turns red rather than tans.

"We've actually already met," Jeff says, sitting down on the couch. "We met for coffee, when was it, Terry?"

"Seven years ago." I avoid the couch, sit in a reclining chair, and take a big swallow of the mimosa.

"Small world," David says, giving me a wink as he sits down next to Terry. "Jeff used to work with Russ, and he just moved back to town."

"I moved to Dallas six years ago." Jeff gives me a huge smile that turns on the spotlights in his brown eyes.

"What do you do?" I ask.

"I'm a graphic designer," he replies just as I remember our conversation at the coffee shop and feel stupid. We'd talked about his desire to paint, and I'd talked about my writing, two artists in different disciplines talking about our drive to create, our need to share our visions of life and the world with everyone.

"Are you painting?"

"One of the reasons I moved back is because I can focus

more on my painting here." He gives me another one of those wonderful smiles. "I actually have a gallery show coming to Royal Street in a few months."

"That's terrific!" I force a smile. He leans forward to place his glass on the coffee table, and I can't help but notice the muscles under his tight shirt. "Definitely let me know and I'll go. I'd love to see your work."

David gives me a look that says plainly *I just bet you would* before going to help Russ in the kitchen, leaving us alone in the living room.

"Terry, they told me about your partner. I'm really sorry."

"Thanks." I shrug. "You didn't tell them we'd already met?"

"No." He sighs. "I wasn't sure if you'd remember anyway, but when Russ said he wanted me to meet a friend, and told me your name, I"—his face flushes red—"I was really glad it was you. I said yes."

"Oh," I say, feeling like an idiot.

"If this is awkward for you—"

"No!" I burst out, and then shake my head. "I'm sorry; you must think I'm an idiot. I mean, I'm glad it's you." I laugh. "I really liked you when we met. I would have called, but—"

"You and your boyfriend worked everything out, didn't you?" He shrugs. "I'd hoped that's what it was. I really liked you, thought we'd connected, but I mean, I could tell you still loved your partner, and...." His voice trails off.

"It's nice to see you again," I say.

"I hope you're hungry!" Russ calls as he brings out a few bowls of food and sets them on the dining room table. "Come on in and eat!"

The food is delicious: a spinach omelet, toast, fresh berries, and coffee with Bailey's. The conversation is lively and animated, and I find myself relaxing as I spoon food into my mouth. Every once in a while, Jeff's and my eyes meet, and we smile at each other. We talk about books, Jeff's coming show, politics, the war, and Jeff is everything I remember from that day at the coffee shop: bright, funny, articulate, and smart. All too soon the food is gone, and the dishes are being cleared.

"I really need to get going," Jeff says. "I have painting to do."

"I should be going, too," I say, although all that's waiting for me is a long afternoon of channel surfing and giving the cat treats when he howls for them. "Are you sure you don't want me to help clean up?"

"Don't be silly," Russ says.

David gives him a look. "You know no one cleans his dishes the way he likes them done."

We say good-bye at the front door, and it shuts behind Jeff and me. "You live just up the street?" he asks.

I nod.

"You mind if I walk you?"

"Not at all."

We walk side by side, not really speaking, and when we reach my gate, he says, "Would you mind if I call you sometime?"

"I'd like that."

He takes out his cell phone and punches my number in as I recite it. He puts his phone in his pocket, and then gives me an awkward hug. "It was nice seeing you again. I'll call."

"Please do."

He turns and starts walking back down the sidewalk. I watch him for a moment, and then call after him, "Jeff!"

He turns, his face questioning.

I walk over to him and swallow. "Are you free Tuesday night?" I die a thousand deaths while I wait the few seconds for him to answer, my mouth and throat dry.

Then that smile spreads across his face again. "Yes. Yes, I am."

"Why don't you come over and I'll make dinner? I'll make a lasagna or something."

"I love lasagna," he replies, and then reaches across and kisses me on the lips. Not a kiss of passion, but a tender, gentle, questioning kiss. I pause for just a second, and then I kiss him back. We stand there for a few moments as the world stops, everything stops moving, and then the spell is broken and time starts again.

He gives me a huge smile. "'Til Tuesday, then."

I nod.

He walks down the sidewalk and unlocks a white car, and then looks back and gives me a wave and another smile before he gets in and drives off.

I stand there for a moment, watching the car disappear down the street. I open my gate and unlock the front door.

The house doesn't seem so empty anymore. Something's changed, I'm not sure what, but the colors seem vibrant again. The sunbeams coming through the windows seem brighter than they did yesterday. The music from the stereo when I turn it on sounds happier, more alive, more joyous.

I sit on the couch and the cat jumps into my lap, and as I stroke his thick fur he starts purring. Maybe it's just a date, maybe it won't lead to anything, who knows? No one knows what the future holds. But it's a start, it's a step back to myself, and maybe it might all work out. I tell myself to take things slowly and see what develops.

I laugh a little, and for the first time in a long time I realize that what I feel is content.

Maybe, just maybe, I'm starting to get over it.

After all, everyone said I'd forget in time.

ANGELS, WHAT YOU MUST HEAR ON HIGH

John H. Roush

One usually doesn't get the opportunity to speak to an angel, so I am totally unprepared on the proper etiquette for what to say and not to say. All my life I grew up hearing that I was going to hell for being gay, so forgive me if I offend. I was always told that I was evil and damned; if it wasn't from the preachers on TV, then it was from family members, friends, Christian right groups—you get the picture. But this doesn't look like Ms. Murphy's high school math class; now that was hell. The stories I could tell you about that class. Sorry, don't mean to ramble, it's just I never talked to an angel before, especially about my sex life, and I guess I'm a little nervous.

Maybe you haven't heard a story like this one, but you did ask me to describe my life for you and, well, while most of my life was so-so, the majority of it was about my sexuality, about me being a devout homosexual. I know I'm rambling. I'm sure you probably hear that from other people. I mean the rambling part, not the gay stuff. Is it okay to talk to an angel like this?

When I was a little boy, I used to sit and think up things. Not the usual things little boys think up, like meeting their favorite baseball player or winning a soapbox derby. No, I was thinking about much grander things. I was thinking about winning the Miss America contest with that gorgeous diamond-encrusted tiara, or better yet, I thought about what it would've been like to walk down a long winding staircase made of beautiful, deep brown mahogany wood with blood-red carpeting so thick that you sink into it when you walk, landing on the bottom stair, and slapping Rhett Butler across his scruffy, five-o'clock-shadowed face for keeping me waiting. Then he would manhandle me the way only he could, pick me up in his massive arms, and carry me up the staircase to our boudoir tastefully decorated in Louis XIV furniture.

Of course, I wasn't sure what happened next. I mean I had some ideas, but I was only a kid in grade school. In my mind, Rhett and I would end up kissing like Streisand and Kristofferson on that album cover, the one where her face is tilted up to his face and his hand is on the back of her head. I think he must have been trying to help her by holding up her head because that position must have really hurt her neck.

In my defense, I did say I wasn't your average little boy.

My full name is William Alexander Washington. My friends call me Alex. Kids teased me because my initials spell out WAW. They called me a crybaby all the time, but I just ignored them and focused on Rhett coming to take me away to our beautiful Georgia plantation with its sweeping verandas and mint julep cocktails. I even practiced my Southern drawl so I'd fit in when I moved down South.

I was an adorable little boy, with reddish brown hair and big, brown warm-puppy eyes with extra-long lashes. No fake eyelashes for me! My parents used to say I could get away with

murder when I looked at someone with my brown eyes. I don't
know about murder, but I did get my own way most of the time.

I was nine years old when I had my first boy-boy experience.
His name was Scott Murphy. God, I thought he was a hunk! He
was an older man—well, an older boy at least. He was thirteen,
and that was almost a man, right? He had the most gorgeous
red hair that he kept long and pulled back into a ponytail, and
he had freckles all over his face. You could play connect the dots
for hours.

Scott was my next-door neighbor. One day he was out
washing his bike in his backyard and I went over to offer assistance. I loved being around him. He was so handsome, standing
there in his cutoff jeans and his wet T-shirt. I could see flashes
of his belly as he stretched to wash parts of his bike. His belly
was flat and toned and had just a little bit of reddish peach fuzz
on it.

I asked if I could sit on his new banana seat, which he'd just
gotten for his bike. At first he stared me up and down, looking
at me like I was something from a freak show. Then he got this
weird grin on his face and said I could sit on it only if I agreed
to do something for him first. He wanted me to go up to his
bedroom with him and help him do his sit-ups. I really wanted
to try out his new bike seat, but the sit-up thing didn't sound
right, even to a nine-year-old.

When we got to his room, Scott locked the door and turned
around to stare at me. I was on the other side of his room looking
around. It was decorated in typical teenager stuff. Posters of
heavy metal rock bands hung everywhere. On one wall he even
had an altar set up.

He told me I was a good-looking kid, and he wanted to see
me with my shirt off. I knew I was something to look at with
my brown hair and eyes, so I took off my shirt and laid it on the

bed. By that time, Scott was standing beside me naked. I stared at him in shock, like I was looking at the Creature from the Black Lagoon.

I'd never really seen other boys without their clothes before, so I was a little scared when I saw his "thing" hard as a rock, peeking out from a mound of fluffy red hair. It didn't look that impressive, but then I didn't have much experience. He asked me if I wanted to touch it, and I practically dropped to my knees. I held out my hand and poked it with my index finger. It bounced up and down like a diving board. I took it in my hands, and Scott gave me instructions. I did as he told me to do, and after about five minutes—well, I thought I'd broken it! I started to apologize and that's when he took me in his arms and kissed me on my mouth. He told me that my hand job was the best ever. I knew this must be what adults were talking about when they mentioned the word *Love*. It just had to be, and I was instantly in *Love,* even without Rhett, the staircase, the slap, and the manhandling.

I became a regular at Scott's house. Then, as some boys do, he grew up and found a girlfriend. Yuck! When Scott told me I couldn't come over anymore, and why, I was devastated. I felt like Rhett had gone off and joined the Rebel army, and I was left to tend the plantation without him. As God was my witness, he would return to me one day.

But he didn't.

I hope I haven't offended you. I get carried away sometimes when I tell a story. I just don't know how to keep my big mouth shut. Let me tell you about high school. Glorious, hormone-filled high school!

The best part was the locker rooms. Can I just say that when God invented locker rooms, He must have been thinking about young gay boys? Where else can a room full of hormone-hyped teenagers slap one another's asses, swing their cocks like battering rams, and make each other sniff their jockstraps? Locker rooms are a gay youth's Garden of Eden, without Eve. I was in heaven. I signed up for all kinds of sweaty sports just so I could see naked boys. Isn't that why all boys sign up for sports? Okay, so God maybe didn't intend for locker rooms to be gay boys' Garden of Eden, but it happened, and I'm sure happy it did.

I was always the first in the showers when the team finished practice or a game. I wasn't even sweaty because most of the time I sat on the bench or carried around the coach's clipboard, but hygiene is important. I was also usually the last one out of the shower, making sure all the spigots were properly turned off because water waste is a horrible thing. You're not buying that and that's okay; the coach didn't, either. He was always telling me to get my pansy ass dressed and out of his locker room.

I met Troy after our big championship game against his high school. He was their quarterback, and he was a god. When I saw him, I fell deeply in love. Some may say it was just a high school crush, but all I can say is he made my heart stop.

Troy was that one guy in high school everyone loved. Tall, blond, perfect teeth, perfect body, and oh, my God, he had a perfect ass. When he wore his tight jeans, I swear you could see the dimples on both of his asscheeks. Sorry, Angel, but you asked me to tell you everything.

After the championship game, we were all headed back to the showers. That's when I saw him walking down the hallway to the opposing team's locker room, which was actually the girls' locker room, but it's all our small school could afford. He walked right by me, looked me in the eye, and said (are you ready for this?), "Hi! How you doin'?" Of course I couldn't speak, so I just stood there with my mouth open, drooling and looking like an ass. Can you believe I was so pathetic? Don't answer that.

I ran to our locker room as fast as I could, took a shower, changed my clothes without anyone noticing my hard-on sticking out of my boxers, and ran to the exit to wait. Some people may say I was stalking him. I prefer to say I was killing time until the man of my dreams came out to meet me.

Almost forty minutes later, Troy emerged with a halo of golden light surrounding his head. Okay, it could have been the halogen light above the doorway, but I do like to think differently, remember? He had on this chocolate-brown sweater that stretched across his broad muscled chest, and a pair of tight-fitting jeans that probably would make you angels cry.

I walked up to him and said hi and gave him the usual great-game talk. Then I went in for the kill and asked him if he wanted to get something to eat. I was so nervous I could have pissed my pants. That's when he said, "Get lost, faggot," and walked away. Now correct me if I'm wrong—which I am usually not—but if he smiled at me and said hello first, doesn't that mean something?

I wasn't sure what to do, so I went after him, stopping him near his cherry red Mustang. I asked why he would call me such a thing, and he said, "'Cause ya are, Blanche." Maybe not in those exact words, but you get the idea. I told him he was wrong, and he told me to get lost. I wasn't going anywhere until I got him to understand what my intentions were. Of course, my intentions were to see him naked.

I told him he needed to take back what he said, or else. At this point of the conversation, I was thinking "or else" would be a nice back massage at his place or even a little spanking on his beautiful ass. He, on the other hand, had a different idea of "or else." Troy got me into a headlock, forced me to the ground, and straddled my chest, pinning my hands behind my head with one hand while he unzipped his pants with the other. Then he pulled out his beautiful, long—sorry, Angel. To this day, I can't drive by the old stadium parking lot without getting a woody.

Ah, the memories of youth, aren't they grand?

When I finally became a man at the ripe old age of twenty-one, I thought the world was my oyster—or at least that I should be wearing a string of pearls. I did the party scene looking all buff and toned. High school sports had finally paid off by giving me a body that was to die for. Rippling abs, strong solid chest, and calves that made men melt. I hate to be called a designer name whore, but I was outfitted in only the best clothes by Kenneth Cole, Armani, and Gucci, to name a few. You're probably wondering how such a young man could afford all the finer things in life. I had what some people call a sugar daddy, but I refer to Philip (with one *L*) as my lover.

I first saw Philip across a crowded room at a friend's party in SoHo. Cliché, huh? Well, it's true. I was sitting on this divine divan made out of purple Muppet fur, and Philip was standing near the fireplace on the other side of the room. I had to find out who he was. He was six feet five inches and had a full head of thick, silver-gray hair. His eyes were so blue they looked like pools of water. Okay, another cliché, but still true. I casually asked around and found out he was just your run-of-the-steel-mill millionaire. Don't look confused; I mean he owned steel mills in Pittsburgh.

Philip was handsome and charming and fell in love with me at first sight. God, I can't stop with the clichés! I fell in love with the bulge in his pants. No, not the front one. His wallet was so thick that I could have loved him forever. He bought me the things I wanted, and did what I wanted when I wanted. Perfect, huh? I thought so.

You're probably thinking I don't have morals. You're thinking that it's wrong to take advantage of a sixty-five-year-old man.

Did I fail to mention that he was sixty-five? He knew what he was getting with me. I was up front and honest from the start, or at least after the first year. A guy's gotta get something, right? This is the part of my life that will send me to hell, right? Come on, Angel, you can give me a hint.

After two years, Daniel came along and it was love at first sight again. Not for me and Daniel, mind you, but for Daniel and Philip. Daniel was younger than I was, cuter than I was (at least he thought so), and gave Philip more attention than I did. So it was out with the old boy toy and in with the new boy toy.

By my thirties, I was looking for a job that paid more than minimum wage. God, I thought life sucked. I'd have stopped going to my AA meetings, but then who would I have talked to? Michael? He and I were together for a couple of years.

We met in a local gay bar called Ballz, where desperate, lonely men went to hook up for one-night stands. It wasn't an impressive place, but it served its purpose. Michael was drinking a beer in one of the booths that ran against the back wall near the jukebox. The way he held the bottle to his lips made me so horny. He kept licking around the top with his long, narrow tongue. I ordered a beer for him and a club soda for me, and then I sat down opposite him and handed him the beer. He smiled and asked my name. We talked for about an hour, and then we went back to my place. Four weeks later, he was moving his stuff into my already crowded apartment.

My apartment consisted of two rooms. One was a bathroom that had a shower stall with a toilet inside it. You could take a shower and then back up three paces, sit down, and take a crap. I think the bathroom must have been a closet in its previous life. The green and orange ceramic tiles were falling off the walls, and I swore that the mold along the bottom edge of the shower moved. The overhead light was a leftover idea that hung from an extension cord plugged into the main room.

The main room seemed even smaller. A Chinese screen blocked off the "kitchen" area, which consisted of a dorm-sized refrigerator and a hot plate. Dishes were washed when I took a shower. The rest of the area—what I called the "grand living room"—held my pull-out couch, a TV, and some bookcases. The carpet was orange shag that must have been superglued to the floor, because I tried to rip it up several times and it wouldn't budge. And I paid seven hundred dollars a month for this! When you wanted a prestigious address, you paid dearly.

Michael and I didn't mind the space in the beginning, because we were all cozy and cuddly. Then little irritating things started to happen. You know the things that rake your last nerve each and every time he does them. Like constantly calling me goofy pet names at the most inopportune times. It drove me nuts!

One time we were out to dinner with my mother (who hated Michael with a passion—but that's *her* story). She called and said she was in town and would love to take me and my "friend" to dinner. She never came to the apartment, because in her mind I was living in a penthouse suite with a fabulous city view, servants waiting on me hand and foot. (See where I get it?)

We met her near the apartment at a little bistro called Shells. This was the kind of place my mother loved. First off, it was all done in pink. The walls, the menus, the uniforms—everything was pink. Imagine a huge Pepto-Bismol bottle throwing up in a restaurant—that was Shells. Second, they only served—you guessed it—pasta shells. Different varieties of pasta shells with different kinds of sauces. My mother loved the place. I, on the other hand, hated themed anything. If I wanted shells with red sauce, I would've gone to the store, bought some Prego and Barilla pasta, and made it myself. Instead, I sat with my mother and lover and ordered a thirty-dollar plate of pasta.

Michael, in his infinite wisdom, started calling me Pookie Bear. Once is cute; twice is nice; but nine times and I was getting pissed off. So was my mother. The tenth time, my mother told him that if he didn't shut up with the names, she was going to puke on him. He thought it was a joke, so he said it again, and she did. She puked all over him. I laughed so hard that my sides hurt for a week. We later found out that my mother had a touch of food poisoning from a sushi breakfast she'd bought earlier that morning at an Asian-themed sidewalk vendor's cart.

That was the end of romance with Michael. I moved not long after that.

I never would've thought I'd make it into my fifties. My body ached, and it took me a few minutes to get up in the morning. Not just in the morning, but at night, too. You probably don't know what I mean, but that's why I loved my little blue pill. My partner, Tom, gave it to me when I started to have some, shall we say, flaccid moments. Who knows what caused it. I was just glad to have my pills!

That's right; I haven't told you about Tom. He's the best.

Tom and I met at a nudist retreat in the hills of West Virginia. He was there from Oregon with some friends, and I was there alone to commune with nature. That's what they were calling screwing in the woods at the time.

On my first day there, it was sunny and warm. I decided to take a walk through the woods on a man-made path that led to a lake. Halfway there, I spotted two guys going at it like bunnies in a little grove of pine trees. It could have looked like an artsy porn film was being made, with the sun filtering through the trees casting shadows on two naked gods. Instead, it was a comedy, because the guy playing bottom—his name was Tank— was so huge that the man behind him looked like he needed a step stool.

The smaller guy was Tom. When he saw me watching them, he stopped screwing Tank, wrapped a towel around his waist, and came over to me with a huge smile on his face like he'd just won something. Tom was definitely a looker. He had coal-black hair and dark eyes that could see into you. He wasn't what you would call a gym god, but his body was well-toned.

We chatted for a few minutes, and then he asked me if I wanted to go back to his cabin with him. I said, "Only if you remove that condom you were using." We both laughed so hard that I actually fell over a rock and had to get three stitches in my head.

We fell in love that week. We were inseparable, and when it was time to go, I asked Tom to move to West Virginia permanently. So here we are, living out our days in true bliss. Just like I dreamed about when I was young: I got my Rhett Butler, the big white mansion, a fleet of cars—and don't forget the dog.

Okay, Angel, I'll tell you the truth. We do have a little two-story Colonial that was built in the 1900s, surrounded by a white picket fence covered in rose vines. It's mortgaged to the gills, and we live paycheck to paycheck. The cars—well, one is in the garage more than at our place and the other needs to be in the garage, but then we wouldn't have anything to drive. We do have a dog, though: a beautiful German shepherd named Tank.

I wouldn't be anywhere else except with Tom. He keeps me grounded. He's the silent type, and you know what they say about the silent type: They're animals in bed! This man could make me praise Jesus in twenty-one different languages. Oh, sorry about that, Angel.

Maybe it's different with Tom because I'm truly in love with him. We've been together twenty-two years. Not bad, huh? We were sitting in our favorite pizza joint in our favorite booth, him nagging me because I didn't order a mushroom-hamburger pizza, and the next thing I knew, I was waking up in the emergency room with Tom crying over me and begging me not to leave him. I didn't want him to be sad. I wanted to see his beautiful smile again.

The funeral was today. I guess that's why you're here, huh, Angel? The service was tastefully done, I might add. Lots and lots of carnations. Tom knows they're my favorite flowers. And lots of color. I hate dry, boring funerals. Tom made sure it was bright and lively.

So, Angel, where do I go from here?

AFTERWORD |

Fool for Love was originally conceived by Greg Herren, who gave it to Timothy and me in a gesture of kindness and trust. After we sought and chose the stories, the collection's original publisher was sold and it languished in limbo. Then Richard Labonté became the matchmaker who introduced the stories to Cleis Press, and a courtship began. When Felice Newman and Frédérique Delacoste accepted the collection for Cleis, as in the best relationships, it became more layered and intriguing, and copy editor Gary Morris took the fear out of fix-ups.

In Houston, there's a House of Pies restaurant more often called "House of Guys." Late at night as the bars are closing and most of the city is asleep, the restaurant's booths and tables are replete with hungry men. As I began reading stories submitted for this collection, I imagined myself sitting in a corner at House of Guys, watching the main characters and trying to figure out what—beyond an omelet, a slice of pie, a bacon cheeseburger—they hungered after. The answer, of course, is that we all hunger for the same things. Love. Kindness. Forgiveness. Passion. Validation. Companionship. Understanding. Trust. Romance. Connection.

There are endless stories at the House of Guys, and Timothy and I have helped serve sixteen of them here to appease your hunger. I hope that some of them will prove to be favorite entrées that you'll devour again and again.

R. D. Cochrane

ABOUT THE AUTHORS

SHAWN ANNISTON loves art, dogs, and photography. He's still trying to decide what he wants to do when he grows up and where he'd like to live while doing it. Though single, Shawn believes in romance and is currently writing his first novel of gay romantic suspense. Shawn's website is shawnanniston.com.

'NATHAN BURGOINE is an expat Brit now living in Ottawa, Canada, with his husband Daniel. 'Nathan runs less often than he should, bakes more often than he needs, and rarely, if ever, fails to say something inappropriate. "Heart" is his first published work. 'Nathan can be found at n8an.livejournal.com.

ROB BYRNES is the author of three novels, all from Kensington: Lambda Literary Award-winning *When the Stars Come Out, Trust Fund Boys,* and *The Night We Met* (2002). A native of upstate New York, he currently lives in the New York City area with his partner, Brady Allen. In his free time, he can be frequently found in bars in Hell's Kitchen, as well as online at robnyc.blogspot.com.

JOEL DERFNER is the author of *Gay Haiku* (Random House) and *Swish: My Quest to Become the Gayest Person Ever* (Random House). Working with Tony Award–winning book writer and lyricist Rachel Sheinkin, he composed the score to *Blood Drive,* produced by the Bridewell Theatre in London; with book writer Peter Ullian and lyricist Len Schiff, he composed the score to *Terezin,* produced in 2007 in Seattle and scheduled for a New York production in 2009. He has also worked as a step aerobics instructor and a stripper. He is currently knitting a 3-D scarf shaped like DNA. He would like to thank Karen Norberg and the Museum of Scientifically Accurate Fabric Brain Art for inspiring this story. He hopes to come to a bad end.

MARK G. HARRIS was born during the Summer of Love in Greensboro, North Carolina, site of the Woolworth's lunch counter sit-ins and the birthplace of O. Henry. He has lived and worked in Los Angeles and New York City and is proud to be included in this anthology. Keep up with Mark online at markgharris.livejournal.com.

TREBOR HEALEY is the author of the Ferro-Grumley and Violet Quill award-winning novel *Through It Came Bright Colors* (Harrington Park Press); a poetry collection, *Sweet Son of Pan* (Suspect Thoughts); and a short story collection, *A Perfect Scar & Other Stories* (Harrington Park Press). Most recently, he co-edited *Queer & Catholic* (Taylor & Francis) with Amie Evans. Trebor lives in Los Angeles where he is working on a second novel. His website is treborhealey.com.

JOSH HELMIN is the co-author of the buddy blog Josh & Josh Are Rich and Famous, co-host of Towleroad TV on Towleroad. com, and a junior editor at a national magazine. His interviews and profiles have been published widely online and in print. He lives in Brooklyn.

GREG HERREN, who lives in New Orleans with his partner, is the author of six novels. His most recent mystery, *Murder in the Rue Chartres,* won the Lambda Literary Award. He has edited numerous anthologies, including the Lambda Literary Award-winning *Love, Bourbon Street,* and has published numerous short stories and essays. He can be reached at gregwrites@gmail.com.

ANDREW HOLLERAN is the author of four novels (*Dancer from the Dance, Nights in Aruba, The Beauty of Men,* and *Grief*), a book of essays (*Ground Zero*), and a collection of short stories (*In September the Light Changes*). His latest book, *Chronicle of a Plague, Revisited,* is a revision of *Ground Zero.* He lives in Florida and Washington, D.C.

PAUL LISICKY is the author of *Lawnboy* and *Famous Builder,* both published by Graywolf Press. Recent work appears in *Five Points, Conjunctions, Gulf Coast, Subtropics, the Seattle Review, the Pinch,* and in the anthologies *Truth in Nonfiction, Diva Complex,* and *Naming the World.* A graduate of the Iowa Writers' Workshop, his awards include fellowships from the National Endowment for the Arts, the James Michener/Copernicus Society, the Henfield Foundation, and the Fine Arts Work Center in Provincetown, where he was twice a Winter Fellow. He has taught in the graduate writing programs at Cornell University, Sarah Lawrence College, and Antioch University Los

Angeles. He currently teaches at NYU and in the low residency MFA program at Fairfield University. A novel and a collection of short prose pieces are forthcoming. He lives in New York City.

BRANDON M. LONG lives with his partner, two dogs, several fish, a bunch of birds, and a tortoise in Salt Lake City. He is not a Mormon.

FELICE PICANO was born in New York and now lives in California. He was the founder of Sea Horse Press and Gay Presses of New York. He was a member of the Violet Quill Club, a literary pioneer in gay fiction. His novel *Like People in History* won the Ferro-Grumley Award for best gay novel, the Gay Times of England Best Novel Award, and was a Lambda Literary Awards finalist. He won the PEN Syndicated Fiction Award for *Why I Do It* and was a finalist for the Ernest Hemingway First Fiction Award for *Smart as the Devil*. His novels *Drylands End, A House on the Ocean, a House on the Bay,* and *The Book of Lies* were Lambda Literary Awards finalists. His memoirs include *Ambidextrous, Men Who Loved Me*, and most recently, *Fred in Love*. His other works include the novels *The Lure* and *Onyx*, numerous short stories, plays, and poetry collections, and nonfiction, including, with Charles Silverstein, *The New Joy of Gay Sex,* and the critically acclaimed *Art & Sex in Greenwich Village*. His plays are produced throughout California.

DAVID PUTERBAUGH's short story "Me Too" was included in Alyson Books' *Best Gay Love Stories 2005*. A lifelong New Yorker, David is currently pursuing an MFA in creative writing at Queens College, CUNY. Keep up with David at davidpnyc.livejournal.com.

JEFFREY RICKER is a writer and graphic designer living in St. Louis, Missouri. His essay "Dakota" was published in *Paws and Reflect* (Alyson Books). He is a graduate of the Missouri School of Journalism.

JOHN H. ROUSH lives in a quiet New England town in Connecticut with his partner. He belongs to a nonprofit organization that goes throughout the United States and Canada raising money for other nonprofit groups. He is one of New England's leading female impersonators. He would like to thank his best friend John G for giving him the push and believing in him.

ROB WILLIAMS is the co-editor (with his husband, writer Ted Gideonse) of the anthology *From Boys To Men: Gay Men Write About Growing Up* (Carroll & Graf). His essays and fiction have appeared in *Maisonneuve, Pindeldyboz, Versal, 400 Words, San Diego Gay and Lesbian Times, San Diego CityBeat Magazine,* and various anthologies including *Fresh Men: New Voices in Gay Fiction, I Do/I Don't: Queers on Marriage,* and *M2M: New Literary Fiction.* After receiving his MFA at Columbia University's School of the Arts, he returned to his home city of San Diego, California, with hubby in tow. He is currently teaching English and creative writing, learning how to surf, and finishing his first novel.

ABOUT THE EDITORS

TIMOTHY J. LAMBERT lives in Houston with his dog Rexford G. Lambert. As part of the writing team publishing as Timothy James Beck for Kensington Publishing, he wrote *It Had to Be You, He's the One, I'm Your Man, Someone Like You* (a Lambda Literary Award finalist), and *When You Don't See Me.* He co-wrote *The Deal* and *Three Fortunes in One Cookie*, both from Alyson Books, with Becky Cochrane. His short stories were anthologized in Alyson's *Best Gay Love Stories 2005* and *Best Gay Love Stories NYC Edition,* as well as Lawrence Schimel's *The Mammoth Book of New Gay Erotica.* He selected stories and introduced Cleis Press's *Best Gay Erotica 2007,* edited by Richard Labonté. Timothy's website is timothyjlambert.com.

R. D. COCHRANE grew up in the South, graduated from the University of Alabama, and now lives in Texas with her husband of twenty years and their two dogs. She co-wrote five novels under the name Timothy James Beck, and wrote two novels with Timothy J. Lambert. She has published short stories and a contemporary romance, *A Coventry Christmas*. Her next novel, *A Coventry Wedding*, will be published by Kensington in 2009. She thanks her husband Tom, and writing partners Timothy J. Lambert, Timothy Forry, and Jim Carter, for their unwavering support. Her website is www.beckycochrane.com, and she shares her thoughts and photos on beckycochrane.livejournal.com.